ARMANDO RETURNS

Book Two in the *Barboza Brothers* Series

By Reeni Austin

Copyright 2013 Reeni Austin

http://www.reeniaustin.com
http://www.facebook.com/ReeniAustin

Published by Gossamer Publishing, LLC

Edited by Laurie Laliberte

TABLE OF CONTENTS

ORDER OF BOOKS IN THE "BARBOZA BROTHERS" SERIES:

Book One: Fresh Temptation

Book Two: Armando Returns

Book Three: More Than a Maid

(Coming Soon – please visit Reeni Austin's website and sign up for her mailing list to receive an email when the book is published)

DEDICATION

Thank you to my beta readers: Joni, Makayla, and Veronica.
Special thanks to Marivett for always checking my Spanish.

CHAPTER 1

"I'll be back in a minute, baby." Armando cupped Katie's chin and gave her a playful smile. "Don't you go anywhere." He winked, then kissed her. He added a quick, "I love you," before opening the door to exit the car.

"Hurry!" Katie giggled with pure glee as she watched her sexy fiance rush to the little convenience store—the first store they had seen in miles in this dry, dusty, Texas landscape.

It was exactly one week after graduation. The day they looked forward to for months was finally here. With only Armando's car, a few suitcases, and their entire combined savings of three thousand dollars, they were halfway to New Mexico where they had an appointment with a judge to get married at a courthouse. A courthouse far from Katie's father's jurisdiction as a judge.

Katie had never been so happy. They were three hours away from home, with three and a half more hours to go until they reached their destination. She would soon be Mrs. Armando Barboza and there was nothing anyone could do to stop her. She planned to call her parents in a few days. By her estimation, her phone call would arrive around the same time they realized she hadn't taken that trip to Galveston with the girls from the church youth group. And by then, she and Armando would be on their honeymoon at a cozy little bed and breakfast.

Smiling, she gazed inside the store. She tucked a lock of her thick red hair behind her ear and turned her entire body to watch him chat with the cashier. *He's perfect,* she thought. Every minute away from him was an eternity. She imagined those strong arms wrapped around her. Succumbing to his kiss. Quenching their need for each other with nobody around to stop them.

Tonight they could finally make love without feeling guilty. They would be husband and wife. No more sneaking around. No more lying.

They would be free.

She watched Armando, entranced. Too swept up in her daydream to give more than a passing thought to the vehicle she heard pulling up beside the car. She saw Armando's jaw drop, then he stormed outside just as she heard an angry voice barely muffled by the closed window and the hum of the air-conditioner.

"Get out of that car right now or I'll break that damn window and drag you out!"

Katie's stomach tied up in one painful knot. Her perfect fantasy shredded into a million pieces at the sound of her father's rage.

This wasn't part of the plan. They were supposed to be a safe seven hours away and married for a few days before she broke the news to Daddy. *He can't tell me what to do anymore.* Mustering her anger, she sat up, crossed her arms over her chest and stared straight ahead, desperate to avoid his stare. She was just about to scream at him when she was interrupted by Armando's voice.

"Whatta you think you're doin'?" Armando dropped the small bag of items he had just purchased and broke into a sprint. "Get away from—"

Katie turned abruptly to the sound of her father's fist now pounding against the door, just below the window.

Armando met the unexpected visitor just as his arm was high in the air, ready for another blow against the metal. "That's enough!" Armando pressed his palms against Mr. McCormack's shoulders with a violent shove, sending the tall, lanky man back a few paces, landing him on his knee as he braced his fall. "We're both eighteen! You can't keep us apart anymore!"

Dwayne McCormack scrambled to his feet. "Really, now?" He rushed forward to pin Armando against the rear window. "You think it's smart to hit a judge, boy? You know what I could do to you?"

Katie's eyes filled with tears as she opened her door and stepped outside. "Daddy! Stop!"

"*Corrupt* judge." Armando snorted and returned Mr. McCormack's glare. "I know exactly who you are and I got the right to defend my girl and my property."

With a sinister chuckle, Dwayne said, "She's *my* girl and she's comin' home with me."

Katie grabbed her father's wrist and pulled it with all of her strength. "No I'm not! You can't tell me what to do anymore!"

Dwayne gritted his teeth and shot his daughter a threatening look, his grip tight on Armando. "The hell I can't."

Armando hooked his leg around Dwayne's and, in one swift motion, brought his heel against the back of Dwayne's knee.

In seconds, the two were on the ground, fighting, as Katie screamed her way to the convenience store to ask the clerk for help. A quick look through the glass door showed her he was nowhere to be found.

That's when she heard the sound of a car entering the parking lot. She turned around and saw a police vehicle. Its tires screeched as it stopped behind Armando's car. The doors instantly opened and two Texas state troopers stepped out.

Katie ran back to the car to see her father helping Armando to his feet, then grabbed him by the back of his shirt, shoving him toward the officers.

One of the troopers said, "We got him, Dwayne," as he put his arm around Armando's shoulders; Dwayne let go.

Dumbfounded, Katie yelled, "What are you doing?" She ran to the vehicle where the officers were now escorting her fiance. "He didn't do anything wrong!"

Armando shook his head, blood running from the side of his mouth. "Katie…" His frightened eyes met hers, but the officers ignored her.

"No!" Katie held out her arms, intent on running to Armando, when she felt her father's arm around her waist, pulling her away. "No! He did nothing wrong! Where are you taking him?"

Dwayne stopped as one of the officers helped Armando into the backseat of the police vehicle. He turned his daughter around and steadied her in front of him, holding her by the shoulders. "It's over. The sooner you accept it, the better off you'll be."

"I don't understand." Her voice and bottom lip both trembled. "What are they arresting him for? How'd they get here? How'd they know your name?" Anger swept through her as a little of her shock wore off. "You did this! Why would you do this to me?" Tears of fury rolled down her cheeks. "I love him!" She wriggled away from her father's grasp and turned around to the car where Armando sat. "Armando! I love you!" She raised her voice, emitting a cry that came from the depths of her soul. "I love you!"

Dwayne grabbed his daughter's waist as she tried to run to the police vehicle again. Thick tears streamed down her face as she watched it back out of the parking lot and head down the road toward home. Over and over, she screamed, "Armando!" at the top of her lungs until she was hoarse.

Katie felt a gentle hand on her shoulder as her father let her go.

"*Katie-bug*."

"Mom?" Katie turned around. "You're here?"

"Yes." Her mom handed Katie a wad of tissues. In a gentle voice, she said, "I'm sorry. I was hiding till it was all over."

"You knew about this?" Katie looked away to see her father open the door to Armando's car, which was still running. She brought the tissues to her eyes. "What *is* this? I don't understand."

"Sweetheart." Mrs. McCormack choked back her own tears as she put her hand on her daughter's face. "Sometimes things just happen and you'll never understand why. You have to trust us. I know it's hard right now, but you'll get over it and find someone else. You'll forget all about him."

"What?" Katie's eyes were wide. "You can't be serious. I deserve an explanation!" In a mocking voice, she said, "*Sometimes things happen and you'll never understand…*" quoting her mom. "I can't believe you! This isn't like that time my cat ran off and went to live at Kayla Murphy's house when I was in the first grade. You think I can just blow this off and forget my parents and the state troopers tracked me and my boyfriend down and had him hauled off to God knows where? This is insane! And it's bullshit!"

Dwayne said, "Watch that language, girl," and marched up to his daughter. "We know what's best for you.

"You're crazy! He didn't do anything wrong. You just had him taken away because you could! Nobody read him his rights or anything! I'm not stupid." She sniffled. "It's true. You really *are* corrupt, aren't you?"

Dwayne produced a grim chuckle and looked in his daughter's angry eyes. "You need to watch the way you speak to me."

Lisa McCormack narrowed her eyes at her husband. "Please, Dwayne. We knew she'd be upset. Let me talk to her."

He shook his head and looked down at the ground, then silently headed back to Armando's car.

Lisa's eyes, filled with pain, stared into Katie's. She glanced at her husband to make sure he was out of earshot, then lowered her voice to a whisper as she focused on her daughter. "Please, sweetie. Trust me this time. I know it's not fair but I can't explain it to you right now. I just can't." She took her hand from Katie's cheek to wipe her own tears away. "Please, for the sake of our family. Forget about this boy."

Katie had never seen her like this. Her mother seemed desperate, like she was begging a friend for help, not like a concerned mother trying to comfort her daughter. "What do you mean, our family?" Katie asked. "Are we in trouble?" She glanced at her dad, who was now pulling luggage out of the back seat of Armando's car. She then asked her mom, whispering, "What could Armando possibly do to our family? Why are you so afraid?"

Her mom sighed. "There's a lot of history with his family...stuff you don't need to know about." Tears fell down her face and she threw herself against Katie, hugging her and sobbing.

Katie's stomach went sour as her mother cried on her shoulder like she was the one who really needed to be soothed. Her mother was the strongest woman Katie knew and she had never seen her like this--vulnerable and desperate, with no explanation.

Her mom took one big breath, calming herself, then whispered in Katie's ear, "I'm so sorry. I didn't know it'd come to this. I thought you only dated for a few weeks." She groaned quietly. "Now I know you were sneaking around this whole time. I thought I kept a better eye on you."

Katie thought back to that wintry night when Daddy caught Armando in her bedroom, just seconds after he'd climbed in through the window. Daddy had forbidden her to see him again and he grounded Katie for a month. Little did her parents know they sneaked around before and after that for months, seeing each other almost every day. "Mom, I love him. No matter what you do, you can't keep us apart forever."

Lisa pulled away and took her daughter's hand, gazing into her eyes with a sad grin. "I know you love him. And I'm sure your dad's gonna rant and rave about you being too young to know what love is, but I can see that look in your eyes. And that's why you've been so happy lately." She sniffled, trying to stop her tears. "Because you knew you were running off to marry him today, right?"

Katie nodded and began to cry again. "Yes."

"Sweetie, I'm sorry. I mean it. Words can't express how much I mean it. But I'm begging you, please try to move on."

"How can I do that if you won't tell me why? I'm worried sick about Armando."

Lisa glanced away to see Dwayne leave the car and head to the store. "You know I wouldn't ask this of you if I didn't have a good reason, right? I hate to see you hurting like this. I want my kids to be happy, and that boy makes you happy. I'm sorry. Please, trust me. If nothing else, do it for your dad."

Katie grunted. "I'm not doing anything for him. I didn't know he could be so mean. I've never seen him like this."

"You better not be thinking about running away. 'Cause if you *do* find a way to run off, you'll never see us again. Not your sister. And not me. Your dad won't allow it."

"What? He can't do that!"

"He was capable of doing this today, wasn't he? He can call in favors just about anywhere."

"Yeah, in Texas." Katie scoffed. "All we have to do is leave the state. That's why we were going to New Mexico, to keep you two from hearing about the wedding. I'm eighteen. Daddy can't stop me anymore."

Her mom's face crumpled as her tears flowed once again. "Oh, sweetie. Don't you understand what I'm trying to say? Your dad *will* keep you and Armando apart." Her eyes widened. "Trust me."

Katie's breath hitched; the haunting look in her mom's eyes chilled her to the bone. "You don't mean…he'd do something… to Armando?"

Her mom's eyes went to the ground as she wept, quietly.

"Mom." Katie's mouth gaped as she waited for her mom to answer. "Surely not. Daddy wouldn't…" Her voice trailed off as her mom's face grew even sadder. "I can't believe this. How can he be so ruthless?" She looked away, nausea building again in her stomach. For years she had heard rumors about Daddy. Occasionally she overheard conversations she knew she wasn't supposed to hear. Ones that made her question his integrity. But she always chalked it up to misunderstanding. She loved her father dearly, and until today, she had never seen him so calculating. He was always strict and overprotective, but never like this. No. Something was very, very wrong. She waited a few moments longer until the disgust coursing through her subsided enough for her to speak. Then she asked, "Mom, why would you stay married to someone like him?"

Lisa took a deep breath and started to answer her, then caught a glimpse of Dwayne heading toward them. Softly, she said, "Sometimes you just gotta take the good with the bad."

Loudly, Dwayne let out a weary sigh and put his hand on Katie's back as soon as he was close enough. His tone was gentle. "I'm sorry I had to do this, darlin'. I love you. You know that. I didn't mean to be so harsh with you."

Katie shrugged away from him, chills going through her body from the touch of his hand. He sounded like her loving, overly protective father again. Except now he was someone Katie didn't know at all. And she was too numb to cry, as though every emotion from horror to devastation flooded her senses at once and she didn't know which was strongest. In a volume barely loud enough for him to hear, and without looking him in the eye, she asked, "Where'd they take him?"

"Don't worry, honey," he said. "They won't hurt him. They'll just scare him a little."

Katie gulped, then nodded, staring straight down at the ground.

"Here." Dwayne handed his keys to Lisa. "You girls take the

truck home. I'm gonna drive this," he nodded toward Armando's car, "back to Turnbrook." He bent down and kissed Katie's forehead. "Tonight we'll go to San Antonio, to that restaurant you like." He gave her another kiss then walked to the car.

Katie closed her eyes, thick with tears. *Yeah. My favorite restaurant. That's gonna smooth everything over?*

It was ten minutes before Katie spoke again. Lisa was content to let her daughter sit beside her in silence as she drove down the highway.

Every time Katie closed her eyes, she saw Armando's face. Blood running from his mouth by the work of her father's fist. Her throat was scratchy from screaming, trying in vain to stop the chaos. She whispered, "I hate this."

"I do too."

"You're still not gonna tell me anything, are you?"

"No." Lisa patted Katie's knee. "It'll get easier. I promise."

Under her breath, Katie muttered, "Yeah, right." She cleared her throat and said louder, "Can you at least tell me where they took him today? When can I see him again? I'm scared."

"You can't see him again."

"But I just wanna know if he's okay!"

Lisa shook her head. "He'll be okay. He'll be even better if you stay away from him."

"I'm sure Daddy'll make sure I stay away, won't he?" Katie quickly began sobbing. "He'll lock me up in my room and threaten me."

"He'll keep a tighter watch on you, that's for sure, but he won't lock you up. There's no need for that. He just wants you to stay away from that boy and his brothers. That's all."

Katie let out a sarcastic laugh as she cried. "So, that means

Armando's younger brother Ramon better not start dating Chelsea, huh? They're about the same age. He's only a year ahead of her in school."

Lisa groaned. "Please don't say such things."

"Well? What if she does? Maybe you and Daddy need to make a list of all the boys we're not allowed to talk to." She wiped her face with a tissue. "There might be family history we don't know about. Sure as heck don't wanna get anyone killed or imprisoned because we fell for 'em…"

In a stern voice, Lisa said, "Katie, it's just *those* boys. And you're such a pretty girl, you could've had your pick of all the guys at Turnbrook High. How were we supposed to know you'd pick one of *them*? Now just calm down." She took a deep breath, trying to keep the tears at bay. "We'll all get through this. Armando's gonna be fine. They'll keep him in a holding cell for a few days until your dad works something out with—"

"A holding cell?" Katie's heart raced with fear. "You mean, jail? For what? He didn't do anything."

"I know. It's just a holding cell. It won't go on his record. He'll be investigated for illegal immigration for a little while, then they'll—"

"Illegal?" She turned to her mother in disbelief. "He's not illegal! Is that what this is about? Daddy hates him because he's from Mexico? He's lived here since he was ten!"

Lisa smirked. "Your daddy doesn't hate anyone from Mexico. You know that. I'm sure they'll find nothing and he'll be let go."

"So, he called in a favor to keep us apart for a little while? Like I'm gonna get over it by then? Take me out to dinner and wait a few days and I'll forget Daddy had my fiance hauled off to jail?"

"Nobody expects you to forget, sweetie." Lisa wiped a tear from her eye. "We love you. I'm so sorry."

CHAPTER 2

Armando's head throbbed as the scorching sun beat down on him. After the three days he spent in that jail cell, he thought his situation couldn't get worse.

But he was wrong.

He woke up on the side of a country road. There were no houses in sight. Just hills and dirt as far as he could see. He had no idea where he was or how he got there. His head hurt and his throat felt like sandpaper. But at least he wasn't in jail anymore.

He trudged slowly up the hill, hoping he was going the right way. From what he saw, the road down the hill only led to more hills. Nothing but more dust and dirt. He swallowed as much saliva as his mouth could produce, and trudged ahead.

Maybe this is all a nightmare...I'll wake up beside her, and everything will be all right.

For ten minutes he walked, praying to God to show him the way home. To erase the miserable days he spent without Katie. The thought of her was all that kept him going.

They won't stop us next time. Fuck 'em. Fuck Dwayne McCormack and all those crooked assholes. I'll expose them for who they really are. They can't get away with this. Katie's mine. She'll always *be mine.*

A few more steps, and Armando's knee buckled as his entire leg seized in a cramp.

"Shit!" He fell against the jagged gravel below, scraping his hands as he tried to brace himself.

Closing his eyes, he contemplated rolling off the road to the dry grass. At least there he could rest until he felt well enough to continue.

Then suddenly, a glimmer of hope. Gravel crunching in the distance. The low hum of a car engine.

"Ow. Damn it…" It took all of his strength, but Armando pushed himself up to stand on wobbly legs and wait for the vehicle. Again, he swallowed, anything to moisten his parched throat.

He closed his eyes and pictured her face once again. Heard her voice screaming his name as they led him away. As much as he desired vengeance, what he wanted more than anything was to collapse in her arms. Then whisk her away in his car to try again.

Through his pain, the thought made him smile.

A cloud of dust from the dry road preceded the vehicle, making it hard to see. As it drew closer, Armando held up his arms, waving. "Help! Help me!"

When the dust died down, he saw a bright red pick-up truck that had obviously seen better days. It had one dark blue door and the shocks emitted a faint squeak with each rotation of the wheels. As it drew closer, Armando heard a mariachi band blasting from the radio. Then he saw two middle-aged Hispanic men inside, both of them staring at him with curiosity.

Armando thought they were going to drive by and leave him alongside the road, but the truck stopped, kicking up more dust. Coughing, he covered his mouth and shuffled toward the truck.

The driver called out, "*Donde te diriges?*"

Armando cleared his throat and made a request to find a phone to call his family. "*Tengo que llamar por teléfono a mi familia. Por favor, ayuda.*"

The men in the truck looked at each other, nodding, then helped Armando climb into the rusty bed of the truck. The way they stared at him meant he must have looked much worse than he realized. He wondered if that was why they asked no questions about how or why he was there. They just drove on down the road for miles, each bump inflicting more pain until they arrived at a small, run down gas station. Along the way, as they neared town, Armando saw signs that alerted him of his location: San Pedro, Mexico.

After the men helped Armando out of the truck, they went inside the tiny cinder block building for a few minutes, then came back outside and proceeded to fill up their gas tank. The driver told Armando to head inside where the lady behind the counter would help him.

Several minutes later, after speaking with the lady, Armando chugged two bottles of water and a bottle of apple juice. He called home on the old rotary phone in the back room of the station.

Henry Platt answered. "*Hello?*"

Armando cringed. He had hoped to talk to Mama. Henry was the benefactor who moved Armando, his brothers, and his mother from Mexico years earlier. Aside from the oldest brother, Victor—who was now in college—they all still lived and worked on Henry's ranch. "It's Armando. I need help."

"*You sound like you're in bad shape, boy.*" Henry chuckled. "*Where the hell are you?*"

"Don't you even care what happened to me?" Armando was confused by Henry's flippant tone. "I've been gone for four days."

"*Yeah, I know.*" Henry let out a slow sigh. "*I told you all along it wasn't gonna work out with you and that girl.*"

Rage swelled inside Armando. He balled up his fist. "If you knew what was going on, why didn't you try to help me?"

"*Now's not the time. Your mama's real sick. Been in bed since yesterday. She's askin' for ya.*"

"Sick? From what?"

"*Just come on home, son. Where are you, anyway?*"

"I'm in San Pedro. Mexico. At a gas station."

"*Shit!*" Henry muttered inaudibly under his breath. "*That's an eight-hour drive, at least.*" More muttering. "*I can send one of the ranch hands down there to getcha. I'll make sure he has your papers so you can get back over the border.*"

"Gee. Thanks," Armando answered, flatly. "So, does that mean you have everything the state troopers took from me? I had it all with me on my way to New Mexico. Driver's license, birth certificate--"

"*Look boy, I'm doin' you a favor. I told you not to get involved with that girl. I've known her daddy for a long, long time. Trust me. You're better off.*"

Armando's pounding headache suddenly returned. He was too tired and in too much pain to argue about Katie or find out what else Henry knew. "Well, whatever. You said someone can be here in the morning? What am I gonna do till then?"

"Well..." Henry paused for a moment, thinking. "You said you're at a gas station? You talkin' on a phone there?"

"Yeah."

"The owner around?"

Henry then had a lengthy conversation with the nice woman at the gas station, who had family nearby where Armando spent a very restless night on a threadbare blanket covering a dirt floor.

The next day, Luis, one of Henry's ranch hands, arrived to give her family some cash to pay for their troubles, and to bring Armando home.

Armando slept through most of the ride home, having spent most of the night awake. For the time he was coherent during the ride, he attempted to pry information from Luis about what Henry told him of Armando's suffering the last few days; Luis knew nothing. All he offered Armando was the same advice, repeatedly: "Do what Henry says." When Armando asked if he knew about Mama being sick, all Luis said was that he heard she was ill and he hadn't seen her in a few days.

When Armando finally arrived home, he took a quick shower, then went straight to his mother's bedroom. She was asleep, with Ramon sitting on the bed by her side.

Ramon took one glance at Armando and said, "She's been like this for days."

"Days?"

Ramon nodded. "A doctor came by. Said it was the flu. Not sure I believe him."

"Should we take her to the hospital?"

With a sad sigh, Ramon said, "She didn't wanna go."

"Why don't you believe the doctor?" Armando went around the bed to the other side and sat down, taking Mama's hand.

"I think Henry knows the truth. He immediately called Victor and told him to come home. Why would he do that if it was just the flu?" Ramon's voice cracked as if he was about to cry.

Armando's head shook with sadness. He gently moved Mama's hair away from her forehead and watched her sleep. "Maybe Henry's just being cautious. What could make her so sick so fast?"

"I think maybe she's been sick for a while but she didn't tell anyone. You know how stubborn she is. You probably didn't notice because you haven't been around much. Too busy sneaking around with your girlfriend." Ramon snorted. "Heard she got you arrested."

Armando shot him a mean look. "Don't start with me. You don't even know half of what I've been through."

"What's jail like, anyway?" Ramon raised an eyebrow. "You find yourself a boyfriend?"

"Grow up, *pendejo*." Armando was too tired to defend himself. He knew his brother was probably only teasing him to distract himself from his own sadness. "I've been through five days of hell. You'll never believe what—"

The bedroom door opened, and Henry walked in, his boots clacking along the hardwood floor. "Armando. Good to have you back in one piece." He walked to the foot of the bed and took off his cowboy hat—a sign of respect—as he gave their mother a glum stare.

The boys weren't stupid. They always knew Mama had a relationship with the old, skinny rancher. It was somewhere in the vicinity of "love," but not quite. And the boys learned long ago not to ask.

But today, Henry's feelings were clear in the concern that clouded his eyes. Valeria Barboza was more than just the woman who lived and worked on his ranch. Henry had a deep fondness for her, and his heart ached to see her like this.

After a few silent moments, Henry cleared his throat and said to Armando, "Can I talk to you?" He nodded toward the door. "Alone?"

Armando answered, "Yeah," and gave Mama's forehead a kiss before hopping off the bed. Ramon eyed him suspiciously as he left the room.

As Henry led Armando to the office downstairs, he looked

around the hallway outside the room to make sure no one was around. Then he shut the door and motioned for Armando to have a seat.

Armando sat in front of the desk, expecting Henry to take his usual seat behind it. But instead, Henry pulled up a chair and sat directly in front of him.

Henry tossed his hat to the desk and bent forward, his weathered eyes focused intently on the boy. "Son, I know you've had a rough couple o' days."

"Couple?" Armando scoffed. "It was more than a couple. I woke up on the side of the road—"

Henry held up his hand, quieting him. "I know. You didn't tell Ramon, did you? Because all I told him was you went to jail and I had to get you out."

Armando's head shook, quickly. "No, that's not what happened at all. That makes it sound like I got arrested. They just held me there like they were *gonna* arrest me. Then I woke up on the ground, feeling like a truck hit me. Didn't even know where I was. I guess they drugged me or something."

Henry nodded. "Probably. But listen, I think it's best you don't tell anyone about all that. Especially your brothers."

Armando's voice was loud and angry. "What? You gotta be kidding. I'm gonna tell everyone! I didn't do anything wrong! I could've been killed out there. That asshole McCormack needs to pay. He's the one whose ass should be locked up."

"Uh-huh." Henry smirked. "And exactly *who* are you gonna tell? Who do you think's gonna make him pay? The cops?"

Armando shrugged. "Yeah."

Henry's eyes were cold. "Really, now? You think the law's on *your* side." He let out a single, sarcastic laugh. "The state troopers who locked you up. You think they're gonna help you?"

"Yeah. They can't *all* be corrupt."

Henry tossed his head back, laughing, then slapped himself on the knee. He quickly calmed down and said, "Who you think they're gonna believe, boy? You, or their buddies? Ain't nobody gonna believe what happened to you. It's gonna sound like some fantastic make-believe tale. You tryin' to run off and marry the judge's daughter then you end up in the desert in Mexico after they drugged you?"

Urgently, Armando nodded. "But that's exactly what happened. Hell, Luis came down and got me. He knows. He can vouch I was there—"

Henry put his hand on Armando's shoulder. "Don't matter. Nobody'll believe how you got there."

Crestfallen, Armando sunk down in his chair as he realized Henry was right.

Silently, Armando hung his face in his hands, considering his options. Pondering the events of the past few days. Less than a week earlier he was overjoyed, expecting a wonderful future with Katie. And now, nothing made sense. Nothing except his love for that girl.

Armando took a deep breath when he was ready to speak again. "Dwayne can't keep us apart forever. Katie's eighteen. She can make her own choices. We're already planning to get an apartment and go to college together this fall and—"

"Is that what you really think?" Henry asked. "Son, it ain't her choice. Trust me. Her daddy's changed her mind by now."

"You don't know that. Besides, what's it matter to him? Why's he hate me so much?"

Henry shrugged. "Does it matter? Men are like that with their daughters. No one's ever good enough." His eyes narrowed, thoughtfully. "You really think you wanna marry that girl? You're only eighteen. You're a kid. You and her both got a world of growin' up to do." Henry laughed. "I guarantee in ten years...hell...five years, you'll forget all about her."

"No I won't."

Henry nodded. "Yes you will. Trust me. You're a smart boy and you're good lookin'. You got the world at your feet. When you go to college this fall, girls'll be throwin' themselves at you. It's better you break up now than break up later when she's naggin' you to death and you got all kinds of hot, young tail prancin' around in front of you at school."

Armando's stomach clenched at Henry's crudeness. "You don't know that. I love Katie. Nobody knows me like she does. She's my best friend."

Henry rolled his eyes. "Yeah, yeah, yeah. I know. I was young and stupid once, too." He set his jaw firmly and gave Armando a stern look. "Tell you what. If she still wants to be with you after all this, you two go on and get married. I'll even help you myself. Pay for the wedding. Take care of Dwayne McCormack. The whole deal."

"Really?"

"Sure."

"Let me call her then—"

"No need." Henry stood, reaching to the desk for his hat. "We'll go over to her house together in a few minutes. Just go upstairs and say hi to your Mama first, in case she's awake."

Dumbfounded, Armando asked, "Huh? You think it's safe for me to show my face around the McCormack's house after what he did to me?"

Henry gave a lighthearted shrug. "I'll be there. That jackass won't do nothin'. Don't let him scare ya. Me and him go way back. Trust me, it's better you show your face in person than do this over the phone." He walked around the desk and put his hand on his phone. "Go on upstairs, now. See if your Mama's awake. And take a shower. I can smell ya from here."

Armando asked, "Who are you calling? Dwayne?"

"Don't you worry about what I'm doin'. Just go on. Meet me outside at the truck in fifteen minutes." His eyes met Armando's. "I ain't gonna let him do nothin' to ya. Trust me."

Armando nodded and went to the shower.

Mama was still asleep when Armando checked on her. He wanted desperately to tell Ramon what was going on, but he could barely make sense of it himself. *What is Henry not telling me?* he wondered.

But as Armando changed clothes and walked outside to Henry's truck, he felt a little happier, realizing he would soon see Katie. She would make everything better. The trauma of the last five days. This new worry about Mama's health. In Katie's arms, his troubles always melted away. She made him feel like he was capable of anything. All the shit that didn't make sense wouldn't matter anymore. They would be together. Somehow.

Henry was wrong—she still wanted him. Armando was absolutely certain of it. Their love was stronger than whatever power her asshole father possessed. Even if Armando had to go through the last five days a million times, that's what he'd do if it meant making her his bride.

Ten minutes later, Henry's truck stopped in front of the McCormack's house. Henry asked, "Want me to go to the door with ya?"

Armando recognized Dwayne's vehicle in the driveway and assumed he was home. He stared at the front door and said, "Yeah," knowing Henry always carried a concealed handgun. But hopefully it wouldn't come to that.

Henry calmly replied, "You got it." Then they both opened their doors and headed to the house.

As soon as Armando rang the doorbell, the door opened. He quickly glanced down at himself to make sure he looked presentable for her. God, he missed her. His heart swelled with joyous anticipation, hoping Katie was the one behind that door.

And she was. She stood there in shorts and a tank top. As pretty as ever. But her eyes were red, like she'd been crying. She stared at Armando for at least five seconds before giving him a shy wave and saying, "Hi."

"Hi." Armando nervously cleared his throat. "Hi Katie. I've missed you. Can we sit down and talk?"

Her head immediately shook. "No." She choked back tears. "You have to go. I can't see you again."

"What?" Armando squinted, trying to look behind her to see if someone was around. "Did your dad threaten you? Did he punish you? Beat you?" He balled up his fists, ready for a fight. "Where is he?"

"No!" Katie held her hand out, as if pushing him away. "We can't see each other anymore. Just go away."

"I know your dad's putting you up to this. Where is he? If he hurt you I'll fuckin' kill him." He took one step toward her.

Lisa, Katie's mom, sidled up to her and put her arm around her daughter's waist. "Armando, you need to leave. Katie's made her choice. It was all her doin'. You kids are too young to know what you want." She sighed. "Now, I'm real sorry about everything that's happened to you, but we thought you needed some distance to reflect on things."

"Distance?" Armando grimaced. "Yeah, San Pedro. That's five hundred fuckin' miles of distance. That was to get me to *reflect*?"

Lisa smirked. "Don't you use that foul language with me." She glanced at Henry, then Armando. "You listen to Katie. She's telling you the truth." Lisa slowly backed away.

Katie nodded and wiped a tear from her cheek. "It's true. Please, just leave. I don't wanna see you anymore. I'm leaving tomorrow to go on a mission with my cousin's church. I'll be gone the rest of the summer." She sniffled. "And I already changed where I'm going to college in the fall. It was your idea to go to the University of Texas. I'm going somewhere else now."

Armando stared into her eyes, looking for a sign. Something to tell him she was lying for her parents' sake, like she had for so many months when they kept their relationship a secret.

But there was something different about her. Where there used to be a spark in her eyes, she was cold and distant. But why was she crying?

Armando said, "Katie, this doesn't make any sense. I love you. And I know you love me. They can't stop us forever."

"They didn't stop us," Katie said. "I did. It was *my* choice. I told you. I'm leaving town tomorrow."

"Where are you going?" he asked. "I'll come with you."

"No, Armando." Katie's voice softened as she wiped away more tears. "No. It's really over. We shouldn't get married so young. I'm sorry for everything you went through. But it's over." She paused for a moment, then added, "I don't think I ever really loved you."

Armando sucked his bottom lip into his mouth, then looked straight down at his feet. Before anyone could see him cry, he turned around, almost knocking Henry down as he bolted to the truck.

A minute later, Henry was driving them both back to the ranch, waiting for Armando to speak. But the boy was too upset. Instead, he slumped against the door, in so much pain that he fantasized about opening the truck door and sending himself tumbling to the ground where he could cut his head open against the hard ground.

However, his next thought was, with his recent bad luck, he'd probably live through it.

But hell. Nothing could be more painful than losing Katie. It hurt so bad he could barely see straight. The pain he felt when he woke up in the dirt yesterday was nothing compared to the agony in his heart right now. To hear her say she never really loved him...

If she never meant it, she sure was one hell of an actor.

Armando steeled himself, refusing to cry in front of Henry. He asked, "You knew about this all along, didn't you? That's why you offered to bring me yourself. You knew what was gonna happen."

With a slow sigh, Henry said, "I knew you had to hear it straight from her mouth."

Armando's voice was soft. "Do you think she really meant it?"

"Sounded like she did, to me." Henry shook his head. "Look boy, I know what you're thinkin'. Her daddy must've put her up to it. But it don't matter. It's over. She's leavin' town tomorrow. The best thing you can do is get on with your life. If she comes crawlin' back in a few months, well...whatever. But it sounds to me like she's gonna do whatever Daddy wants her to do."

Tears filled Armando's eyes but he blinked until they went away.

Henry continued. "And remember what I said. Don't tell your brothers or your mama about what happened. Let 'em think you got arrested and I bailed you out. No use gettin' everyone all worked up about takin' revenge on Dwayne McCormack. Trust me. He ain't nothin' to be scared of. And he can be real useful, sometimes."

"He could've killed me."

Henry huffed a breath out of the side of his mouth. "Nah. He was just sendin' you a message. Throwin' his weight around. He'd never kill nobody."

Armando sighed. "Whatever."

For the rest of the trip home, Armando sat with his eyes closed and his palm stuck to his forehead, trying to make sense of it all. Praying for a way to ease his sorrow. Her callous words repeated in his thoughts, hurting him more each time. Nothing in his life made sense anymore. And maybe nothing would ever make sense again.

When Armando got home, he went against Henry's admonition to keep the past five days under wraps. A furious Ramon received the same speech from Henry, encouraging him to keep it a secret.

Victor was dumbfounded to hear Armando's story, but after a few fruitless days of calling the authorities, the brothers turned their attention to their mother. She confessed to them that she was dying of liver cancer and she had known about it for a while. But by the time she found out, she was beyond treatment. All she wanted was to spend her remaining days surrounded by her precious boys, and that's what she did.

CHAPTER 3

Ten Years Later

"Katie?" Jennifer, a bubbly blond server, snapped her fingers and waved to get Katie's attention. "You busy? There's a man at the front who wants to rent the patio."

"I'll be there shortly." Katie was in the kitchen, discussing the evening special with the chef. Her official title was, "Events Coordinator," at Cortez Inn, a restaurant on the San Antonio Riverwalk. She had worked there for two years, and with the recent, abrupt departure of the restaurant's general manager, the employees now looked to her for guidance. Her title and pay had not officially changed—yet—but she was currently the restaurant's day manager. In addition to her new duties, she always had to attend to customers who wanted to reserve the restaurant for a party.

Jennifer giggled uncomfortably, knowing she was about to give Katie some bad news. "He wants it Friday evening."

Katie nodded a quick approval to the chef, then turned her attention to Jennifer, her eyes widening. "*This* Friday evening? Did you tell him we need more notice?"

"Yeah, but he's here from out of town. I didn't know what to say."

Katie started toward the front of the restaurant with Jennifer following along. "Did you get his name?"

"He told me but I forget. It was something Hispanic." Jennifer let out an unconcerned sigh and veered off to the main dining room. "Oh well. I think he's sitting at the bar. Good luck."

Katie rolled her eyes and kept going. It was the middle of the afternoon, the slowest time of the day. At least this customer hadn't shown up during the middle of the dinner rush.

She arrived at the bar area, seeing only empty chairs. She was just about to get the bartender's attention when out of the corner of her eye she saw a man hovering nearby, his back to her as he scanned the sparsely populated restaurant. She cleared her throat and turned in his direction. "Sir, may I—"

That's when he turned around.

Katie's pulse quickened and she forgot what she was saying. Dear Lord, the resemblance. Those warm brown eyes. She'd never forget those eyes. Victor was away in college when she dated Armando. They had never been formally introduced, but she knew him instantly.

He extended his hand, smiling as he walked up to her. "Hi. I'm—"

"You're Armando's brother." The words slipped past her lips as if they had a mind of their own.

He laughed for a moment, nodding. "Yeah. I hope that's a good thing. My name's Victor."

Katie gulped and reached numbly for his hand to shake it. "Katie. Katie McCormack."

"Nice to meet you." Victor met her eyes with a quizzical stare as he let go of her hand. "So, you know my brother well?"

"Oh." She felt her cheeks flush with embarrassment, aware that she had been gaping at him. *He doesn't even recognize my name?* The thought that maybe she wasn't important enough for Armando to mention to his older brother made her heart sink. "We were...uh... close...in high school. Senior year. You'd moved away by then. I haven't seen him in years. How's he doing?"

She nodded along as Victor caught her up on Armando's life, telling her what she already knew. Armando Barboza was not hard to find online. She knew he had done well for himself as a venture capitalist and he was currently living in Los Angeles. She did an occasional search for his name, finding a picture of him once in a while, attending events or having dinner with various celebrities. But those pictures were nothing like seeing Victor in person. They didn't look exactly the same, but there was no mistaking they were brothers.

Unlike Ramon. Katie scowled inside as she thought about him. She had seen Ramon in passing a few times since she moved back to the area after college. Maybe it was just the cold silence he always shot her way. Maybe that's why she didn't see Armando's face in Ramon's on those rare instances. She naturally assumed Ramon would hate her and her family forever.

Victor, on the other hand, seemed blissfully unaware of their sordid history. He paused, lifting his eyebrows as he proposed an innocent question. "He's single as far as I know."

"Oh." Katie flashed him a huge smile, caught off guard by her own relief at this bit of information. But she immediately shook her head and glanced down at her hand where a new engagement ring adorned her finger. "That's okay. I just got engaged."

"Oh. I'm sorry. I didn't mean to assume—"

"No, no, it's okay." Katie fidgeted mindlessly with a lock of her long red hair, feeling guilty about her giddiness. "It just happened a few weeks ago. He's a lawyer." She took a deep breath. "So, are you here to reserve the patio?"

"Yeah, hopefully. I tried another place but they were booked and they told me to check here."

Katie took another breath to steady herself, then motioned toward a table close by where they sat. Victor explained that he wanted to propose to his girlfriend, Cara, at sunset on the river. If it had been anyone else, Katie may have told him to go elsewhere with such short notice.

But when she handed her business card to Victor, she secretly hoped it would find its way to Armando. And she knew she shouldn't feel that way. Heck, what would she even say if he called? She had no idea. And as a result, she struggled to keep her mind on the conversation with Victor. Thankfully, all he wanted was a private dinner for two with some added romantic ambience. It would be easy to arrange.

Before Victor left, he gave Katie his private cell phone number and said, "Please, call me if something changes, even at the last minute."

"I will."

"Good. I appreciate you letting me do this on short notice. Do you want me to say hi to Armando for you?"

"Yes. Please," Katie said without missing a beat.

"Sure thing. It was Katie," he paused as if he was trying to remember, "McCormack, right?" Victor nodded and narrowed his eyes, reaching out to shake her hand.

She took his hand and said, "Yes."

His eyes lit up with a hint of familiarity. "It was nice meeting you, Katie."

"Likewise. Thanks." She watched him turn around and exit the restaurant.

Then she rushed off to the restroom to have a moment alone with her thoughts. They flooded her mind like a tidal wave. *Maybe Victor will mention me. If this Cara chick accepts his proposal, maybe I can get invited to the wedding and see Armando there. What would I say? What would he say?*

Oh crap…what would Mitch say?

She turned her wrist to see the brand new, two carat, pear-shaped diamond solitaire ring, twinkling brightly. Her beautiful engagement ring from Mitch. Two weeks earlier all she wanted to do was sit and gawk at the back of her hand as co-workers showered her with compliments. But now, she nearly forgot she was wearing it.

And then she looked at her watch. She had to get through the last hour of her workday without anyone noticing her mind was a milllion miles away.

Thirty minutes later, as Katie was lost in thought, rearranging chairs around a large, round table, she gasped at a sudden tap on her shoulder. "Ah!"

"Sorry. Didn't mean to scare you." Jennifer giggled nervously. "You seem pretty stressed out today."

"Oh." Katie drew in a massive breath and straightened her posture. "Sorry. I have a lot on my mind, I guess."

"I'm sure you do!" Jennifer nodded. "There were a million things we had to do for my sister's wedding last summer. You need to start preparing the guest list as soon as possible. Don't put it off. Also, make sure you register for gifts early, too, because some of your relatives may want to shower you with presents right away, the second you tell 'em you're engaged." Her eyes popped open wide, her words flowing faster. "Oh! And make sure you…"

As Jennifer wound down, her eyes darted thoughtfully around the room. "Hmm. I think that's about it for now. If I remember anything else I'll let you know."

"Thanks. I've helped out with so many weddings the past few years I feel like I already know it all. My little sister's wedding was so stressful. But it's good to have another perspective."

"You have a little sister?" Jennifer's eyebrows furrowed. "How old was she when she got married? Aren't you only, like, twenty?"

"No." Katie cleared her throat, thankful for the compliment. "I'm twenty-eight. My sister's twenty-five."

"Whoa." Jennifer's jaw dropped. "You're twenty-eight and you're just *now* getting married?"

Katie stammered. "Uh…"

"I'm sorry. I didn't mean to imply you were an old maid or anything. It's just that…" Jennifer mindlessly twirled a strand of her blond hair. "I don't know. I'm twenty-two and I think I'll probably kill myself if I hit twenty-five and I'm not engaged by then."

Katie rolled her eyes and went back to her task of moving chairs. "Wow. So much for the feminist movement…"

"Listen, I can only speak for *me*." She brought her hand to her chest. "And I wanna get married, for sure. I'm so sorry. I didn't mean to hurt your feelings. It's nothing to be ashamed of. And you know, my great Gram-Gram had this saying. 'Sometimes, the older the cow, the sweeter the milk.'" Then she smirked. "But Gram-Gram never touched a single cow in her life, so I don't know—"

"I was engaged once."

"Oh," Jennifer said, with quiet sympathy. "What happened? Was it one of those long engagements that broke up at the last minute? Took up most of your good years and then fizzled out?" She pouted. "It's so sad when that happens."

Katie sighed. "No. It was a long time ago." She took a deep breath, catching herself before accidentally spilling her guts to Jennifer. Katie was dying to talk to someone about what happened all those years ago. It was a secret outside of her immediate family.

Katie hadn't told anyone of the engagement, including her high school friends, for fear that one of them would open their big mouths and the secret would find its way back to her parents. Even the tiny bit of information she just shared with Jennifer nearly gave Katie chills as she thought about how angry her father was that day. And how adamant he was that they never speak of it again.

Katie continued. "Never mind. Was there a reason you came out here to find me?"

"Oh yeah, *that*." Jennifer giggled. "I get so distracted. Some other guy just showed up at the front, asking about renting the ballroom for a party—"

"And you're just *now* telling me? You left him standing there while we were talking?" Katie turned around and immediately began walking to the front.

Jennifer followed along. "He said it was no rush. Said he'd sit down at the bar to have a drink while he waits. Kinda reminds of that really cute guy who came in earlier to rent the patio."

Katie's heart raced. *Could it possibly be Armando? Somehow?* "Are you sure? Did you get his name?"

"Yeah, but I can't remember it now."

Katie groaned. *She's worthless.* "Okay. Let me just…" She squinted as the bar came into view. "Is it that guy in the white shirt?"

"Yeah."

"Oh." Even from the back, Katie could tell the guy was too old and too short to be Armando. *So much for getting my hopes up.*

"Like, he could totally pass for that guy's dad. I swear, he could," Jennifer said. "Oh, and remember, I'm leaving five minutes early today. So, I guess I'll see you tomorrow. Have a good night." Jennifer's face lit up with glee.

Ignoring her, Katie forced a smile and approached the stranger, shoving her disappointment and irritation aside.

After thirty minutes discussing catering options with the customer, Katie exited the back door of the restaurant, bound for her car. Finally, she was sufficiently distracted from her thoughts.

That is, until she fished through her purse for her keys, catching a glimpse of her shiny new engagement ring. It was nothing like the dainty little ring she used to wear on a chain around her neck when she was secretly engaged her senior year of high school. Katie chuckled as she thought about it. Funny how she wore that necklace for months and her parents never once asked where she got the ring or why she was wearing it. Mom later admitted she thought it was just one of those cheap rings from the flea market, and maybe all the girls were wearing them as necklaces. *If Mom only knew.* Katie treasured that little gold-plated ring with its single, tiny diamond chip. After much tearful begging, Daddy surprised Katie by letting her keep it. Even though it was now dark with tarnish, it was still proudly on display in her jewelry box like it belonged there.

Tears came to her eyes, and she fanned her face with her free hand in a sorry effort to dry them.

Is it normal to pine away after your high school sweetheart for ten years? What the heck's wrong with me?

Katie opened her car door and sat down, wishing there was someone she could call who may understand. Although there were at least ten girls in her contact list who would probably drop everything to give her a shoulder to cry on, that nagging fear was still there. The fear that kept her from telling even her closest friends about the boy she almost married. She shuddered to think about what Daddy could still be capable of. Surely nothing as bad as what she had always imagined.

Nonetheless, the Armando chapter in her life was forcibly closed long ago, and she knew she needed to accept it. They were kids back then. Stupid kids who thought they were ready for a lifelong commitment. Katie chuckled and wiped away the last of her tears as she considered how foolish it was to think of him as the same Armando she fell in love with ten whole years ago, at the tender age of eighteen. Ridiculous.

Push it out of your head, girl. Shake it off.

She took a deep breath and started the car, feeling a little relieved that Mitch was working late again tonight and she had the evening to herself.

And once again, the guilt crept in. She should want to spend time with her own fiance, right? But why was he the last person she wanted to see tonight?

Crap. Katie already knew why. And she couldn't wait to get home and type Armando's name into a search box.

* * * * *

She's getting married?" Armando grabbed his jacket. He held his phone to his ear, ready to run to the exit. "To whom?"

"What?" Victor asked. *"Is it the same girl? The one you were engaged to? I was too preoccupied to recognize her name at first."*

Armando pressed his lips together tightly, suppressing his sudden urge to scream. He also waved goodbye to his associates, trying not to make it obvious that he was suddenly leaving for reasons he wouldn't explain. It was the biggest Lakers basketball game of the season, and he was there entertaining a room full of clients in a private suite. Just another day at work for Armando. But after the news he just heard, work would have to take a back seat for a while. "Yeah. It's her."

"You sound a little frantic. Are you okay?"

"Did she mention me?" Armando's pace increased to a light jog outside the suite as he headed to his car.

"*I already told you. She knew who I was, immediately. Asked if I was your brother.*"

"That's all she said?"

"*She said to tell you 'hi.'*" Victor chuckled. "*So...you gonna tell me why it's such a big deal to you, now? After all this time?*"

"Do you know who she's marrying?"

"*No. Oh wait. He's a lawyer. I know that much. I don't remember what else she said.*"

Armando sighed. "Okay. You said she's working at Cortez Inn? Where's that?"

"*It's on the Riverwalk. Nice place.*"

"Why don't you propose to Cara at a nice spot somewhere on the ranch? Seems a lot more personal than a restaurant."

"*She'll suspect that, and I wanna surprise her. Besides, she's a city girl. I don't think she likes walking around in the country all that much.*"

"And Katie's helping you get the room set up? What, like flowers and candles or something?"

"*We'll have a private deck overlooking the river at sunset. Just us. Katie's an event coordinator, I think. She'll make sure everything's set up just right. Music, food. Flowers. You want me to tell her you said hi?*"

"No!" Armando cleared his throat. "I mean, no. Please. Don't say a word about me, okay?"

"*Uh...okay. Are you running? Sounds like you're breathing hard.*"

"Yeah. Hey, can I call you back tomorrow?"

"*Of course.*"

"And remember what I said. Don't breathe a word about me to Katie."

"I already told her you live in Los Angeles and—"

"That's fine. Just don't tell her we spoke. Talk to you soon." Armando hung up and put his phone in his pocket. As much as he wanted to talk to his older brother, he was already too distracted with the task at hand. First, he'd have to rearrange some meetings, or maybe hold them all via teleconference.

Two, he had to book a private jet.

And three, he'd have to figure out what exactly to do about Katie McCormack.

CHAPTER 4

Victor chuckled and walked into the the house, hearing silence on the other end of the phone after Armando abruptly hung up.

Armando was always the most introspective of the three brothers...and the most secretive. Katie McCormack was obviously still very special to Armando. Victor had never heard him react that way about a woman before.

He walked past the room where Isaac lay sound asleep. A big smile spread across Victor's face. The boy was usually awake until at least eight o'clock, but today was their second day at the ranch, and Ramon let Isaac wear himself out with small, routine chores. And even though Isaac was exhausted by the time it was over, he told Victor and Cara at dinner that he's a cowboy now, and tomorrow he needs to wear the right hat.

Just as Victor was about to ascend the stairs where the lovely Cara awaited him, he heard Ramon typing at the end of the hall. So he walked down to his brother's office for a little talk, stopping just inside the door. "Hey."

Ramon looked up from his computer. "Hey. Thought you were already down for the night."

"No. Just Isaac. I don't know what you put him through today but he's out like a light way before his usual bedtime."

Ramon chuckled. "No doubt. I turned him over to Silas, one of the ranch hands. He's great with kids. Said Isaac did a good job today. Need me to keep him busy tomorrow, too?"

Victor shrugged. "I don't think you could keep him away from helping, after all the fun he had today. Seems like he took to the animals, fast."

"Hmm." Ramon nodded, thoughtfully. "So, does that mean there's a chance my oldest brother might relocate his new little family soon? There's plenty of room here to build a house or two."

"Nah, you're getting ahead of me."

"No, I'm not. You're still proposing on Friday night, aren't you?"

"Shh!" Victor glanced over his shoulder to make sure Cara hadn't quietly wandered downstairs. "Not so loud. It's a surprise."

Ramon smirked. "You really think she doesn't suspect?"

"No. Not at all. I wanted it to be a surprise, and that's how it's gonna be." Victor's eyes narrowed as he pondered his conversation with the woman he met today. "Speaking of Friday..." He shut the door behind him and took a seat in front of Ramon's desk. "You remember Katie McCormack?"

Ramon winced. "Of course I do."

"I met her for the first time today. She works at the restaurant where I'm proposing to Cara. When I introduced myself, the very first thing she said to me was, 'You're Armando's brother.'"

Ramon snorted. "Yeah. She probably heard what she was missing out on."

"Maybe." Victor shrugged. "Armando had the weirdest reaction when I mentioned her name. It sounded like he left the basketball game and went running out to his car."

Ramon's eyes rolled. "Damn. I can't believe he's *still* hung up on that girl." Then he produced a big yawn.

As Victor watched his tired brother, he was thankful he decided to take an extended leave from work. Originally it was to spend more time with Cara and Isaac. But this week, after seeing how much Ramon worked and how little care he took of himself, Victor realized he needed to use that time to be a better brother to Ramon. It was obvious that since Henry Platt sold out of the ranch and took off for a long vacation, Ramon was in over his head, trying to keep the business going.

This was only Victor's second day on the ranch in Turnbrook. And already, he was more worried about his youngest brother than he wanted to show. But knowing Ramon and his pride, he'd probably tell Victor to pack up and leave if he knew how concerned he was.

Victor planned to keep his eyes open and watch out for Ramon. And after tonight's phone call, he wondered if he needed to do the same for Armando.

"So," Victor said, "You ever take any time off? You look exhausted. I've barely seen you since I got here."

"Yeah." Ramon nodded. "Saturday. I try to take the whole day off. Sunday's a different story. It's the one day I'm usually not bogged down in paperwork and I actually get to go out back and make sure the boys are doing their jobs when I'm not here."

Victor frowned. His brother was obviously much more overworked than he wanted to admit. "Well, let me know if I can help. It can't be easy running two other ranches in addition to this one. I don't know how you do it."

Ramon smirked. "A lot of coffee and reliable employees. That's how." Then he sighed. "I'll try to be home earlier from now on."

"Good. Again, if you need my help, please tell me. Especially with the business end of things. That's sorta one of my specialties, you know?"

Ramon cocked his head to the side. "I'm all right, Victor. Now go on upstairs and take care of your woman." He yawned again. "I gotta get a few things sorted out before I go to bed."

With a glum nod, Victor said, "Okay. Don't stay up too late," as he headed for the door.

Ramon responded with a half-hearted wave.

* * * * *

It was Thursday, the day after Katie met Victor, and her constant thoughts of Armando were still going strong. She had not seen her fiancé, Mitch, since dinner on Tuesday evening and she dreaded lunch with him and her parents today. Memories she locked away years ago now seemed fresh, in the front of her mind.

How could she possibly look Mitch in the eye when she was fantasizing about another man?

Katie sat at the bar at five minutes till noon, nursing a glass of ice water as she waited for them to arrive. All she really wanted to do was take the week off and stay in bed, pretending she was sick. And honestly, ever since her thoughts of Armando started, "sick" was exactly how she felt.

Sick that she spent more time thinking about Armando than she did Mitch. Sick that she had to face her father today and pretend—as she had for years—that Daddy was actually a nice guy. That he hadn't ripped her away from her first love without explaining why.

She sat at the bar, trying not to appear tense, when she heard her Dad and Mitch laughing, then felt her mom's hand on her shoulder.

"Katie." Her mom, Lisa, shook her gently. "Katie-bug. You all right?"

Katie took a deep breath then slowly swiveled around on the bar stool. "Uh-huh. Hi Mom."

Suspicious, Lisa gave her daughter a once-over. "Are you sure? You look like you're off in dream land. Better be careful sitting at the bar like this or they'll think you're slacking off at work."

"It's okay. I'm on lunch break and my boss knows how hard I work. It's fine."

Lisa shook her head as she took her daughter's arm, leading off to the table where Mitch and Dwayne were already sitting down. "No matter what, you always need to do your best. Especially if you become a senator's wife someday. The last thing you'll want are your old co-workers coming forward, saying you're lazy, making up rumors because of all the extra work they had to do on your account."

Katie sighed. "Mom, I put in more hours than anyone else here." Then she stopped talking, fearful that in her anxiety she would let out the wrong words slip and start an argument with her. *Appearances.* They were all her parents seemed to care about. Katie and her little sister, Chelsea, had always silently rolled their eyes at the constant admonitions. *People judge you by the company you keep. Do you think the First Lady of the United States of America would wear a skirt that short? Whatever you do, don't let anyone take your picture tonight.*

Katie's jaw tightened as she drew closer to the table where Daddy was still laughing with Mitch.

Mitch...perfect, educated, Daddy-approved...All these years, Katie knew that had to be why Daddy hated Armando. Dwayne McCormack wanted his two girls to marry men he could respect as if they were his own sons, and Armando didn't fit his idyllic mold.

Mitch was so into his conversation with Dwayne, he barely noticed Katie standing there. "Oh, hey honey."

Mitch and Dwayne both stood from their chairs long enough

to be courteous as their companions took seats. Dwayne went a step further and pulled out Lisa's chair for her. But Mitch simply leaned forward and gave Katie a peck on the cheek as she sat.

Katie said, "Hi hon," to Mitch, and with a weak grin said, "Hi Daddy," to Dwayne.

Dwayne, oblivious to his daughter's hesitance, put his elbows on the table and said to her, "Mitch here tells me you two been lookin' at houses already."

Katie shrugged, feeling defensive. "Yeah. What's the big deal?"

Dwayne sighed. "I wish you'd let me know. Our wedding gift to you's gonna be your down payment, just like we gave your sister when she got married."

Mitch patted Katie's hand. "Yeah. You should've said something." His eyebrows rose. "We may have a higher price range than we thought."

Katie stifled her groan. "Daddy, I told you I don't want that." She thought about her sister, Chelsea, and how often she complained that Daddy and Mom reminded her of that big down payment "gift." And Katie was in no mood to hold her tongue. "Daddy, I'll feel like I owe you for it for the rest of my life. Please, just keep your money."

Mitch scoffed. "Speak for yourself."

Then he and Dwayne burst into laughter.

Lisa spoke up from across the table. "Sweetie, it's only fair. We did it for Chelsea. We can do it for you, too. Unless you'd rather we spend that money on the wedding instead."

"No." Dwayne put his elbows on the table, leaning forward. "Now, I know girls always want a nice, big wedding, but after it's all said and done, it just ain't worth it." Dwayne grunted and looked at Mitch. "You wouldn't believe what I spent on her sister's wedding. If anything I should've put my foot down then and said we'd give her a bigger down payment on her house instead. That's the better way to do it. You can have a perfectly nice wedding for a lot less money without feeding half the county at the reception."

Katie said, "It's okay, Daddy. I don't want a big wedding like that. It was too much hassle."

Mitch nodded. "Yeah, we've talked about one of those getaway weddings. That's what my cousin in Tennessee did a few years ago. They were gonna have a big church wedding but after they added up what everything was gonna cost, they went to Cancun instead. Said it was less than half the price and they got a nice vacation out of it."

"Hmm," Dwayne said, with a thoughtful nod. "Sounds like a good idea after that fiasco with Chelsea's wedding." He sighed. "So much money. Seemed like I wrote checks for weeks. A deposit for this, a deposit for that."

Lisa smiled at her husband. "It's whatever Katie wants, dear. Let's just be glad..." Lisa glanced at Katie, then reached for her glass of water, opting not to finish her sentence.

But Katie knew that look on her mother's face. It was meant to inflict guilt for the years Katie had spent in college, using her inheritance from her grandmother to get three undergraduate degrees at three different colleges that she would probably never use. That's what Katie had been doing for most of her life since high school: learning. A perpetual student, her parents called her. And since then she had heard the speech a thousand times: "We're just glad you're finally out of college." Katie was sure the offer of a down payment on a house was about more than Dwayne keeping his daughters under his thumb. It was about helping them find a place to live so they would be more likely to raise their families nearby. Katie's final degree—in business administration—came from a private college four hours away in Fort Worth. Her parents were unhappy when Katie briefly considered staying in

Fort Worth for a man she was dating, but the relationship ended and she moved to San Antonio after graduation to work at the restaurant.

Katie looked at her mother. "Thanks. But I actually don't mind the idea of a getaway wedding. It's like you're already on your honeymoon when you get there."

Dwayne let out a sigh of relief and reached for his water. "Good. I wish Chelsea'd had the sense to do that."

Katie laughed as Mom rolled her eyes. Daddy could complain all he wanted, but Katie knew the wedding was mostly their idea, not Chelsea's. Appearances, appearances. Lavish wedding, big write-up in the tiny local "Turnbrook Times" newspaper. Politicians and friends of the family the girls had never heard of were invited. It was all for show.

Already angry, and growing tired of her father's complaints, Katie decided to test the waters. What would Daddy possibly say, in public? Especially in front of Mitch? She cleared her throat, then calmly said, "Well, if you think it makes sense to have one of those getaway weddings, forget about Cancun. You can go right over to New Mexico and get married, fast. They don't have a waiting period or anything. Just show up and get married."

Lisa glared at Katie.

Dwayne lifted one eyebrow at her then tilted his glass of water up to the ceiling as he took a sip.

Mitch turned to her. "You want that? I think I'd rather go to Cancun and stay in a resort."

Katie smiled. "Yeah. We'll have to look into it."

And then their server, Jennifer, bounded to the table, giving the group her familiar greeting. "Hey guys! You're getting to be regulars now, huh? Good to have you back."

Dwayne and Mitch both started talking to her at once, remarking about Jennifer wearing her hair in pigtails today, to which she giggled and flirted like she did with all the customers.

Lisa took her napkin from her lap and put it on the table as she rose from her seat. "I'm heading to the ladies' room. Katie? Care to join me?"

Katie knew she was about to be scolded. And she also knew her dad and fiance were too busy flirting harmlessly with Jennifer to notice they were leaving the table. She shrugged and stood. "Sure."

Katie and her mother walked along in silence to the restroom. When they got there, Katie crossed her arms over her chest and waited as Lisa looked under the stalls to make sure they were alone.

With her hands on her hips, Lisa faced Katie. "What do you think you were doing out there? Were you trying to be cute? Trying to upset your father after he's offered to pay for your wedding and give you a substantial down payment on a house?"

Katie's eyes and mouth both flew open. "What? All I did was mention New Mexico. It's not that big a deal. Seems like Daddy really wants to save money. Thought I'd help."

"Oh, you and that smart mouth." Lisa fumed. "We both know why you brought it up. It's been years since we kept you from making that mistake. And now you have a nice, respectable fiance and you wanna make a scene in front of him?"

"A scene? That's all you and Daddy care about, Mom. How things look to other people. God forbid I do anything to make you both look bad."

Lisa grabbed Katie's arm and gave her a stern stare. "We love you and we want the best for your future. That's all we've ever wanted. And you need to be a little more grateful." Lisa inched closer, narrowing her eyes. "If you were little I would've brought you in here and taken you over my knee for that little stunt out there."

Katie huffed and pulled away from her mother's grasp. "Well, I'm twenty-eight years old. I'm not a little girl and I don't appreciate being spoken to like one."

Through her gritted teeth, Lisa said, "No matter how mature you think you are I'll always be your mother and I'll speak to you however I please."

Katie felt her blood pressure rising as she grew angrier by the second. "Speaking of respectable, did you know Armando Barboza's a successful venture capitalist now? How's *that* for respectable?"

Lisa squared her shoulders. "Well, he probably wouldn't be if you'd run off and married him like you wanted. You were too young and stupid to know any better. You both probably would've dropped outta college because you'd have a bunch of babies you couldn't afford."

The door opened, and two women entered. Katie immediately exited the room with the intention of going directly back to the table when Lisa put her hand on her shoulder, stopping her just outside the door.

Quieting her voice to just above a whisper, Lisa said, "Katie, look, I know you'll never understand it but we've always just wanted what's best for you."

"No, Mom. You want what's best for *you*."

"No." Tears filled Lisa's eyes as she put her hands on Katie's shoulders. "No, that's not true. We love you and your sister more than anything in the world." She inhaled deeply and looked around the restaurant as though she were afraid her husband might hear from this far away. She continued, whispering, "If I really thought you would've been happy with that boy, I would've fought with Daddy to let you marry him. The last thing any mother wants to do is watch her baby girl's heart get broken."

Katie watched her mother, dumbfounded. She could count on one hand the number of times she had seen her well up with tears.

Lisa took in a deep breath, then smoothed her hands down the front of her dress before taking her daughter's shoulders again. "Please, Katie. It was a painful time for all of us. Even your father. We don't need to talk about it again, even in jest. You went on to get an education and now you're getting married. And it sounds like..." Her voice got even softer, as if she was afraid to speak his name, "the Barboza boy went on to better things, too. So please, just be grateful and let it go."

Katie's stomach went raw. Her mom's grave tone reminded her of that day all over again, the day Katie screamed until her voice was hoarse, asking where they were taking Armando. Getting few answers.

She stared into her mother's watery eyes for a few more seconds, then in silent agreement, they both turned and headed back to their table where Dwayne and Mitch were both looking over the menu.

The rest of the meal went on as if the conversation in the bathroom never took place. After they placed their orders, Dwayne got Mitch talking about some cases he was working on. Mitch was thirty-four. He had recently become the youngest partner at a respected San Antonio law firm.

As often as possible, Dwayne tried to encourage Mitch to think about running for district judge someday; it always gave Katie a twinge of anxiety. She was glad, on one hand, to find someone Daddy liked so much. It would certainly make her life easier. But on the other hand, she didn't want to marry a man who was anything like her father. In fact, when she first met Mitch at a bar a year earlier, she had to hide her disappointment that he was a lawyer. And she procrastinated about introducing Daddy and Mitch, afraid that Daddy would make too big of a deal out of it. And, of course, he did.

When lunch ended, Katie and Mitch walked Dwayne and Lisa to the restaurant's main entrance to say goodbye.

Dwayne adjusted his hat and said, "We should make this a regular thing. Every Thursday."

Katie forced herself to smile and nod, already dreading next Thursday. Then she looked at her watch. "Oh no. I have to get back to work." She waved goodbye to everyone and gave Mitch a quick peck on the lips, then turned around to head to the main dining room.

CHAPTER 5

Armando tilted the seat of his rented SUV back as far as it would go and kept his body still. Hopefully Katie hadn't seen him from the door of the restaurant. And now, he hoped like hell her parents wouldn't glance over and see him either.

No one could know the anger boiling inside him, directed at the man two cars over: Dwayne McCormack. The *honorable* judge. Armando snorted at the thought, amazed by how quickly his anger resurfaced just by seeing him today. That old asshole still wore a cowboy hat like a bad Texas cliche. His gut was a little paunchy now and he had a few more wrinkles. But no matter how much he aged, he would always be the same prick who tried to ruin Armando's life.

Tears came to Armando's eyes as he watched Mr. and Mrs. McCormack talking to each other in the car. It looked like casual chatter. Probably about something they discussed with Katie and her fucking fiance at lunch in that fancy restaurant. And now they were going about the rest of their sweet, perfect day as if they hadn't just driven past the guy they left for dead in the middle of nowhere ten years earlier.

Armando made a fist and hit the outside of his steering wheel. They were lucky it happened that summer Mama got sick. Lucky Armando had something else to occupy his sorrow over what they did to him. Otherwise...well, Armando was afraid to think about *otherwise*. Mama begged him to move on. She said no girl was worth going to prison. *Please, go on and make me proud, 'Mando. That kind of revenge will end up killing you.*

He could still hear her pleading voice in his thoughts.

Armando wiped his eyes and resolved to maintain his composure. *I'll go visit her grave site today. Mama, if you can hear me, please forgive me for these evil thoughts. I'd do anything to make you proud.*

Just as he was about to put the car in reverse to leave the parking lot, Armando caught a glimpse in his peripheral vision. Mitch. The tall, geeky white boy that he had just seen with Katie moments earlier at the entrance of the restaurant. Mitch left the restaurant without Katie, but with a big smile spread across his idiot face. He headed toward the back of the parking lot, oblivious to Armando's scowl.

Hmm...is it just me or does that guy look like a weasel? No. A snake. Like one of those garter snakes we used to find on the ranch. Or maybe a rat...

Oh well. At least Daddy approves of him, right Katie? Armando snarled to himself, but he couldn't take his eyes off of Mitch, who was now in his rear-view mirror.

In a moment of clarity, Armando looked away. *It was ten years ago. You're a grown man now. You're successful. It doesn't matter what any of these people think of you.*

Logically, he knew how immature his thoughts sounded, but Armando couldn't keep his eyes off of that rear-view mirror, and from fantasizing about how fast his fist could knock the smile off of Mitch's face.

Armando cracked his knuckles, took a deep breath, then reached for the gear shift when his peripheral vision caught something new. His breath hitched. At the restaurant's entrance Armando spotted a young woman with her hair in pigtails, waving excitedly as she held the door open. She was on her cell phone, waving at someone in the back of the parking lot.

Wait. Waving at...Mitch?

Armando glanced up at the rearview mirror to see Mitch holding a phone to his ear, happily returning the blonde's wave.

Armando's jaw dropped. *Is he cheating on Katie?* He sat there for a little while, stunned, but quickly shook it off. Maybe they were just friends. Hell, even if he was cheating, what would Armando do with that information? Run inside the restaurant and tell Katie? Maybe he should hire someone to follow Mitch around to find out for sure.

But even if he had a chance with Katie again, Armando didn't want to win her back that way. He wanted Katie to choose him. Wanted her to go against her big, bad father for once, and not because she was heartbroken and on the rebound.

But shit, why would she do that? Armando let his forehead hit the steering wheel. *How do I know she'd even want me? And how do I know I'd want* her?

He felt like such a fool, canceling everything and rushing here from Los Angeles because his high school sweetheart was getting married. Nobody would ever understand. Not his brothers, not his friends.

And certainly not Katie.

Armando took a deep breath and sat up straight. He didn't look at Mitch in the rear-view mirror this time. He simply pulled his car out of the parking lot and headed down the street in the direction of Turnbrook, the small town thirty minutes away where he spent his teenage years. The town where he fell in love with Katie, and where his dear Mama was buried.

And he had to pray his brothers wouldn't see him on the way

to the cemetery; it was only a few miles away from the ranch. He was in no mood to explain to either of them why he had been in the area for days without telling them. No way they would ever let him live it down.

* * * * *

"Okay, sweetie," Cara said to Isaac. "Let's try again if you want. You almost had it."

Isaac puffed out his bottom lip and let his fork drop to his empty plate. His eyes went around the dinner table, to Ramon, then Victor, then to Cara. "Okay."

The three adults shared a look, then Cara spoke, clearly enunciating Ramon's name. "Ruh-moan. Try it. Ruh…" She widened her eyes at Isaac, waiting.

Isaac glanced across the dinner table at Ramon, then looked down at his lap, shyly. His voice was soft. "Wuh-moan…Wuh…"

Ramon smiled. "Hey Isaac. Try this. Put your teeth against your lips when you say it. Rrrr…Ruh…"

Isaac let out a determined sigh, gnashing his teeth in frustration. "Wuh…Wuh…"

Sensing Isaac had probably had enough of this, Victor stood and walked around the large table to take the empty seat beside him. "It's okay, buddy. You're doin' good." He patted Isaac's shoulder.

Isaac exhaled with great relief.

And then an idea occurred to Victor. It was a perfect time to sneak outside with Isaac for a little talk. "Hey, I know what'll make you feel better. There's a pond I'll bet you haven't seen yet."

"A pond?" Isaac asked.

"Uh…" Ramon winced. "It's been really dry lately. It's more like a big mud puddle right now. I need to get someone out here to take care of it."

"That's okay," Victor said. "I think he'll like it. Come on, let's go." He glanced at Cara, lifting one eyebrow as if asking her permission; she quickly nodded.

Victor was thrilled when nobody offered to tag along.

Isaac smiled and immediately followed him outside.

As they walked along through the field next to the house, Victor asked, "So, you like it here in Texas?"

"Yes," Isaac answered, matter-of-fact.

"Are you sure it's not too hot for you?"

Isaac shrugged. "I don't know. It's weawy hot but it's okay. I wike the animaws."

"I like the animals too."

They walked on as Isaac began a story about a cow named Becky he met today when he was "helping" Silas again.

What Isaac didn't know was that Mommy was always watching him as he "helped" on the ranch. Sometimes she would hang back out of sight, ducking into a corner just far enough away to be unnoticed. Other times, she was in the house, watching him over a surveillance monitor. She and Victor had already talked about how much Isaac was enjoying himself here. And Victor knew it was a long shot, but he had just begun to wonder if maybe he could talk her into moving. Even though he hadn't lived here in years, this ranch was home to Victor. And if he were to retire early as a bachelor, that was definitely the place he wanted to move to spend the majority of his time. But hopefully he wouldn't be a bachelor for long. The decision to retire and move was one he hoped to make with his wife in the not-too-distant future.

When they arrived at the pond, Victor took a seat on a big rock and said, "You and I need to have a talk."

Isaac scowled at the pond. "I don't think that's a pond."

"Well, it used to be."

"Wed the pond go?"

Victor chuckled. "It evaporated. Ramon will probably get it filled with water again soon. He'll put some ducks out here—"

"No! Ducks aw scawy. I got chased by a duck at the zoo." Fear clouded Isaac's eyes. "I had some food in my hand to feed him and he stawted wunning at me and—"

"Okay, no ducks. I'm sorry. I didn't know that happened to you. It sounds terrible." Victor would usually love to listen to one of Isaac's stories but today he had his own agenda, and he wanted to make sure they got down to business, quickly. "Listen, buddy. We need to have a talk." He gave Isaac a stern look. "Man to man."

Isaac smiled and sat beside Victor on a smaller rock. "Okay. Man to man."

Victor took a deep breath and looked in his eyes, now realizing he had no idea how to broach this subject with a small child. But he had to try. "First, this is a secret. You can't tell anyone about this, okay? Especially not Mommy."

"Hmm." Isaac's lips pressed together, thoughtfully. "I'm not s'posed to have secwets. That's what Mommy and Gwammah say."

"It's only for a couple days. Then you can tell Mommy. It's a good secret, I promise."

"I don't know…"

"No, really. You can tell Mommy soon." Victor hesitated as he thought of a way to change his terminology and ease the situation. "Actually, it's not really a secret. It's a surprise. A big surprise. For Mommy."

"Oh! Wike a buthday pawty? With cake?"

Victor nodded. "Something like that." He hesitated. *This seemed like a much better idea in my head.* Still, he pressed on. He wouldn't feel right proposing to Cara without first talking it over with the most important guy in her life, even if it put his surprise proposal at risk. He placed a gentle hand on Isaac's back. "I want to marry your Mommy. Do you know what that means?"

Isaac's eyebrows knitted tightly. "Huh?"

Victor sighed. He could already imagine Isaac asking Cara all about it when they went back to the house. He took a deep breath. "Okay. Let me think. You remember last month when Grandma married Tom?"

"Yes. I had to walk in fwont of people. I don't wike that."

"That's fine. You don't have to do that again." Victor paused to think of a way to rephrase his request once again. "Okay, forget I said that. How would you feel if I was with you and Mommy for a long, long time? Like, for the rest of our lives. Would that be okay with you?"

"Oh!" He gasped with a sudden realization. "Okay. You mean I could have a baby bwothow?"

Stunned by the question, Victor stared in Isaac's eyes before answering. "Yeah. Maybe. If that's what your mom wants. Or maybe a sister—"

"No!" Isaac's head shook. "A bwothow!"

"Why a brother?"

"Because *you* have a bwothow. You cawed him 'baby bwothow.'" Isaac's face set smugly. "So I need a baby bwothow, too."

Victor laughed. "Yes. I have two brothers."

"Two?"

"Uh-huh. You already know Ramon who lives here at the ranch. But I have another brother named Armando and you haven't met him yet."

"Aw!" Isaac's lifted his hands dramatically. "I heawd of him. Okay. So I need *two* bwothows."

Victor put his elbows on his knees and hung his head in his hands, chuckling. "You don't *need* two brothers."

"Yes. I need two." He put a hand on Victor's arm. "Pwease?"

Victor tried his best to rein in his surprise as he gazed at Isaac's pleading face. "Well, buddy, I need to talk to your mommy about it first but—"

"Can I have one bwothow for my buthday?"

"Your birthday? Six weeks from now?"

Isaac nodded frantically, his eyes wide.

"Uh..." Victor stammered as a flurry of thoughts ran through his mind. *How in the world do I answer this question?* Then he had an idea. "Isaac, I wish I could help you but it's gonna take more time to give you a brother. But how about next year for your fifth birthday instead?"

"I don't know. I want—"

Victor interrupted Isaac, fearing the young boy would ask too many questions. The last thing he wanted was to turn this into a discussion of where babies come from. "For your birthday next month I'll get you a race car instead, okay? One small enough for you to drive, with big wheels. And we can come here to the ranch sometime and you can drive it all through the fields. Just don't take it around back to the animals because they'll get scared."

Isaac gasped. "Can I have a wace caw *and* a baby bwothow?"

"No." Victor ruffled the hair on the back of Isaac's head. "I'm sorry. You can have a race car this year and maybe a baby brother next year. That's the best I can do." *Oh shit, how am I going to explain either of these requests to Cara?*

Sadly, Isaac sighed and looked out at the muddy hole where the pond once was. Then his face suddenly lit up. "A wace caw, huh?"

"Yep. A car of your very own." Victor winced as he thought a little more about how wrong it was to make this promise before discussing it with Cara. And how stupid he was to try to have this conversation with Isaac in the first place. "Now, you have to promise me you won't go back to the house tonight and tell Mommy what we talked about. But you can tell her all about it in a few days, okay?"

"It's a supwise fuh Mommy." Isaac grinned. "Wight?"

"Yes. A surprise for Mommy." Victor let out a long, quiet sigh, doubtful that Isaac would keep anything secret for long. But at least Victor hadn't mentioned any of his specific plans. "Come on, let's go back to the house. It's time for dessert."

"*Ooh*!" Isaac hopped up and started toward the house as Victor followed along.

On the way there, Victor asked Isaac more about his day at the ranch and all the animals he had met. Hopefully he could distract Isaac enough to make him forget all about their talk.

For the rest of the evening, Victor was able to successfully divert Isaac's attention. All he had to do was get the boy talking about something else, or walking around the ranch with him and Ramon while Cara stayed inside and made some phone calls. The next day, Victor knew he would have to distract Isaac during breakfast, but after that, Isaac would be running around the ranch most of the day. And at dinner time, Victor's plans were to whisk Cara away for a romantic evening alone.

All things considered, Victor felt like the secret of his proposal was intact. That night he lay in bed with the covers turned down, waiting for Cara to come upstairs after tucking Isaac in for the night.

Victor smiled and propped himself up on his arm when Cara entered the room. "What happened? Was he already asleep, like last night? He really wears himself out during the day."

"No." Cara squinted in confusion as she took off her robe and draped it over the back of a chair. Wearing only a short, silky nightgown, she slipped under the covers beside Victor. "He was really sleepy but he was still awake. And he said the strangest thing."

Oh no, Victor thought. "What was it?"

"He said he's gonna name his baby brother 'Texas,' and call him 'Tex' for short." Cara chuckled. "I guess he really likes it here in Texas." She sat up, giving Victor a serious stare. "Do you know where he got the idea that he has a baby brother in his future? When I asked him about it, he just yawned and said, 'it's a surprise,' and then he said 'good night.'"

Victor laughed as he reached over to the night stand to turn off the light. "A baby named 'Tex.' Sounds like the star of one of those old western movies. Where's he come up with this stuff?"

"I don't know. He never said anything to me about a brother before. It must have to do with meeting Ramon. Maybe he thinks he needs a brother because *you* have a brother."

"Yeah, that's probably it." Victor put one arm around her shoulders and drew her to his side. "So, what about you?" Victor thought back to that day months earlier when he asked her if she thought about having more children. Her response had been hesitant. He decided not to ask again for a while. But now that he was about to present her with an engagement ring, he hoped it would be a good time to bring it up again. "What do you think about giving him a baby brother?"

Cara sighed. "Why not a sister? It's not like there's a way to choose which one you get."

"Ah." He kissed her cheek. "So you *have* thought about it."

She let out a shy giggle. "Maybe just a little. I told you before. It all depends on...you know...the future..."

"Yeah. I know. And I want you to make no mistake about my feelings. I'm in love with you, *querida*." He kissed her cheek again, then her ear, where he stopped to whisper, "And maybe we should take our chances tonight and see what happens."

Before Cara could process what he said, his mouth went down to her neck, nibbling her in that spot he knew would drive her wild. "Oh...Victor...yes..." She let him ease her onto her back, enjoying the sensation of his lips and tongue as his hand went up the bottom of her nightgown.

"I love you so much, Cara." He whispered in between kisses.

"I love you too."

Cara turned toward him, kissing him, her hands wandering all over him. Stopping at his underwear, tugging them down.

Victor broke away from her kiss with a deep moan. Usually he took his time and truly made love to her, but she was more aggressive than usual tonight. And Victor loved it. He moaned once again in response to the movement of her hand, then whispered, "Does this mean you like that baby idea?"

Cara let out a nervous giggle. In a soft voice, she said, "Maybe."

"Mmm." He grinned. "Yeah, I think you do."

And then Victor kissed her as he reached for the bottom of her nightgown to pull it off.

Soon, they were both naked. Victor pulled Cara across his lap, grateful that his eyes had adjusted to the darkness enough to look in her eyes as her body descended on top of him.

"*Ooh*. Yes," he whispered. It was his first time inside her without a condom. Victor was turned on not only by the physical sensation, but by the knowledge that their intimacy tonight was in the hopes of getting her pregnant.

As they went on a while longer, Victor grabbed her hips, moving her faster.

Cara flashed him a big smile, and Victor sensed she enjoyed the idea of having his baby much more than she originally let on. She grabbed his shoulders and threw her head back as he worked himself deeper inside her.

He held, moving her body faster and faster, then surprised her by lifting her away from him and easing her onto her back.

She smiled up at him as he hovered over her. Then he leaned down to give her a kiss as he entered her once again.

Victor broke the kiss and moved faster, unable to restrain his desire for her. He gazed down at the woman he loved, knowing she loved him, too.

She moaned his name as her head thrashed on the pillow.

He sensed a new closeness between them. A new passion. Like something had finally broken free in Cara, and she was truly letting him in for the very first time.

Victor couldn't stop his body's reaction. He called out her name as he released, and he heard her yelling his name, too.

As soon as he collapsed in a heap beside her, he said, "I hope nobody heard that downstairs."

Cara sighed. "Too late now if they did."

He took a few shallow breaths and said, "I love you."

"I love you, too."

CHAPTER 6

"Are you sure I'm not overdressed?" Cara asked as she watched a group of casually dressed people cross the street. She and Victor were stopped at a red light a few blocks from their destination on the Riverwalk in San Antonio. "I feel overdressed." She wore a navy blue cocktail dress that skimmed her knees. Adorning her neck was a sparkling diamond necklace—a present from Victor earlier that evening.

Victor smiled and reached across the front seat to give her knee a reassuring squeeze. "You're not overdressed. I'm taking you someplace where you'll fit right in." He waited until she looked over and their eyes met. "You look absolutely stunning tonight."

Her voice softened as a shy grin passed across her lips. "Thank you."

He held her gaze for another second before turning his attention to the road. The light turned green a moment later, and Victor realized his knee was bouncing just a little. Hopefully she couldn't sense his nervous excitement.

As they accelerated through the intersection, Victor took notice of his surroundings to try to calm himself down. Some of the names had changed, but the area looked the same as he remembered. It was such a treat to come here with his brothers and Mama, especially the hot summer nights when she would bring them here for ice cream. Three rambunctious adolescent boys, oblivious to those romantic surroundings...until they grew up a little. One night when Victor was fourteen, he saw a man propose to a woman in a small cafe along the river. All of the patrons eating there clapped and cheered when they saw her squeal, "Yes!" He remembered Mama's eyes welling up as she watched. If he hadn't been around his ornery brothers, he may have asked how their father proposed to her. Mama was always secretive about him, reluctant to volunteer information unless they wore her down with questions.

But Victor remembered that night in vivid detail. And he knew, if he ever found that special woman, he would bring her here to propose if he could. And he wanted to, with Alexis. He was disappointed when she refused to take the trip. Something about the high humidity making her hair frizzy. Tonight, Victor was thankful he hadn't brought that woman here. Instead, this would be a special place where he would propose to the one, true love of his life: Cara.

Victor took a deep breath when he caught a clear view of their destination. "Here it is. At the end of the block."

"It's a hotel?"

"Yes, but the restaurant has a separate entrance. We'll be on the upstairs patio, overlooking the river." Victor slowed down and pulled off the street as a parking attendant approached.

A few moments later, after handing off his keys, Victor was holding Cara's hand and stepping up on the curb when he put his other hand in his pocket and let out an abrupt, "Shit!" He couldn't feel the tiny box that held the engagement ring.

Cara stopped walking, her eyes widening. "What's wrong?"

"Uh..." He turned fully around to see the Mercedes he borrowed from Ramon heading onto the street. He gritted his teeth. "Damn it. I left something...uh...my wallet." He cleared his throat. "Can't very well pay for dinner without that, can I?" He smiled and tried to appear calm as he scanned the pavement to see if the ring had fallen out of his pocket.

A second attendant approached. "Is everything all right, sir? Did I hear you say you left your wallet in your car? We can look for it if you want to go on inside and—"

"No," Victor said. "No, please. I insist. Just tell me where it's being parked and I'll run and get it myself."

Cara said, "I'll come with you."

The attendant shook his head. "That's not necessary, sir. I can send him a message right now and have him bring the car back around."

"No...uh..." He squinted at the parking lot across the street. "You park the cars right over there?" He had to think of a way to keep both the helpful valets and Cara from finding out about the ring, which was probably wedged somewhere below the driver's seat after falling out of his pocket. *Think fast...think...you're usually so good at this...* He kept his eyes on the parking lot, afraid to turn around and let Cara see his anxiety. All he wanted was to give her a perfect, romantic evening, and he refused to let his stupid mistake ruin his big secret.

As Victor wiped his sweaty palm down the front of his suit, he gasped, then chuckled as a wave of relief washed over him. The ring was there all along. He had completely forgotten about moving it to his coat pocket at the very last minute, before they left the house. *This woman has no idea how flustered she makes me.* His usual calm, logical reasoning evaded him tonight, replaced by anxiety-ridden forgetfulness.

"Sir?" The parking attendant asked. "Are you sure there's nothing we can do to help?"

Victor was just about to answer when his eyes caught something in the parking lot. A man behind the wheel of an SUV in the front row, only a few spaces from where Victor's borrowed car was now parked. The man had been staring at Victor, but now his head was turned the other way and his hand covered the side of his face as if he were trying to hide himself from view. A man with a familiar silhouette. *Is that...? No, it couldn't be...*

Again, the attendant asked, "Sir?"

Cara grabbed his arm. "Victor? You okay?"

"Um..." Victor let out a concerned sigh, then said, "*Querida*, will you please wait for me in the lobby of the hotel? I just remembered something." He cut her off as she opened her mouth to protest. "I promise I'll explain later. Please, darling." He cupped both of his hands around one of hers. "Just relax in the lobby for a moment. I'll come get you and escort you into the restaurant. I'll only be a few minutes."

"Uh." Cara's eyebrows furrowed. "Sure, I guess?"

Victor leaned forward to give her cheek a quick peck. "I can see I'm confusing you. I just want us to have a special evening tonight. It'll make sense later." He nodded to the attendant. "Could you please see her inside the hotel lobby for me?"

The attendant nodded and stepped forward. "Absolutely, sir. Right this way, ma'am."

Victor waited until their backs were turned before rolling his eyes in frustration. This evening was carefully planned to go off without a hitch, and now it seemed to be falling apart. He turned toward the parking lot and broke into a sprint, heading toward the blue SUV on the front row. The man inside was still turned away from him, covering his face, but Victor would know him anywhere.

Victor knocked on the window. "Armando!" *Knock, knock, knock.* "Armando! What are you doing here?"

Armando grunted, then muttered, "Shit," before turning to face his brother. When their eyes met, Armando took a deep breath, hesitantly opened his door, and stepped out.

In momentary disbelief, Victor looked him up and down before pulling him into a quick embrace. Then he stepped back, his hands on Armando's shoulders. This was the first time he had seen him in nearly a year. Armando was dressed nicely in a crisp Armani suit, similar to the one Victor wore. From first glance, Armando appeared normal. But his expression was sobering. The color had drained from his face, and there were deep bags under his eyes. Victor shook him a little, staring at him with concern. "What the hell, man? Did you come here the other night after I told you I met Katie? It sounded like you ran out to your car when we were on the phone."

Armando's voice was scratchy from not speaking in several hours. "You weren't supposed to see me."

"Well, I'm glad I did. You look terrible. Tell me what's goin' on." Victor gave his arm a soft smack. "Come on. You're worrying me."

"Damn it." Armando cleared his throat. "Just go back and pretend you didn't see me. You're gonna propose to Cara in there, right?"

"Yes, but we're a little early." Victor turned his wrist to see the time. "I got exactly five minutes before my reservation officially starts. Seriously, talk to me. I'm worried."

"I'm sorry. I didn't mean to derail your plans. Guess I should've hidden myself a little better. Come on inside." Armando opened his door and sat down.

Victor instantly rushed around to the other side of the car and slid into the front passenger seat. He waited for Armando to continue, but instead, his brother stared straight ahead with a blank look. Victor said, "Please start talking. I'll be distracted and worried about you the rest of the evening unless you tell me what's wrong."

In a weak voice, Armando said, "It's hard to explain."

"I can see that." Victor waited as Armando hesitated once again. "Why don't you start with how long you've been here?"

"You mean, in the parking lot?"

"That too, I guess. But I meant, when did you leave L.A.?"

In a flat tone, Armando said, "I got here yesterday morning. The day after you called."

Victor's jaw dropped. "And you didn't tell anyone? You should've come to the ranch."

"No." Armando gave him a quick glance. "I haven't figured out what I'm gonna do yet."

"When are you going back to L.A.?"

"No idea."

"Okay, then. Come out to the ranch tomorrow. You can finally meet the woman who'll hopefully be my fiancee after tonight." Victor chuckled. "And you can explain to me why you're so worked up about this Katie girl."

Armando gritted his teeth and hit the steering wheel with his palm. "Shit! See, that's why I didn't wanna tell you about it. I knew you wouldn't understand."

Victor softened his voice. "Sorry, man. Didn't mean to upset you. Did you come here to talk to her? You want her back?"

Armando groaned. "Haven't spoken to her yet."

"Want me to talk to her for you? Tell her you're here?" Victor watched as thoughts quietly passed across Armando's face. He had never seen him like this before. "Maybe she wants to talk to you, too."

"No. I need to do this myself." Armando faced Victor. "I really wish you hadn't seen me out here. I don't want your help. I'll be just fine. Go on back to the restaurant and propose to your girlfriend. Please."

"Okay. But promise me you'll come out to the ranch tomorrow, for lunch."

"I don't know…"

"Come on. I want you to meet Cara and Isaac." Victor narrowed his eyes at Armando and gave his arm a playful slap. "Don't make me track you down and drag you out there myself."

"All right." With a light shrug, Armando added, "I'll be there tomorrow."

"Good. Where've you been staying?"

With reluctance, Armando casually gestured toward the hotel across the street.

Victor nodded. "I hope you'll think about staying at the ranch instead. It's been too long since I had my two brothers with me under one roof."

Armando nearly grinned. "I know. I'll think about it."

"Good." Victor peered thoughtfully in his brother's eyes. "Let me know if I can do anything to help. But I should leave now before Cara thinks I forgot about her."

"Okay. Good luck tonight."

Victor gave Armando one last slap on the shoulder, then exited the car and headed across the street.

* * * * *

Cara sat in the hotel lobby, her eyes fixed on the entrance. What in the world was taking Victor so long? He had been acting a little strange for days, but she chalked it up to being back on his home turf for the first time in a while. San Antonio had more of a city feel, but the small town of Turnbrook—where the ranch was located—felt much slower and more laid back. Cara had lived in urban areas like Chicago and Newark for most of her life, and if she felt like a fish out of water, she imagined Victor might feel the same way.

But there was something different in the air tonight. Victor had presented her with a brand new diamond necklace and helped her pick out the dress she was wearing. He was always full of surprises, never telling her where they were going until they got there. Maybe it would all make sense once they entered the restaurant.

Cara was just about to go outside and look for him when finally, he appeared outside the glass door and pushed his way in. She instantly grabbed her purse and stood. *Oh, he's so gorgeous in that suit. Heck, he's gorgeous in anything, or nothing at all. How did I get so lucky?*

Victor rushed to her, taking her hand and kissing it. "I'm so sorry, *amor*. I didn't mean to keep you waiting."

"It's okay." Smiling, Cara tucked a lock of her blond hair behind her ear. "I'm glad you're here now. I already missed you."

He slid his arms around her. "I missed you too." Softly, he kissed her lips then pulled back, smiling. "I was afraid you'd grow impatient and ask for our table without me. But I'm so glad you didn't. I love to make an entrance with you."

Cara felt a warmth rush to her cheeks as she took his hand. No matter how often he complimented her, there were times when his sweet words made her feel like she was blushing from head to toe.

Victor escorted her to the hostess, who led them through a crowded room to a small set of wooden stairs. When they reached the top, Cara gasped at the beautiful room.

"Wow." She brought her hand to her chest. "What's this?"

The hostess smiled and quickly exited the room as Cara took inventory of her surroundings. The room was dimly lit, with candles placed strategically amidst large, bright bouquets of flowers. To their right the room opened to a patio, where there was a cozy table for two.

With his arm around her waist, Victor guided her to the patio. He asked, "Isn't it lovely?"

"Yes." Cara gazed out at the river below. She heard the hum of mingling voices as people dined at nearby restaurants along the Riverwalk at sunset, but she felt as though she and Victor had their own private island away from everyone. "Is it just us?"

"Yes." Victor motioned toward the small table. "Care for some champagne?"

"Oh." She had been too distracted by her surroundings to notice the bottle of chilled champagne on the table. "Yes."

Victor poured each of them a glass as the soft sound of an acoustic guitar filled the room, emanating both from within the building and from outside. Victor informed Cara that there was live music downstairs. He left the glasses on the table and put his hands on her waist, pulling her into a rhythmic dance. Her hips instinctively matched his movements. She giggled when his hands moved down her body, and she looked shyly around the room to make sure they were still alone.

"What is it, *querida*?" Victor pressed his forehead to hers.

"I didn't know you could move like this."

He smiled. "Well, now you know." Then he bent his head down to give her a passionate kiss as they danced.

When the song finished, he kissed her again then scanned the room behind her, his face tightening.

"What's wrong?" she asked. "Is something wrong?" She looked behind her at the candles and flowers, noticing they were still alone. "Shouldn't there be a waiter by now? Do they know we're up here?"

"You're so sweet. Everything's fine. They know we're here."

"Well, what's going on?" Her eyes widened, concerned. "Are you sure they didn't forget about us?"

A deep, happy laugh escaped Victor's throat but he instantly forced himself calm. He looked deep into her eyes as he stroked the side of her face. "Cara. My darling Cara. Everything's fine." He took a deep breath and reached down, each of his hands taking one of hers. "I just wanted you to have a lovely evening."

"I am."

"Good." He held her gaze. "And I hope you'll always know how sorry I am for how our relationship began. Taking advantage of you so intimately, so quickly..."

Confused, Cara shook her head. "It's okay. You know that by now."

"But I need to make sure. I want you to know I truly enjoy your company. I appreciate you for everything you are. It's been my intention to move slower since then and show you how I really feel about you. It's not superficial. It's real. You're the most wonderful woman I've ever known."

Cara blinked against tears that formed at the sound of his unexpected sincerity. And suddenly, she had an inkling about why he had brought her here tonight but she dare not let herself think it just yet.

Victor continued. "You've made my life infinitely better in ways I didn't know were possible before you. Each day is special with you. You're the woman I imagine myself waking up to every morning. I hope to still wake up to you for years to come. I love you and I intend to spend the rest of my life with you." He reached into his suit pocket. "If you'll let me."

And suddenly, he knelt down. Cara's hands lifted to cover her gaping mouth.

"Cara, my darling Cara." He pulled a tiny red box out of his pocket and opened it, exposing the ring. "Will you please be my wife?"

With tears trickling slowly down her cheeks, she put her hands down and took a deep breath to whisper, "Yes."

Victor instantly jumped to his feet to kiss her.

Cara threw her arms around him, her mind and body tingling with bliss.

When he pulled away, Victor said, "I'm sorry. I planned to put the ring on your finger before I kissed you but I got excited."

Cara laughed and wiped tears from her cheeks as Victor took the ring from the box, then reached for her hand. "It's okay."

He slowly worked the ring down her finger. "I think it's too big. We'll get it sized. Hell, we'll get you another ring if you don't like this one."

"No." She held out her hand to look at it. "No, it's the most beautiful ring I've ever seen."

"Great." Victor let out a big sigh. "But honestly, if you change your mind—"

"No." She smiled at him, shaking her head. "I love it, I promise."

"I'm so glad." He took her face in his hands. "You've made me so happy, Cara. I swear I'm the happiest man in the world right now."

"Wow." Her voice was soft. She could barely speak. "I don't know what to say."

"You already said yes." He touched her lips. "You don't need to say anything else."

CHAPTER 7

Katie watched from the shadows, waiting until she saw Victor get down on one knee to propose. It was her cue to leave the room and send a waiter to take their orders in ten minutes.

From Katie's location in the back of the room, Victor's words were muffled, and she was glad. It was a constant struggle to keep herself from thinking about Armando's proposal at sunset in the park. She remembered feeling like she was glowing with euphoria, and the thought still made her heart skip a beat.

Mitch's proposal was nice too, I suppose, she thought with a melancholy sigh. He proposed at his birthday party in front of friends and family, and Katie had already picked out the ring a few weeks earlier. But still, it was nice.

Katie watched Victor and Cara for another second, then inched quietly to the back stairs to find the server who was assigned to the patio tonight.

Katie's original plan had been to stay until after dinner was served to congratulate the happy couple, but now she just wanted to leave. And since her shift was over, that's what she decided to do, afraid that she would become a blubbering mess in front of Victor.

And so, careful not to get held up by idle banter with co-workers, Katie headed out the back door to find her car. She was grateful Mitch had plans with work buddies tonight that didn't involve her. All she wanted to do was go to her apartment, slip on some comfy pajamas, and polish off the last of the wine in her fridge. Maybe now that her involvement in Victor's proposal was over, she wouldn't have to see him again. He'd go back to New York City, and so would the constant reminder of Armando. She exhaled with relief as she thought about it.

My thoughts will return to normal...soon...I hope...

As she strolled through the employee parking area, she reached into her purse for her keys. *Damn it!* It was the third time this week she had mindlessly tossed them inside instead of stashing them in the little pocket where they could easily be found. No wonder. She hadn't been thinking straight for the past few days.

She stopped walking and opened her purse, thankful there was enough light from the street to let her see inside. She held up her purse and shook it, hoping to catch a glimmer of the shiny keys, when suddenly she heard footsteps behind her.

Her stomach leaped to her throat. *Oh no.* She was petrified to turn around. The footsteps were slow, but they were steady and getting closer.

Pepper spray! I know it's in here somewhere...

She rifled through the contents of the purse and found it, quickly. Her mouth formed a little smirk and her pulse quickened with newly found boldness as she prepared to turn around and pull out the little can of spray. But before she could, a man's voice sliced through the darkness.

"Need a ride, Katie?"

A chill shot up her spine. She let go of the pepper spray and nearly dropped her purse. It didn't matter that she hadn't heard his voice since he was eighteen. She would have recognized it anywhere.

With a thin layer of tears in her eyes, she turned around. Her whisper was almost too quiet to hear. "Armando?"

He took one more step and emerged from the shadows, staring at her with a quiet fixation.

Katie stared back at him, her mouth gaping. She had longed to see him, and now here he was right there in a form-fitting black suit. His face looked sad, but he was just as sexy and debonair as the pictures of him she had fawned over online. It was like he had stepped right out of her dreams and onto the pavement. She waited a moment and wiped her hand across her eyes to dry them. "You...scared me."

Armando let out a long, weary sigh. "I know. Sorry."

"It's all right."

Their eyes met for a while, but neither spoke. Katie was unprepared for the obvious sadness in his eyes, his stance, his being. There were so many questions she wanted to ask. *Why are you so sad? Did you come here for me? Do you still think about me?*

But then she saw him blink, and tears ran down his chiseled face. Without thinking, she let her purse drop to the pavement with a *bang* and held out her arms, rushing him tearfully. "Armando!"

He eagerly accepted her embrace, holding her so tight she didn't even notice her own difficulty breathing. She squeezed him back just as tight, crying against his lapel. Neither was prepared for the torrent of emotions unleashed by the other's touch.

As she attempted to calm down, Katie made a conscious decision to drink him in. Memorize everything. His cologne, his body, the strength of his arms around her.

His hand slowly wandered to the nape of her neck, weaving

through her long red hair as he cradled her head against his chest. His warm lips grazed her forehead, making her breath splinter and her knees weak.

She grabbed a fistful of the back of his jacket with each hand and let out a soft gasp as she tried to steady herself.

"Katie," he whispered. "I thought I'd never get to hold you again."

She let herself collapse fully in his arms as his words sunk in. In a weak voice she said, "Me neither. I can't believe this is happening."

"Someone told me I'd forget all about you in five or ten years. I'd grow up and forget all about you." Armando lowered his lips to her ear. "But I've never forgotten about you, Katie."

She sniffled and said, "I never forgot about you, either," her voice cracking.

Armando gritted his teeth and took a few shallow breaths until he could speak without crying. Finally, he whispered, "Why didn't you try to reach me?"

"What?" Katie pulled away enough to look up into his eyes. "You mean, contact you? Why didn't *you* try to contact *me*? I made sure everyone in town knew what college I went to. You could've found me anytime you wanted."

His brows went up. "You're the one who told me you didn't want me anymore. You looked straight in my eyes and said it." He let go of her, his tone now serious. "Do you know what that does to a guy? I thought you loved me and you broke my heart in front of Henry, your mom. Probably your whole family listening inside your house."

"They made me do it! Couldn't you see that?" Katie's wide eyes pierced Armando's. "I didn't mean a word of it."

"I figured if you didn't mean it you would've let me know. Gotten word to me somehow. I had no idea how to reach you for the rest of the summer. And my mom was dying. I needed you." He paused, shaking his head. "It was the worst time of my life. Losing you, losing Mama."

Tears ran down her face but she didn't wipe them away. "I'm so sorry." Like a reflex, her hands both went to her mouth, covering it in shame. Her vision blurred with tears, she stared into his questioning eyes, wishing she had a better reason for rejecting him than, "I was scared." Wondering now if she could have changed the course of their future if she hadn't been so afraid of her father. She cried for a while longer as Armando waited patiently for her to speak. She pulled a tissue out of her purse to wipe her eyes, then said in an unsteady voice, "I was afraid of what Daddy would do to you. But I've spent all these years wishing you'd come back for me."

"Maybe I should've. But for all I knew you moved on and found someone else. You're a beautiful girl. You could've had anyone." He grimaced. "Shit, Katie. You're the one who told me you didn't want me anymore. Broke my heart after I'd already been through hell. Was I supposed to read your mind?"

Their heads both turned to the back door of the restaurant where a cook and a server had both just stepped outside for a cigarette. They were laughing and talking with each other, oblivious to the emotional discussion a few feet away.

Armando gave them a glance and quietly said to Katie, "Let's go to my room. I'm staying here at the hotel."

"I don't know if that's appropriate." The idea of being alone with Armando made her heart race, but it also brought her back to reality. "I'm...with...someone else," she stammered. "I'm engaged. I can't be alone with you in a hotel room. It's not right. My fiance wouldn't approve."

"You were engaged to me first, remember?" Armando lifted a brow. "I think that gives me rights. I'm calling dibs."

Katie bit her lip and looked away, ashamed of herself for wanting to go to his room. "I don't know."

Armando continued his argument. "We need to hash this out. Talk about things we should've talked about years ago. That means you need to come upstairs." He put his hand under her chin and tilted her face up. "You'd be married to me right now if I had my way."

A quiet gasp slipped past her lips. "Oh." And her knees felt weak again, like they had when he held her. But the sound of her co-workers' chatter snapped her out of her trance. She pushed his hand away. "No. This is how rumors start. Everyone here knows my fiancé. They'll say something."

Armando gave her a flat stare. "You worry too much about what people think."

"No. I just can't be seen going up to your room, okay?"

A wry grin passed across his lips. "Maybe you're afraid of what'll happen if you get me alone. You don't trust yourself."

She let out an abrupt chuckle, surprised by the sudden glimpse of his sense of humor. This was the Armando she remembered. "I just...can't."

"We could have dinner in public. At a different restaurant. Where everyone doesn't know you and your fiancé."

She sighed. "I don't know. This town's a lot smaller than you think."

"Okay, what about this. You come out to the ranch tomorrow and we can talk in private." Armando handed her his business card. "I'm probably gonna check out of the hotel in the morning and stay there instead."

"I have to work tomorrow."

"Then come over after work. We'll have dinner." He cocked his head to the side. "Unless you have big plans with the fiancé."

"No, actually. He had to go out of town for work at the last minute."

"Hmm. Leaving you all alone on a Saturday night." Armando slowly shook his head. "Shame on him. Call me tomorrow when you're on your way."

Katie stashed the business card safely in a pocket inside her purse, her hand gently trembling. Here he was, back in her life again. Exciting and terrifying all at the same time. She cleared her throat and steadied herself. "I'll think about it."

Then his eyes fixed on hers. And Katie felt as though she was in a trance, unable to look away. Wondering if he was real or a figment of her imagination. She didn't want to go home. Didn't want to leave him again. Katie wanted to go to his room, like he'd asked.

And for a second she envisioned them in his car on that fateful day. Those warm brown eyes full of life and love, peering into her soul. The same way he looked at her tonight. Maybe they should run off again and leave their lives behind.

But she snapped back to the present as soon as his eyes broke contact.

"Tomorrow," Armando said. "I'll be waiting."

In silence, Katie watched him walk away. Knowing she would soon have to make a choice.

CHAPTER 8

It was early Saturday morning. Sunlight cut through a tiny gap between the curtains and threatened to wake Victor several times. But every time his eyes opened, he put his arm around Cara and sank once again into his peaceful slumber. They stayed up late the night before, celebrating their engagement.

She said yes. That's all he cared about. They could finally start planning a real future together. Vague, "someday" wants could now be fulfilled with more permanent plans. He felt safe, knowing the woman he loved would be his, for life.

The room was just cold enough to require the use of a blanket as he spooned Cara underneath it. Her blond hair gently tickled his chin as she nestled against him. He awoke for a second, but quickly fell asleep once again.

Until he heard the sound of tiny, loud footsteps, followed by the smell of coffee wafting in from the kitchen directly below them. Still his eyes remained shut, hoping he was having a dream.

Then the door creaked open, and the footsteps came into the room. And then the mattress springs squeaked at the same time he heard, "Suh-pwize!"

"Hmm?" Cara winced against the sunlight, her voice weak. "What's going on?"

Isaac again yelled, "Suh-pwize!"

Victor opened his eyes to see Isaac in his Spiderman pajamas, jumping up and down on the bed near Cara's feet. He rubbed his eyes and sat up. "Isaac, buddy, don't jump on the bed. You're gonna hurt yourself."

Cara extended her arms to Isaac. "He's right. Come here."

Isaac giggled and ran down the bed, flopping into his mother's arms. "Suh-pwize, Mommy!"

Cara chuckled and kissed his forehead. "Okay. Good morning, sweetie. You're surprising us by waking us up at," she glanced at the clock, "six o'clock on a Saturday morning?"

Isaac smiled. "I can have my baby bwothow now, okay Bictow?"

Cara's eyebrows furrowed at Victor. "What?"

"Oh." Victor closed his eyes and used one hand to rub his temples. He dreaded explaining this to Cara. "Let me go downstairs and have some coffee first, okay?"

"Okay!" Isaac tore away from Cara and hopped out of bed. "I see if it's weddy." He instantly ran out of the room. They heard him yell, "Wuh-moan!" as soon as his feet hit the stairs.

Cara yawned and let her head fall down to the pillow, her eyes wide open. "You mind telling me what that's about?"

Victor propped himself up on his elbow. "You have a very intelligent child who remembers everything you tell him. That's what." He sighed. "You see, I made the boneheaded decision to ask Isaac's permission to marry you."

"What?"

"Well, maybe not his permission, exactly. But I just felt like having a talk with him was the right thing to do, since he's the most special guy in your life. I wanted to know what he thought about me being in your lives, for a long, long time."

"Did he know what you were talking about?"

"Well…" Victor winced. "I don't know. I didn't think he did, then all of a sudden he asked if he could have a baby brother. Like, somehow he connected *that* to marriage but I didn't ask how. I was afraid it'd lead to a conversation we didn't need to have right then. I don't know when you're supposed to talk to kids about sex and I'll be ready to talk to him someday if you want me to, but that wasn't the time."

"Aww." Cara rolled on her side to face him. "You'd do that?"

Victor shrugged. "If you want me to. I figure that's the dad's job. Or, well, stepdad in my case."

Cara smiled. "Stepdad." Tears filled her eyes, but she continued to smile. "It seems so real now."

Victor leaned forward to kiss her, then sat up, peering into her eyes. "I guess I've never said it out loud before. But you know how I feel about Isaac. I'd like to adopt him, if that's okay with you."

Cara blinked and tears ran down her face, which she immediately wiped away. "Yes." Her eyes darted around the room. "If I didn't want you in his life I never would've started seeing you. But… somehow, now that we're engaged…I…" Her voice trailed off as she stared blankly up at the ceiling.

"Are you sure it's okay? Did I do something wrong? I didn't mean to rush you."

She let out a small chuckle. "No, it's good. It's just…I don't know. He won't just be *mine* anymore. He'll be someone else's. I guess I never really thought about it." She looked at Victor. "But it's good. Really good."

Victor let out a relieved sigh. "I'm glad."

She laughed and wiped away the last of her tears. "I don't know if he'll ever call you Daddy. You may be 'Big Toe' forever."

Victor laughed. "That's fine. And it's also perfectly fine if you don't want me to have the sex talk with him someday. Just thought I'd put it out there."

She sighed. "Okay then, back to *that* subject. What's this about a baby brother?"

"Oh. Yeah." Victor cleared his throat. "He told me he wants a baby brother because he heard me call Ramon 'baby brother.' Then I told him I actually have *two* brothers, so Isaac said he wanted *two* baby brothers. And somehow we made a deal where he promised not to tell you about our little talk until today, and in return I'd see about getting him a baby brother."

Cara smirked. "Well, I'm glad the two of you decided to include *me* in this decision." She sighed. "So that's why he made that weird comment the other night."

"Yes. It was the same day we had that talk."

"But he wants *two* brothers."

"Yes." Victor chuckled. "No sisters. And he wanted the first brother as a birthday present next month."

Cara laughed. "Oh no. What'd you tell him?"

Victor mentally winced. "I told him maybe next year he could have a brother, but this year he'd have to settle for a race car instead. Something he can ride around the ranch."

"Huh?" Cara sat up, scared. "No."

"Why not? They make these cool little cars for kids his age. Kinda like a souped-up tricycle."

She shook her head. "You don't mean one of those little four wheelers, do you? The ones with a motor? They go way too fast."

"No. It's nothing like that. They have pedals."

Cara let out a sigh of relief. "Well, please be careful what you promise him. You don't have to buy his love. And I'm absolutely determined not to spoil him. He needs to appreciate what he has."

Victor nodded in agreement. "Yes, absolutely. Look, I was desperate, trying to keep him from ruining the surprise. I can't believe he didn't ruin it anyway." He looked in Cara's eyes. "I know I have a lot to learn about being a parent but I swear to you, from now on I'll talk to you before I promise to buy him anything."

"Or promise him a brother or two?" Her eyes grew wide.

Victor grinned. "What? Seemed like you were okay with it the other night."

Cara blushed, thinking about it. "I know."

Victor cradled her cheek with his hand. "Cara, my love. I want a big family. With you." He kissed her, then pulled back. "If Isaac gets sisters, I guess he'll deal with it." His ears perked up at the sound of feet quickly ascending the stairs. "Speaking of Isaac…"

"Yeah." Cara covered her mouth as she yawned. "I knew I wouldn't get to sleep in today."

Victor gave her a peck on the cheek then threw the covers off and headed to the dresser. "I need to go downstairs and have a talk with Ramon anyway. Saw Armando last night. He's supposed to come out here today."

Cara walked to the closet. "Armando? Last night? How? Why are you just now telling me?"

Victor laughed. "Didn't seem as important as asking you to marry me."

Right then, Isaac entered the room. "Hey! Coffee's weddy!"

Victor and Cara talked Isaac into returning downstairs to help Ramon with breakfast, then locked the bedroom door and sneaked into their bathroom for a quick shower…

Five minutes later, the fringes of his hair damp, Victor went downstairs in jeans, a T-shirt, and socks while Cara stayed to finish getting ready. The first thing he noticed in the kitchen was Isaac struggling to open the refrigerator with his arms wrapped around a gallon of milk.

"Hold on there," Victor said as he took the milk from Isaac. "You're gonna drop it." He looked over his shoulder at Ramon, who was standing over the stove. "Hey, be a little more careful with him."

Ramon wiggled a spatula inside a skillet of bacon. "What? He's helping. He can handle putting the milk in the fridge."

Isaac nodded proudly. "Yeah. I'm a big boy."

Victor sniffed, then squinted in Ramon's direction as he headed to the coffee pot. "What's burning?"

Ramon shot Victor a mean glance over his shoulder. "Nothing. This is what good food smells like."

Under his breath, Victor muttered, "If you say so." Then louder, "Need me to help with something?"

"Nah, I got it." Ramon looked at Isaac, who was now standing close by. "Hey, go get me a roll of paper towels. They're in that big cabinet." He nodded behind him toward the other side of the large kitchen.

"Okay!" Isaac took off to fulfill the request.

"So." Ramon placed the spatula on the stove. "How'd it go last night?"

Victor smiled as he poured himself a cup of coffee. "She said yes."

Ramon chuckled. "So, it went well then?"

"Yes. Very." He took a long sip then put his mug on the counter. "In other news, did you know Armando's in town?"

"What?" Ramon's eyebrows shot up. He turned around to face Victor. "No. Are you sure?"

"Yeah. I spoke to him. He's here about that Katie girl."

Ramon shook his head, his eyes wandering aimlessly around the room. His voice was quiet. "Well I'll be damned. He didn't even call me."

"Didn't call me either." Victor shrugged, then picked up his coffee. "I happened to see him before dinner. He was just sitting there in an SUV in the parking lot across the street from the restaurant. Wouldn't tell me what was going on. But I told him to come out here today for lunch."

Ramon let out a disbelieving sigh and reached into the pocket of his jeans. "I'm gonna call him."

* * * * *

Armando eased onto the brake pedal when he heard his phone ring. He hit the speaker phone button. "Hello?"

Ramon said, *"Are you really here in town? Why didn't you tell anyone?"*

Armando wished for a moment that he had stayed at the hotel. He kept his groan to himself and said, "I'm on my way to see you right now. Be there in a few minutes. Bye." And then he hung up.

In no mood for his brothers' goodhearted ribbing, he regretted that he hadn't been able to hide from Victor the previous night. All he wanted to do today was collect his thoughts. Maybe have a few beers. Hopefully talk to Katie again.

He took the long way from San Antonio to Turnbrook this morning to avoid passing the house where Dwayne McCormack still lived with his wife. It felt like it all happened yesterday. Armando's rage was closer to the surface than ever, after a decade of lying dormant. Especially after seeing Katie last night.

He felt a spasm of dread in his stomach. There would surely be a million questions today. He could already imagine the worst one: Why are you still pining away over your high school sweetheart, *pendejo*?

Armando had already asked himself the same question more times than he wanted to admit. He had stayed awake all night, staring at the ceiling, seeing only her pretty face in his mind. Hearing only her voice.

It took every ounce of his self-control not to kiss her last night.

Maybe I'm not still in love with her...maybe I just need closure. Maybe that's why she's all I can think about.

Armando took a deep breath as he turned down the long driveway that led to his destination. A few seconds later, he gritted his teeth and jerked the steering wheel as his vehicle hit a pothole he didn't notice. A little further on, he noticed a large portion of a wooden fence that was broken and splintered. "Shit, Ramon. You're lettin' the place go to hell." Armando squinted and looked in the rear-view mirror, trying unsuccessfully to see that pothole. When he turned to the expanse of road in front of him, he saw another one, but this time he was able to swerve around it in time.

Soon, he was heading up the circular driveway where he parked close to the porch and sat there for a second with the engine off, bracing himself for the day ahead of him.

Finally, knowing he couldn't avoid them forever, he stepped out of the vehicle and headed to the front door. It swung open before he could knock, with his brother Victor standing there to greet him. A precocious wide-eyed young boy with blond hair, who Armando assumed was Isaac, peeked out from behind Victor's leg.

"You're early!" Victor welcomed him with a hug, patting him heartily on the back. "Glad you came. Been worried about you."

Armando pulled away and looked into Victor's eyes. "You don't need to worry."

Ramon stepped out of the kitchen, immediately giving Armando's shoulder a smack. "*Pendejo*. First you don't tell me you're comin' to town. And today you hang up on me? So rude."

Armando rolled his eyes and put his arms out to give Ramon a quick hug. "Nice to see you, too." He quickly let him go, sniffing the air. "What's that? Smells like someone's burning breakfast in there."

Ramon groaned and turned around to the kitchen. "Shut up."

Armando looked down to see the little boy staring up at him, still hiding behind Victor's leg. In a soft voice, he said, "Hi there. Are you Isaac?"

Isaac grinned, nodding vigorously.

Victor put his hand on Isaac's shoulder and said, "This is my brother, Armando."

Isaac let out a tiny giggle then whispered, "Baby bwothow."

Victor smiled and said, "Isaac, don't be shy. Shake Armando's hand and introduce yourself. Come on, you can do it."

Isaac looked up at Armando, smiling, after Victor gave his shoulder another friendly squeeze. He extended his hand. "I'm Isaac."

Armando took the miniature hand in his, surprised by the boy's firm grip. "Hi. I'm Armando. It's nice to meet you. That's a very firm handshake."

Victor nodded proudly. "I taught him that. Firm handshakes go a long way in this world. It's good to learn early."

Armando let go of Isaac's hand and smirked at his brother. "Oh really? You're turning him into a stuffy old businessman? Already?"

Isaac's eyes narrowed as he examined Armando. "You wook wike Bictow."

Seeing the confusion on Armando's face, Victor spoke up. "He said, 'You look like Victor.'"

Armando slowly nodded. "Ah. Yeah, that's what they tell me. Personally, I don't see it."

Victor was about to reply to his comment when he heard the stairs creaking. "Cara's on her way down."

Armando said, "So, how'd it go last night?"

Victor smiled. "Very well."

"Good. I'm happy for you." Armando nodded and waited patiently as Cara entered the room.

"Hi," she said, extending her hand as she neared him. "Armando? It's nice to meet you."

Armando smiled and opted for hugging her instead of shaking her hand. "Cara. It's good to finally meet you. Congratulations."

"Thank you," Cara said.

Armando pulled away and said, "Welcome to the family."

Isaac patted Cara's leg and looked up at her, loudly whispering, "He wooks wike Bictow."

Cara nodded. "Yeah. I've seen pictures and you two looked a little bit similar but in person it's much more prominent."

Armando shrugged, shaking his head. "I don't really see it. When I look at him," he gestured at Victor, "it doesn't feel like I'm looking in a mirror."

Cara's eyes darted between the two brothers. "No, you don't look identical, but there's a strong resemblance. Your eyes and the way you smile. There's a resemblance with Ramon too but not nearly as strong."

Victor sighed. "That reminds me." He walked off to the kitchen. "Hey! You still cookin' in here?"

Armando, Cara, and Isaac followed Victor into the kitchen where a tray of biscuits sat on top of the counter, burnt to a crisp and emitting a thin layer of smoke.

Ramon took some plates from a cabinet. "Nah. Just about done. I hope you all like your eggs scrambled."

Cara took the plates from Ramon. "Let me and Isaac set the table." She glanced around the kitchen. "Need help with anything else?"

Ramon shook his head and opened the drawer to get a spatula. "Nah. I'm good."

As Cara and Isaac went off to the dining room, Armando surveyed the kitchen, noticing a cabinet door dangling precariously a few feet above the stove. Then he looked around at the food, all of which appeared to be either burnt or undercooked. He eyed an unusually greasy plate of bacon and said, "Uh, you sure you're all right, Ramon?"

"Yeah." Ramon narrowed one eye at him. "It tastes a lot better than it looks."

Armando asked, "What happened to your housekeeper, Elsa?"

Ramon sighed and started prying the charred biscuits out of their pan. "She disappeared last year when Henry did. Guess they're on an extended vacation together." He chuckled. "She was never *my* housekeeper to begin with."

Armando gave Victor a suspicious look, which Victor met with wide eyes, telling Armando he had probably already asked Ramon these questions. But Armando pressed on. "So, you're living here all alone in the big house?"

Ramon snorted. "Yeah. So?"

"Have you thought about hiring another housekeeper?" Armando asked. "Seems like maybe you're a little too busy trying to run the ranch with Henry gone and—"

Ramon let the spatula drop to the pan and glared at Armando, his jaw firmly set. "What're you doin'? Trying to keep the attention off yourself and why you came runnin' back to town for Dwayne McCormack's daughter? Is that why you're startin' shit with me in my house? You got a lot of explaining to do."

Armando took a step toward Ramon, startled by his younger brother's unusually short fuse. "I'm not trying to start shit with you. I'm just a little concerned, that's all. You never told me Elsa wasn't here anymore."

"So?" Ramon huffed. "Like I need some old lady hangin' around, pickin' up after me like she's my mom? I'm not some pampered little pretty boy, like the both of you." He shot a glance at Victor. "I know you both got people to make your beds and do all your cookin' but I like to do things myself. Nothing wrong with hard work."

Victor groaned and gave Armando a massive eye roll.

Armando swallowed his urge to scream. "It's not about that. We *all* work hard. I know you get up early every morning and take care of things around here. I can't imagine how you still have time to cook and clean and take care of yourself. There's nothing wrong with hiring someone to come in and help. People need jobs. And what about those potholes—"

"Shut up." Ramon glared at Armando. "Now you sound like Henry. He calls at least every two weeks to bark at me about the potholes, the landscaping, the fences, making sure that stupid pond out back doesn't dry up." He brought his hand to his chest. "This is *my* ranch now. I decide what gets fixed and how things run around here."

Armando took in a very deep breath and tried to keep his voice gentle. "Do you need money?"

Victor's eyes widened at Armando just as Ramon gritted his teeth, ready to yell.

Right then, Cara and Isaac entered the kitchen. The guys immediately calmed down.

Cara went for the greasy plate of bacon. "I'll start taking everything to the table."

Breakfast was awkward. The table was full of barely-edible food. Ramon appeared oblivious to the fact that everyone besides him had opted for a bowl of cereal as he crunched through his burnt biscuits.

After breakfast was over, Ramon, Cara, and Isaac were in the kitchen, cleaning, when Victor saw an opportunity to take Armando upstairs for a private talk in an empty bedroom.

As Victor shut the door, he said, "You know better than to *ever* ask Ramon about money."

"Well, I'm worried. Couldn't help it."

"I know. I thought all the same things. But he showed me his financial statements. Unless he's really good at fraud, he's doing all right."

"Well, if he has money, he shouldn't get so pissed when I ask about it." Armando shrugged.

"It's about more than that. He's really defensive about the house, the personal property. But if you go out there," Victor gestured toward the back part of the property where the livestock was kept, "it's impeccable. New equipment, happy workers, healthy cattle. But he won't even ask any of the ranch hands to help fill in the potholes out front. I guess he still thinks of this as Henry's house, and he's got a big chip on his shoulder about Henry. It's almost like he's trying to let the place get run down, on purpose."

"Don't you think that's kinda weird? Even for him?"

"Yeah." Victor nodded. "It's concerning. That's why I'm gonna stay awhile longer. I have a feeling it has something to do with Henry taking off eight months ago. I still have no idea what happened." Then Victor tilted his head to the side, calmly asking, "So what about you? Are you ever gonna talk to Katie?"

Armando groaned. He hoped their troubles with Ramon had

been enough of a distraction that he could avoid the questions for a bit longer. "Actually, I spoke to her last night. Invited her to come out here today after she gets off work."

"Huh." Victor folded his arms across his chest and gave Armando a thoughtful look. "So you're gonna go for it. What about the fiance?"

Armando shrugged. "What about him?"

"Shit, man."

Widening his eyes, Armando repeated himself. "No, really. What about him? She belonged to me first."

Victor took a deep breath, his eyes darting around the room. "Well, I guess that's one way to look at it. So you really wanna try to win her back after all this time?"

Armando sighed heavily. "Like I said. She was *mine* first."

CHAPTER 9

Katie's stomach fluttered every time she glanced at her watch. She usually had Sundays and Mondays off, so Saturdays passed much slower as her anticipation built for the weekend.

But not today. No, this Saturday was different. The minutes raced by as she counted down to that moment when she would make a crucial decision about where to go after work. Today she had received eight text messages from friends and family—including her sister, Chelsea—to hang out tonight, since Mitch had to go out of town on short notice. But she hadn't replied to anyone. The invitation to visit Armando dominated her thoughts. And to think, he was practically casual..."*Come out to the ranch. We'll catch up.*"

Oh, but there was nothing casual about it to Katie. His touch... his voice...his sweet face. It was like he'd stepped out of her wildest dreams and derailed her life. When she imagined seeing him again in person, she never anticipated feeling this way about him. It was chaotic and beautiful and, at the same time, sickening. It chased away all thoughts of the man who was supposed to be the current love of her life.

A week earlier she would have pined away over Mitch. She would have already left him at least one voicemail telling him she would miss him and think of him tonight. But today she hadn't called him, and he hadn't bothered to call her either.

And Katie was perfectly fine with that.

Maybe I just need to see Armando one more time to sort out how I feel. Surely it was just the excitement of seeing him again after so long. The shock of him approaching me when I least expected it. Maybe that's why I'm feeling this way.

She took a deep breath to steady herself as she strolled into the dining room on her final walk-through before leaving for the night. There was absolutely no way she could tell anyone where she was headed. Not her sister, not her friends. And especially not Mitch.

Her stomach twinged.

Crap. Yes, I have to tell Mitch. After all, what if I see Armando again and feel nothing and I actually start thinking about Mitch again?

She scowled to herself, then found an empty table in a lonely corner of the bar. Usually this time of day was when Jennifer, the dim-witted server, approached her with a last-minute dilemma that took up the rest of Katie's shift. But Jennifer had called in sick today, and Katie had now finished her daily tasks with time to spare. She took out her cell phone and started to send Mitch a text message, but changed her mind and chose to call him instead.

His phone rang four times and she was already silently rehearsing what she would say on his voicemail, when suddenly he picked up.

"*Hey babe.*" Mitch's quick greeting was almost drowned out by the sound of a bustling crowd around him.

Katie cleared her throat. "Oh, hey. Didn't expect to get you."

His tone was slightly anxious. "*Yeah. So what's up?*"

"Sorry. It sounds like you're busy. Are you at dinner?"

"*Uh-huh. The clients chose the restaurant. I'm just waiting for them to get here. What's up? You find something to keep you busy tonight?*"

"Actually, yes." Katie tried to make her voice sound breezy as not to alarm him. "But I wanted to check with you first. See, there's an ex-boyfriend in town and he asked if I wanted to have dinner."

Mitch paused, then his voice was muffled as if he had his hand over his phone and he was talking to someone else. When he came back to the phone he said, "*I'm sorry. What was that? Did you say an ex-boyfriend asked you to dinner?*"

"Yes."

"*Uh…*" Mitch paused again in the same fashion, like he was having another conversation. When he spoke he said, "*How long ago did you date?*"

"High school."

"*High school?*" He chuckled, and Katie swore she heard a female voice chuckling along with him. "*That's fine. I'm Facebook friends with most of my high school girlfriends. I don't see the big deal.*"

"You are?" Stunned, Katie held the phone tighter in an effort to make sure she heard him correctly. She swore she heard a woman's laughter a little too close by. "Is there someone there with you? Are you telling her what we're talking about?"

"*No! You're paranoid.*" He produced a tiny gasp. "*Hey, my client just got here. I gotta go. Have a good time at dinner tonight. Love you.*"

Before she could say, "Love you, too," he hung up.

Relieved, Katie stood and slipped her phone into her skirt pocket. Instantly, she felt like a liar. Armando was more than an ex-boyfriend; he was an ex-fiance. And she would have said so to Mitch if she wasn't afraid he would casually mention it to her parents, who would immediately know who she had dinner with.

She groaned aloud as she headed to the kitchen. After all this time, she still had to hide Armando from her parents.

Five minutes later, Katie was in her car, poised to pull out onto the street from the parking lot. Heading to her apartment would require a right turn. But the road to Turnbrook required a left turn. She sat there looking both ways, contemplating her decision once again.

Oh, who am I kidding with this? I know exactly where I'm going.

Surprisingly, the left turn calmed her. The decision felt final now.

Katie put her Bluetooth headset on her ear and took her phone out of her purse. At the first stoplight, she dialed his number, at the very beginning of her contacts list. She had sneakily programmed it into her phone simply as "A" for "Armando."

He picked up on the second ring. "*Is this Katie?*"

"Yes." She chuckled, startled by his greeting. "You still want me to come out to the ranch?"

He let out a relieved breath. "*Yes. Absolutely. I can't wait to see you again.*"

Warmth slowly spread through her extremities. She fumbled for something to say, but he cut her off before she could speak.

"*Oh, be careful when you come up the long driveway to the house. Potholes. Ramon isn't keeping the place up very well—*"

"Oh no. Ramon's there?"

"*Yeah. Why?*"

"He hates me. He's made that perfectly clear."

Armando grunted. "*Don't worry about it. You're coming here to see me, not my brothers.*"

"Oh crap. Victor." She sighed. "He didn't know who I was when he came to the restaurant earlier this week. I assume he knows now?"

"*Yes, but he's fine.*" He chuckled. "*He's a hell of a lot more mature than Ramon."* His voice softened. *"Please Katie, don't be nervous. Just come on out. I'm gonna hang up and let you drive uninterrupted, okay?"*

"It's fine. I have Bluetooth."

"Doesn't matter. It's still a driving distraction. And after I finally found you again…" His voice trailed off and he let out a deep sigh. *"Please, just be careful. See you soon."* And then he hung up.

Katie blushed at his sweet overprotectiveness, then tightened her grip on the steering wheel. He was the same way in high school. Always watching out for her. Always putting her comfort before his. She had forgotten how that felt, until now.

* * * * *

Thirty minutes passed and there was still no sign of Katie. Armando sat on the couch and looked at the clock above the fireplace. Then he glanced at his watch.

Ramon, sitting beside him, snorted and said, "You're pathetic."

They had all just eaten dinner and were now resting in the living room. Isaac was on the floor, playing with some toy cars. Victor and Cara sat on a loveseat, watching him.

It was Armando's idea to eat before Katie arrived, since he wasn't sure if she would even show up. And he was doubly sure of his decision after hearing Ramon's attitude about her.

Armando rolled his eyes. "For the last time, leave me alone. This has nothing to do with you."

Again, Ramon snorted. He put his hands behind his neck and his heels up on the coffee table. "Yes it does. Someone hurts my brother, I take it personally. End of story."

Victor gave Armando a sympathetic look and said, "When's she supposed to be here?"

Armando shrugged. "Don't know. She should've been here already."

Isaac put his cars down and looked at Victor. "Who?"

Victor said, "Armando's friend, Katie."

His lips bunched in confusion, Isaac asked, "A guhl?"

Ramon nodded. "Yep. A girl." He put his hands in his lap and his feet on the floor, then leaned forward for emphasis. "Let me tell you something, Isaac. Girls are trouble. You're better off to leave 'em all alone. Trust me."

At the same time, Victor and Cara shot Ramon an angry look. Armando just smirked.

Isaac's eyes lit up at Ramon. He pointed his thumb at himself. "I know. That's why *I'm* getting a baby bwothow." He shook his head. "I don't wike guhls."

Victor said, "Hold on a second. Your mommy's a girl."

"No," Isaac said. "She's a mommy. I wike Mommy."

Cara sat up straight and reached out for her son. "Come here. You like girls. You play with girls at the playground all the time."

Isaac frowned as he walked to his mom for a hug. "I wike boys bettow."

Victor laughed and stretched his arm around Cara's back. "That'll change, buddy. I promise."

Peeking at Ramon, Isaac shook his head as he hugged his mom.

Armando chuckled as they shared a look of agreement. He slapped Ramon's leg with the back of his hand. "You're a bad influence."

And then all heads turned in the direction of the car they heard driving up the gravel driveway.

Armando immediately stood, his heart racing as he went to the front door. "You guys just stay here. Don't scare her."

Victor laughed and followed him. "Geez, man. Stop being so nervous. She really has you worked up, huh?"

"It's not that." Armando glanced over his shoulder at Ramon in the living room, then lowered his voice. "I don't want anyone giving her a rough time. What happened back then wasn't her fault."

Victor sighed and gave his brother's shoulder a compassionate smack. "I know. And you have nothing to worry about from me. I'll be nice to her. But in a way, I have to agree with Ramon. Someone hurts my brother, they hurt me. Until this week I hadn't thought about what happened to you in a long, long time. Really pisses me off. Makes me wonder if we should do something about it, now that we got the means." He widened his eyes.

Armando scoffed. "Yeah, like what? How would we ever prove it after all this time? Henry sure as hell won't speak up for me."

Victor shrugged then quickly glanced behind him to make sure no one was listening. His voice was quiet. "I guarantee we have more money than Dwayne McCormack's ever seen in his entire lifetime. We could think of something. It'd be worth it after what he did to you."

"I don't know." Immediately, Armando thought of Mama, and her admonition to forget about it and resist the urge for revenge. For that reason alone—to appease their dying mother—Armando had spent years trying to forget. "Let me see what happens with Katie first. I don't wanna do something to make her hate me."

Victor nodded.

Armando turned away from his brother to the sound of footsteps on the front porch. As soon as he heard a knock, he opened the door.

And there she was. Katie. The sweet, innocent girl he had fallen for so long ago. Damn. She was even more beautiful now, wearing a nice blue dress, looking shyly down at the floor as the gentle breeze rustled her long, red hair. Then she let out a nervous giggle.

"Oh, sorry. Hi." Armando extended his hand, then changed his mind and stepped outside the door to put his arms around her. Near her ear, in a gentle voice, he said, "I have no manners today. I'm so sorry."

She buried her face against his cotton T-shirt and held him tight, inhaling his scent. Her voice was a soft purr. "It's okay."

After a little while, Armando heard Victor's throat clear behind him from inside the house. Slowly, Armando peeled himself away, keeping one hand on her back as he motioned toward the front door. He took a deep breath. "Katie. You remember Victor?"

Katie nodded and took Victor's hand as she stepped through the door. "Yes. Hello again."

"Hello." Victor put both of his hands around hers. "Please forgive me for not realizing who you were when we met this week. I had a lot on my mind and I didn't remember your name. I thought about bringing it up yesterday but—"

Quickly, Katie shook her head. "It wasn't the right time, I know. There's no reason to apologize. It's a strange...uh..." she gulped, "*situation*, I guess you could say."

Victor nodded. "Yes. That it is. But anyway," he let go of her hand and stepped back, gesturing toward Cara, "this is Cara, my fiancee as of last night."

"Oh!" Katie smiled and shook Cara's hand. "Congratulations!"

"Thank you." Cara beamed. "Seriously, I mean it, thank you. I heard you were responsible for our lovely evening last night. Everything was wonderful."

"No big deal," Katie said. "Just doing my job. But I'm glad you enjoyed it." She peered down at Cara's ring, trying not to gape at the enormous, glistening cluster of diamonds. Victor obviously spared no expense. "Wow. This ring is amazing."

"Yes. He did very well." Cara glanced at Katie's hand and almost made a comment about the lovely ring she saw, but stopped as she sneaked an uncomfortable look at Armando. To change the subject, she looked around for Isaac and saw him lingering in the living room with Ramon. "Come here," she said as she waved him into the foyer.

Isaac hesitated, looking up at Ramon for approval.

Cara groaned, and in a stern voice, said, "Come here, Isaac. We have a guest. Don't be rude." Her eyes narrowed briefly at Ramon.

Isaac ran to the door and wedged himself in between Cara and Victor, giving Katie a shy grin. When Victor prompted Isaac by patting his shoulder, he extended his hand. "Hi. I'm Isaac."

Katie smiled down at him and took his hand. "I'm Katie. It's very nice to meet you, Isaac."

When Isaac let go, he skulked backward to stand next to Ramon—who hovered behind them, shooting Katie an icy glare. Cara shared a knowing look with Victor, then said to Katie, "I'm sorry. My son's usually a bit more talkative but he's had an unusual week."

Victor cleared his throat. "Yes. He's spent the whole week helping out here at the ranch. I'm sure he misses his friends at home."

Katie acted like she didn't notice Ramon's angry eyes. "I don't know if you're interested, but if you're staying for a while, my sister, Chelsea, works at a daycare just outside San Antonio." Ramon grunted at Katie's mention of Chelsea, but she ignored him and continued. "They have a great pre-school program and you could probably get him right in without a wait. It has a stellar reputation and kids love it there. He'd probably fit right in."

Cara's eyes perked up. "Hmm. I may have to take a look. We're not sure how long we're staying just yet."

Determined to break the uncomfortable tension in the room— courtesy of Ramon—Armando touched Katie's shoulder and said, "Let's go outside. It's a nice day."

Relief passed across Katie's face, and she nodded.

Cara and Victor quietly went to the living room with Ramon and Isaac as Armando opened the front door. On the porch, he stopped and asked, "Are you hungry? I'm so sorry, I didn't even offer you dinner. We ordered pizza and there's plenty left over."

She shook her head and fidgeted mindlessly with her engagement ring. "No. I couldn't possibly eat right now. Maybe I shouldn't have come."

"Why? Because of Ramon?" Armando rolled his eyes, then slowly started down the porch steps, making sure Katie was following beside him. "Please, don't let him get to you. He's been acting like a jerk to everyone since I got here today. Has nothing to do with you."

Katie sighed, anxious. "No, I'm sure it does. He's acted that way toward me and my family ever since…" she paused, her voice trailing off for a moment. "I don't blame him, I guess. If someone did all that to my sister I'd probably never forgive 'em."

Armando shrugged as they headed toward a flat, empty field. "Well, I can't speak to that. I can only tell you Ramon's too young to turn into a crotchety old man. I think he's just working himself too hard and he's too proud to ask for help. He's got this place," he gestured toward the back area of the vast property where the barns and stables were located, "and he's somehow managing two other ranches he acquired last year. I think today's the first day he's taken off in a long time. Victor said the only way he's been able to spend any time with him all week is if he helped him work."

Katie chuckled as she stepped over a large rock. "That's funny to me. Don't you and Victor have these big careers of your own?

He's in New York. You're in Los Angeles. And now, here you are, walking along in your jeans and a T-shirt, staying here at Ramon's house in Turnbrook."

"What's so funny about that?" Armando gave her a playful smirk. "I spent my best years in that house. And now, I'm just a regular guy, visiting my brothers on the weekend—"

Katie laughed, hard. "You're *not* just a regular guy, Armando. I know *that* much. I've seen that big, fancy bio you have online."

Armando squinted as he thought about it. "You mean, at the Hightower Investments website?" He huffed. "That's all for show. Don't believe everything you read."

"Yeah, sure. So you don't have a collection of sports cars, or a private jet, or a controlling interest in the largest hotel franchise in North America? And you're never seen eating dinner with beautiful women. TV stars and models, and—"

"Okay, okay." Armando stopped walking and turned to face her. "The sports cars, yes. The private jet, not exactly. I have *access* to a private jet anytime I need it, but I figured there was no reason to buy my own unless I just wanted to look like a rich, wasteful jackass."

Katie burst into laughter.

Armando continued. "The hotel franchise." He shook his head. "Too much headache. I sold most of my equity and now I'm just a shareholder. A silent partner, really. And as for the T.V. stars and models," he let out a defeated sigh and shook his head, "yeah, that might've happened a few times. When you have money in L.A. you tend to run in the same circles as some of the more recognizable people in our society. But it never takes me long to see through a phony, bullshit exterior to the woman inside."

Her eyes narrowed. "Is that why you're still single?"

"I guess so." His eyes narrowed, matching her expression. "Wait a minute. How'd you know about the women I've been seen with? I'm not usually named in those pictures because I'm not a," he used air quotes for his next word, "*celebrity*." Even when Armando had a serious relationship with a famous model several years earlier, he prided himself on staying in the background and keeping a low profile.

Katie shrugged. "You have to know where to look, I guess. But I've always kept tabs on you." She briefly looked in his eyes, then gazed off in the distance. "Well, if you wanna call searching the internet, 'keeping tabs,' that is. Sorry if that seems creepy. I know you've been successful and I think you deserve it."

"Thank you. And for the record, that's probably no creepier than me scaring you in the parking lot last night. Or finding your little wedding website."

"Oh." Katie winced and groaned. "*That*. I wish you hadn't seen it. My sister and her husband did it without my consent, as a gift. They're dorks."

Armando chuckled. "It's okay. No reason to be embarrassed. It told me everything I wanted to know about where you've been since high school. You went to a few colleges. Got a few degrees. Moved back here to Bexar County, and," he inhaled dramatically and brought his hand to his chest in a sarcastic display, "found the dreamiest dreamy dreamboat hunk of a man you'd ever laid eyes upon, who's a lawyer, like Daddy. And you found him just in time, too, because the whole family was holding their breath, afraid you'd still be single when you turn thirty in a couple years."

Katie grimaced. "I told you, they're dorks. Most of it was written in jest."

"Most of it, huh?" Armando cocked his head to the side. "How much of it's true? You don't seem very happy about marrying this guy. Don't let the pressure get to you."

She looked down and gently nudged a rock with the side of her leather pump. Her voice was soft. "I'm not. He's a good guy. He works hard. We have a lot in common."

"So, *that's* why you're marrying him. Good guy. Hard worker.

Common interests. It has nothing to do with the fact that he's a lawyer who, according to the bio on *his* firm's website, has some political aspirations? You know, like your dad, the district judge?"

"Daddy and Mitch are nothing alike, aside from that." Katie set her lips in a straight line and crossed her arms over her chest, glaring at Armando. "Do you know how offensive that is? That you think of me as some weak, simple-minded girl who wants to marry someone exactly like her father?"

Armando's voice was deliberately calm. "I don't think you're weak or simple-minded. You sure weren't in high school. It seems that maybe after what happened with me, you only dated guys you thought Daddy would approve of. And since Daddy's a jerk, guys who live up to his standards probably don't come along very often. That's why you got engaged."

She sighed, then bit the inside of her cheek and looked again at the rock on the ground. She took a long pause, then answered, "No."

"Well, is it the pressure to get hitched before you turn thirty? Is that why you're marrying this guy?"

Katie took a deep breath and met Armando's gaze. "There isn't that much pressure. It's mostly just Mom. She's a little old-fashioned. She thinks I'm gonna shrivel up and die if I don't settle down and start a family soon."

Armando scowled. "It doesn't matter what she thinks. You need to do what's best for *you*." His face brightened with an evil grin. "Maybe you should remind her that you could've already had that, with me. Who knows where we'd be right now if they hadn't stopped us?"

Katie drew in an unsteady breath and looked away, blinking fast to stop the tears that unexpectedly filled her eyes.

Concerned, he took a step forward, watching her. Waiting to see if she would respond. He gave her another moment, then gently asked, "Are you okay?"

She sniffled and wiped her palm across her eye. "I don't know." She paused for a breath. "It's like it's all fresh again. Crazy. Feels like it happened last week, not ten years ago."

"I know." Armando gritted his teeth. His own rage and sadness lingered much closer to the surface than he wanted to show. He inhaled and exhaled slowly, trying to calm down.

Katie sniffled again and hesitantly said, "A couple days ago I actually *did* mention it to Mom, for the first time in years. She went off on me and scolded me like a child."

"Oh no, I'm sorry. Did that scare you?"

Anger replaced the sadness in Katie's eyes. "No, it didn't scare me. It pissed me off!" Katie groaned and wiped away a stray tear that lingered on her cheek. "I've been on an emotional roller coaster for days. I'm sorry. I don't know what I'm supposed to be feeling." She let out a heavy sigh. "And there's no one I can talk to. No one who'd understand—"

"I understand." He placed a hand on each of her shoulders, staring deep into her eyes.

One side of her mouth quirked up with a hint of a smile. Her voice was soft. "Yeah. I guess you would."

Their eyes locked. The scent of her perfume was intoxicating. Her lips were so close, it would have taken little effort to tilt his head down and kiss her. And that's what Armando desperately wanted to do.

And he would have...if only she wasn't engaged.

But she was mine first! he told himself. Unfortunately, he knew it was a weak argument. Although there was undeniable familiarity and an instant attraction, too much time had passed. They weren't the same people they were when they concocted that crazy plan to run away after graduation.

And yet, there she was. His first love. The same beautiful girl who claimed his heart so long ago.

Would it really be so wrong to kiss her? Just one little kiss? Or maybe two. Or maybe he'd take her to that shady spot on the ground about twenty feet away where he could rip that pretty dress off and show her just how much she still meant to him and—

Shit.

Armando dropped his arms to his sides and turned his face up to the sky, then took a deep breath, trying to think about anything else.

Katie asked, "Are you all right?"

"Yeah." He closed his eyes and took another breath, blowing it out slowly.

"I'm sorry. Did I upset you?"

He kept his eyelids shut and shook his head. "No, it's fine."

"Okay. So..." Katie twirled her hair with her fingers. "Do you want me to go home then?"

"No." Armando looked in her eyes. "Please, no. I asked you to come out here because I wanted to finish our conversation from last night but..." his voice trailed off.

She giggled. "But...you don't know where to start?"

"No. I sure don't."

"Well, could we maybe start with finding a place to sit?" She shifted her weight from one leg to the other. "My heels are starting to sink down in the dirt."

"Oh, shit! I'm sorry. I didn't even think about that." Frantically, he looked around, wishing they could go back to the house, but there would surely be ears listening in every corner. "There's a pond right over there. Or at least, there used to be."

Katie nodded. "I remember."

"Oh. Yeah." Armando smiled at her and started in the direction of the pond. It used to be one of their favorite make-out spots. How could he have forgotten?

After a few steps, Katie stumbled. "*Ooh*. No, my shoes don't like this at all."

Quickly, Armando bent down and put his arm under her shoulders. "Does this help?"

CHAPTER 10

Katie hobbled along through the field, with help from Armando. Her heart raced from the feel of his strong bicep against her back. She hoped he wouldn't notice her labored breathing.

Damn it. The heat of his body awakened every part of her. Whipped her thoughts into a frenzy of rebellious desire.

Mitch had sure as hell never made her feel like this.

"You okay?" Armando asked. "Is it too hot out here for you? You're still all dressed up from work and I'm just wearing this T-shirt."

Oh yes, you certainly are wearing that T-shirt... It was perfectly fitted but not too tight, nicely displaying the lines of his muscles. "You must work out a lot," she said.

He laughed for a bit as he tightened his arm around her, then he answered, "Yeah. Every morning. I'm addicted. Can't start my day without it."

Katie blushed, realizing she had ignored his question. "That's nice."

"Uh-huh. So, the heat isn't getting to you? I wish I could take you inside the house but I really don't want them listening."

I wish you could take me, too. Yes, take me... She breathed deeply and tried not to appear distracted. "It's not that hot. It's actually kinda nice."

"Good."

A few more steps and they reached the pond. Or, rather, what was left of it.

Katie eased herself down to sit on one of the large rocks that served as benches. She scanned the pond. "Geez. It's kinda sad to see it like this."

"Yeah it is," Armando said. "Ramon could have some water hauled in but," he sighed, "he's Ramon."

"Remember those cute little baby ducks? And there were rose bushes over there," she pointed, "and some really pretty trees—"

Armando groaned and sat down beside her. "I know. Henry prided himself on the landscaping around here. Ramon thinks it's all a waste of time. He just let it all go."

"Why can't Mr. Platt just have it done anyway?"

"He doesn't live here anymore. He's off traveling the country or something. Ramon owns the whole place now."

"You mean, you don't even know where he is?"

"No. He calls Ramon once in a while." Armando shrugged. "Last I heard he was at a campground near the Grand Canyon for a few weeks. Before that, he was in Reno. And he apparently took the housekeeper with him. Elsa. That's why the house is such a disaster."

Katie chuckled as she gave the ground a light kick. "Well, I hope they're having a good time."

"Me too. He's earned it after all these years."

"So, you don't keep in touch with him? He was like a father to you, wasn't he?"

"Eh…" Armando winced. "It was a strange thing. We all respected him but we never really crossed that line to father-son relationship. And, of course, we knew he and Mama had something going on but there was never any talk of marriage as far as we know. So, he was always just the nice man who moved us to Texas and let us live in his house."

"And you never asked if he and your mom were together?"

Armando's eyes widened and he shook his head, rapidly. "No. Mama made it very clear right away that it was none of our concern."

"Oh!" Katie gasped. "Remember that time you sneaked me into your room really late at night and we had to go past Henry's bedroom and we heard—"

Armando held up his hand, quieting her. He groaned. "Please don't remind me. It was bad enough living there, pretending like nothing was going on."

"Well, for what it's worth, your mom always seemed happy, to me. Maybe she was the one who didn't want a commitment, but Mr. Platt wanted more."

He let out a pensive sigh. "Yeah, maybe."

Before they veered off to another subject, Katie knew it was time to bring up something. "Speaking of Mr. Platt." She gulped and fidgeted with her hands for a moment. "I sorta hate to bring this up because I don't wanna start crying again but…"

"What? Tell me." Armando's brown eyes flashed with interest.

She hesitated, then said, "Well, Mom told me back then, right after we got stopped at the gas station, that they didn't want me dating you because of some kind of family history."

"What exactly?"

"She wouldn't tell me. But she made it sound like our family would be devastated if you and I got married. Said that's why they tried to keep us from dating in the first place."

"What's Henry have to do with it?"

"I don't know for sure. The next few days there was a whole lot of arguing in our house. Usually me versus Mom and Dad. But a few times, it was just Mom and Dad arguing with each other, always behind closed doors. They'd even turn on the radio to try to keep me and Chelsea from eavesdropping. But they had this one argument in the den where Mom screamed loud enough to hear. She told Dad he never should've taken money from Henry Platt. Said it was like making a deal with the devil and it'd follow them the rest of their lives as long as they stayed here in this part of Texas." She sighed. "Then they went back and forth for a while with some words that would've gotten my mouth washed out with soap if I'd said 'em. And right after that, Dad opened the door and found me listening and we started arguing again. They would never answer me when I asked about Mr. Platt."

"So, you never asked them later? Like, days or weeks later after they calmed down?"

Gently, she said, "Armando. I don't think you understand. When it all blew over, my parents acted like it never happened. My sister and I were *forced* to act like it never happened. And since I didn't hear from you, I just went along with it. It was easier that way. I didn't wanna think about all that pain."

His voice was sad. "Yeah, I know."

"Whatever happened, with your family, with Mr. Platt," she shrugged, "it was bad enough that my parents *still* won't talk about it. It's this huge, shameful family secret we're all supposed to take with us to the grave. Like, a few years ago when my fourteen-year-old cousin got pregnant and my aunt and uncle sent her to a Baptist group home in El Paso for five months where she gave the baby up for adoption, and now they all pretend it never happened. You know, one of *those* secrets?"

"That's really sad."

"I know. Her parents won't even talk about it. The same way my parents won't talk about what happened with you."

"So it's *that* bad. I'm a shameful secret they won't even talk about." Armando shook his head and looked away. "Shit. And Henry knew the whole time. That's why he didn't want me dating you. He told me it was because your dad would never approve. Told me that the day he drove me over to your house, too. When we left he told me he knew it was coming. Your daddy got to you. That's what he said."

Katie's eyebrows furrowed. "Mr. Platt didn't want me dating you? He didn't say anything when I came over here. He even invited me to stay for dinner one night and he never said anything to my parents about me being here. I thought he liked me."

Armando folded his hands together and looked down at the dry grass. "He *did* like you. So did Mama. But Henry always had a long talk with me after you left. I didn't say anything because I figured you'd get upset." He faced her. "Didn't you ever wonder why we had to sneak around so much here at my house?"

She frowned. "I don't know. I guess I didn't realize we were sneaking around. I was just happy to be with you." She paused, going through a few memories in her mind. "Dang. I hope I've gotten more observant since then. I feel so dumb now."

He smiled and put his hand on her knee. "You're not dumb. Not then, not now. You were in love. It makes you overlook a lot of things." He gave her a sympathetic stare. "How do you think *I* feel? I'm sure I overlooked a lotta stuff too. Here we were, two kids, sneaking around, having a great time, planning a future. Had no idea what a big deal it'd turn out to be."

"They made fools out of both of us," Katie said, glumly. She felt her eyes welling up with tears. "I swear, I'm just so dang stupid." She put her elbows on her knees and hung her face in her hands. "How the hell did I graduate college?"

"Aw, Katie." Armando drew closer, his arm around her shoulders. "You graduated three times, right? Three degrees? A stupid person couldn't do that."

She sniffled. "They could if they went to three dumb colleges! Geez. Who gets three *undergraduate* degrees anyway? Maybe I was too stupid for grad school and I knew it subconsciously. Maybe that's why I always just went for another undergrad degree."

He pulled her closer, resting his cheek against the top of her head. "No, honey. Maybe you just didn't wanna go to grad school. We had almost every class together our senior year of high school. Trust me, I know you're not stupid."

Tears flowed freely down her face. "Yes I am! I should've reached out to you years ago. Why didn't I do that?"

"You told me last night, you were afraid. Don't be so hard on yourself."

"I know." She passed her wrist across her eyes. "But I missed you so much. I thought about you all the time. We should've had this talk long ago. I'm sorry we're only having it now." She stopped to sniffle. "After I'm engaged to someone else."

Armando let out a breath against her hair then kissed her temple. "I wish I'd contacted you, too. You should be mine right now. We never should've let 'em rip us apart."

Katie closed her eyes, enjoying the feel of his hot breath. His soft lips lingered along her cheek, then pressed against her skin in a slow kiss. Her tears dried up. All she could think of was his gentle kiss. His muscular arms holding her tight. The scent of an alluring, unfamiliar cologne…

Slowly, Armando trailed kisses along her skin until he was dangerously close to her lips.

Instinctively, Katie turned her face toward him, and his mouth went to hers. His lips were warm and skillful, drawing her bottom lip between his, then massaging it with his tongue.

She gasped into his mouth and threw her arms around his back, desperate for more. Her chest went weak as the breath slipped from her lungs. Her body tingled with pleasure from head to toe, radiating from his lips against hers, his hands sliding up and down her back. Fingers pressing roughly against the fabric of her dress like he wanted to peel it off.

His lips got faster. His tongue, more aggressive. Katie slid her hand up to his thick, dark hair, pulling him closer.

Armando released her lips long enough to whisper, "Mmm. Katie…"

She could barely take a breath when he kissed her again, harder than before. She held his face there and used her other hand to give his back a firm rub, loving the feel of his solid body through his shirt.

His hand moved to the small of her back, then lower. She moaned when she felt his palm on her backside, then sliding around to the front of her thigh.

Armando stopped to whisper, "I thought I'd never get to kiss you again." Then he attached his lips to hers once again. His hand almost went under her dress, but he changed course and slid up to the small of her back again.

Katie opened her mouth wider, giving his tongue room to explore. She wanted to lose herself in Armando. This passionate boy she once knew had grown into the man of her fantasies. She wanted to soak up every second with him. Make up for lost time.

She needed to be closer to him as they kissed. In a dreamlike state, she grabbed the back of his shoulders and slowly hoisted her leg across his.

Not breaking the kiss, Armando's hands went to her bottom to guide her into place.

Soon, she was straddling him, as he held her as tight against him as possible, and they continued their kiss. His hands moved slowly up her thighs until he was kneading her pantied cheeks with his fingers.

Katie lowered her hips and felt his arousal pressing against her panties through his jeans. She moved her mouth for a moment just to catch her breath and have a look in his luscious brown eyes, then she kissed him again.

She was just about to take off her panties when she was startled by a man's laughter in the distance. Then a child's loud squeal.

Her head shot up. "Oh no."

Armando craned his neck, listening for a moment. "They're not close by. Sounds like they're in the front yard."

But it was too late. Katie looked down to see her dress hiked up to her waist, and she snapped back to reality. *This wasn't supposed to happen.* "Oh, sweet Jesus, this is *so* wrong!" She whispered loudly, then slowly backed away from him on her knees. "I've gotta get outta here."

Armando reached forward and took her hand as she stepped to the ground. "I'm so sorry."

She jerked away from him and pulled the hem of her dress down, immediately bolting in the direction her car. Tears fell down her cheeks. "No, it's my fault. I knew better. This is why I shouldn't be alone with you."

Armando rushed to block her path, his hands on her shoulders, stopping her. "You were *mine* first. Remember that."

"Please, let me go." Katie pushed against him and tucked her head down, trying to hide her crying face. "I can't believe I let that happen."

He pulled her to his chest.

She collapsed against him, in tears.

"Katie." Armando cradled the back of her head as he whispered in her ear. "I'd never use you. Never. Please, let me make love to you."

His plea made her swoon. Made her wish, now more than ever, that she wasn't engaged. She took a deep breath and said, "I don't know what to say."

"You're confused." He kissed her ear. "I understand that. Just let me get to know you again. We can take it slow."

She cried against him, unsure how to respond.

"Please think about it," he whispered. "What they did to us wasn't fair. This could be our second chance." He strengthened his embrace. "I came back here the second I heard you were engaged. I don't know why I waited so long. Should've come back earlier."

Softly, she asked, "That's why you came here?"

"Yes. I know it's crazy. For all I knew you moved away and got married to someone else years ago." He moved his hand to her hair. "But knowing you were right there in San Antonio, engaged to some other guy. I don't know. It hit me in a way I didn't expect. I had to see you. And I almost never come to Texas, after what happened with us. It's just too painful."

She stayed there in his arms, searching for something to say. The same thought repeated on a continual loop in her mind: *I wish I wasn't engaged.*

After a few silent minutes, Isaac's laughter rang out, much closer this time.

Armando pulled away from her. "Sorry. We've been found."

"It's okay." She sniffled for the last time. "Just help me get to my car, okay?"

"Yes. But only if you promise to call me. We can have lunch or dinner. With chaperones. I won't ask you to be alone with me." He grinned. "Unless you *want* to be alone with me."

She let out a nervous giggle, then asked, "How long are you staying?"

He shrugged. "Don't know yet. Probably a while. I can work from here. Fly out for a meeting if necessary."

Katie's eyes widened. "Am I the reason you're staying here?"

Smiling, he hooked an arm around her shoulders. But his tone was too sober to be kidding. "Of course you are."

Right then, they heard footsteps. Isaac appeared from behind a tree. "A-mando!" He turned around and yelled, "I found 'em!"

Victor chuckled and slowly came up behind Isaac. "Sorry, you guys. We're just out for a walk. Didn't mean to bother you."

"It's okay," Katie said, pulling away from Armando. "I was just leaving."

Katie walked unsteadily on her high heels through the rocky field, grateful Victor and Isaac were there to ease the tension between her and Armando. When they arrived at her car, Victor and Isaac waved goodbye and walked off in another direction.

Soon she was in her car, saying goodbye to Armando through the open window. He kissed her forehead and told her he was expecting her call. As she drove off, she looked in her rear-view mirror and saw him standing there, watching.

And Katie wondered why she was driving off, at all.

* * * * *

Katie drove fast, tapping her fingernails on the steering wheel. She was bound to go crazy if she didn't tell someone what she was going through.

And she knew there was only one person she could tell. The one person who lived through the nightmare with her, who knew what a huge family secret it was: her little sister, Chelsea.

Katie tried several times to call her sister, but it went straight to voicemail. She finally gave up and just drove to Chelsea's house as quickly as possible.

Chelsea and her husband, Eric, lived in a four bedroom house in a nice neighborhood. It was the kind of home they could only afford with a massive down payment "gift" from Mr. and Mrs. McCormack. Chelsea regularly complained to Katie that she wished she had never taken that money, in favor of buying a smaller place. The money made both Chelsea and Eric feel indebted to her parents. That feeling was made worse by the fact that Dwayne and Lisa often stopped by unannounced to drop subtle reminders of their generosity.

Katie parked her car in the driveway and ran to the front door to ring the doorbell.

Eric answered the door with a smile. "Hey sis! What's goin' on?"

"Hey. Is Chelsea home?" Katie returned his smile. Eric was a sweet guy with a sunny disposition. A very welcome addition to their family. But right now, Katie was too frantic to talk to anyone but her sister.

As he stepped back to welcome her into the house, Chelsea traipsed in from the kitchen. "Hey!" Her face immediately fell the instant she caught a glimpse of her frazzled sister. "Are you all right?"

"Can I talk to you alone?" Katie asked.

"Ah. A sister thing." Eric winked at Katie, then excused himself, giving Chelsea a kiss on the cheek before heading upstairs.

Chelsea and Katie sat down on the couch in the living room.

Katie waited until she heard Eric's footsteps on the second

floor before speaking. And she decided to bring up the subject of the website before she forgot. "Okay. You've got to do something about that website. *Now*. Right now."

"Oh, come on. It's funny. Is that what this is about? Nobody's even seen it yet. Eric'll get it all fixed before you mail your invitations—"

"Someone's already found it! I was so embarrassed. I swear, I could choke you right now."

"Katie, it's not that bad. Anyone who knows you—"

"Just change the damn thing!" Katie lifted her hands for emphasis. "Please!"

"Okay, what the heck happened? You're way too panicky about this. Most people know how to take a joke."

"You just don't get it. I have to tell you something and you can't tell Mom or Dad."

"Sure. Fine."

"You can't tell Eric either. I'm serious. I can't take any chances and I'm only telling you because I'll go crazy if I don't talk to someone about it and I really really *really* need you to fix that damn website."

"Fine. I won't tell Eric or Mom or Dad or anyone. Please, calm down. You're scaring me."

"It was Armando. He found the website. Read everything, too. He's here in town. I just spoke to him."

"Armando?" Chelsea shrugged. "In *this* part of Texas? I know like, six Armandos. You'll have to be more specific."

"Barboza!" Katie glanced around the room, paranoid, then lowered her voice. "Armando *Barboza*. Remember him?"

Chelsea gasped. "You mean Ramon's brother? *That* Armando?"

"Yes. *That* Armando."

"Oh…" Chelsea got quiet for a second, straightening her back against the couch. She stared straight ahead, dumbfounded. "Do Mom and Dad know?"

Katie gritted her teeth and let out a growl. "No! Why do you think I just told you not to tell them?"

"Oh, Katie…" Chelsea clucked her tongue against the roof of her mouth, thinking back to that summer. "I haven't thought about that in a *long* time…"

Katie took her sister's hand, pleading. "You've gotta listen to me. I'm going crazy. There's no one else I can talk to. I can't even tell my friends. You're the only one who knows about it and understands what a huge deal it is."

Chelsea nodded, numbly. "Uh-huh."

"First things first, you need to take down the website. Or change it or something."

Chelsea raised a brow. "Didn't you say he already saw it? What's it matter if we change it now?"

Katie hit her forehead with her palm. "Just change it. Please. It'll make me feel better. It was so embarrassing to know he found it."

Chelsea shifted around to look directly at Katie, then took both of her hands. "Sweetie, you've gotta calm down. This probably isn't the huge deal you're making it out to be. So what if he's back in town? You're both adults now. He's probably just here visiting his brother. I doubt Mom and Dad would even care."

The corners of Katie's mouth turned straight down. "I kissed him."

"What?"

"Yeah. I kissed him." She stared into her sister's wide eyes. "It was actually a bit more than kissing. I don't know what would've happened if we hadn't been interrupted."

Chelsea's jaw dropped. "No!" She glanced down at Katie's engagement ring. "Does Mitch know?"

Katie shook her head, tears filling her eyes. "No. It just happened a little while ago. I'm a terrible person." She collapsed against her sister's shoulder, crying.

Trying to soothe her sister, Chelsea held her close and said, "You're not a terrible person. You're human. People make mistakes."

Katie instantly sat up straight. "I'm not so sure it *was* a mistake. I don't know how something can feel that good and be wrong."

Chelsea smirked. "I'm pretty sure cheating feels pretty darn good to the people who do it. It's still wrong."

Sniffling, Katie said, "See? I'm a terrible person." Tears ran down her face. "I told you."

"Oh no." Chelsea sighed. She had never seen Katie quite like this before. "Why don't you just start at the beginning? Has this been going on for a while?"

"No." Katie reached into her purse for a tissue, then wiped her nose. "Just today. I met his older brother, Victor. He came to the restaurant earlier this week to rent the upstairs patio to propose to his girlfriend."

"Victor? I don't think I knew they had a brother named Victor."

"Yeah. He's the oldest. He was away in college before I dated Armando and he just sorta stayed away. I remembered him from high school but he didn't remember me. Didn't even recognize my name." Katie dabbed her eyes. "He's lived in New York for years and barely ever comes here, from what I understand." She gave Chelsea a pleading look. "Oh...but he looks and sounds *so* much like Armando."

Chelsea nodded, listening. "Okay. So, what happened?"

Katie took a deep breath. "Well, after that, I couldn't stop thinking about Armando. There was only one degree of separation between us, you know? Kinda freaked me out. I wondered if I should relay a message through Victor—"

"Hold up. You could've contacted him through Ramon anytime you wanted."

Katie scowled. "Really? You think *he* would've helped me?"

Chelsea sighed. "No, you're right. He's an asshole."

"He wouldn't even talk to me tonight when I went to the ranch. He stood there and glared at me, just like he does when I see him around."

"Okay, back up a second. So, you went to the ranch tonight?"

"Yeah. Armando asked me to come out there. He approached me after work last night. In the parking lot."

"Huh?"

"Yeah. Totally surprised me. It was the first time I'd seen him since...you know...that summer..." Katie paused. "I was shocked. He said he came here to find me when Victor told him I was getting married."

"What?" Chelsea drew her hand to her chest. "Is he actively trying to break up you and Mitch?"

Katie shrugged as her eyes darted anxiously around the room. "I guess so, yeah."

"All right. Let me think." Chelsea studied her sister's distraught face, desperate to find a solution. "What is it *you* want, exactly? Do you wanna break up with Mitch for a guy you haven't seen since high school? That sounds like a bad idea to me."

"I know. Especially when you put it like that." Katie frowned and took a moment to collect her thoughts. "I think I just wish I wasn't engaged right now. I'd love to give it a shot with Armando and see what happens."

"It's probably better you're engaged. It's protection. It's the only thing keeping you from rushing in."

"I wouldn't rush in. I just wish I had the freedom to *think* about rushing in." Katie suddenly balled up her fists. "Damn it! Why couldn't this have happened sooner? Like, even a month ago?"

"A month ago?" Chelsea asked. "You mean, right before Mitch proposed? Are you saying you would've broken up with him *that* easily, for Armando? It sounds to me like you just don't wanna marry Mitch." Chelsea groaned and shook her head. "It doesn't help that he's working so much. Always going out of town, leaving you alone at night. On the weekends. Would you have gone to visit Armando tonight if Mitch had been in town?"

"Probably not. But that doesn't prove—"

"Shh." Chelsea put her hand on Katie's arm. "You need to calm down before you make a crazy, impulsive decision. You've been with Mitch for over a year now. I remember when you were *really* excited about him, too. I think you just need to spend some quality time together. Remind yourself why you said yes."

Katie produced a long sigh. "Maybe you're right."

"When's he coming back from Dallas?"

"Monday morning."

"Okay." Chelsea nodded. "Have a date night on Monday evening."

"I think he has to work."

Chelsea gasped. "Again? Seems like every time I talk to you lately, Mitch has to work."

Katie shrugged. "I know. It's because he just made partner at the law firm. They expect a lot more out of him. He has to prove himself."

Chelsea's eyes rolled. "Whatever. It's not a great way to start an engagement. Have you thought about traveling with him? Why can't you just get up early and drive to Dallas in the morning?"

"We talked about it. Four hours there, and four hours back. Doesn't give us much time together, and I'd just get in the way of his work."

"Well, I hate to be the bearer of bad news, but you need to see him soon. You have to tell him what happened with Armando."

Katie's posture crumpled. "Yeah. You're right." Then her eyes perked up a little. "Do you think he'll break up with me over it?"

"Oh my God!" Chelsea's mouth dropped open and she smacked her sister's arm. "It sounds like you *want* him to break up with you."

"You don't know what I'm going through, Chelsea." Katie's sank back against the couch, her hand over her eyes. "I'd be with Armando right now if we hadn't been torn apart. Everything would be different. I feel like I need to see what would've happened."

"There's no way to know what would've happened. Your marriage might have already ended by now. You could've both been miserable."

Katie brought her hand down to her lap and faced her sister. "Or maybe not."

CHAPTER 11

After Katie left, Armando took a cold shower. As much as he wanted her physically, he knew damn well it was more than that. It had always been more than that. She was the only woman who sparked that kind of desire in him. Made it difficult for him to restrain the sexual impulses that accompanied his love for her.

All these years, he convinced himself the reason no woman could live up to Katie was because she was his first. He smiled, thinking about that night. Their senior year of high school, just before Christmas. It was the one time Mr. and Mrs. McCormack let Katie date Armando. Obviously, they thought the relationship was nothing serious and Katie would quickly move on. What they didn't know was that Katie and Armando showed up at the dance just long enough to have some pictures taken, then they sneaked off to Katie's aunt's empty house fifteen minutes away.

And there, in a spare bedroom, Armando learned how it felt to make love to a woman.

He chuckled, remembering how bad his technique was, but they were both virgins with nothing to compare it to. Making love to her for the first time was still the greatest moment of his life. And now, after all the women he'd been with over the years, that night still played through his mind in exquisite detail.

And it was because he still loved Katie.

A few hours later, after Isaac was sound asleep and Cara was reading in bed, Armando told his brothers they needed to have a talk. They went to Ramon's office and shut the door.

Armando and Victor sat in chairs in front of the desk, while Ramon sat behind the desk, leaning on his forearms and smirking at Armando.

Armando glared at Ramon. "What?"

Ramon shrugged. "Nothing. Just waiting for you to start, that's all."

Sighing, Armando said, "You know, you'd think since we haven't seen each other in a while, you'd at least be civil toward me?"

Ramon scoffed. "I *am* being civil. I told you, I'm waiting for you to start."

Victor shook his head. "No, you're waiting for a chance to argue. You've been an ass ever since Armando showed up this morning. I thought we were all grown men here, but apparently not. Maybe it wasn't right for me to bring Isaac. You're rubbing off on each other."

Armando snickered.

Seething, Ramon narrowed his eyes at Victor, cleared his throat, then calmly said, "It pisses me off that he came here without telling anyone and it was only to see that bitch who could've gotten him killed."

Before Armando could respond to Ramon's comment about Katie, Victor interjected. "Well, you need to get over it. I, for one, am just glad to see my brother." He glanced at Armando, then turned again to Ramon. "I'm glad to see *both* of you, in fact. So, instead of being an asshole, how 'bout you just be grateful that we're all under the same roof. It's been a while."

Ramon pursed his lips and looked up at the ceiling, angrily mulling over what Victor said.

Armando took a deep breath and quietly said, "Listen guys, I know my actions don't make a lot of sense right now. Not even to me." He folded his hands together and stared down at the floor. No way was he telling his brothers about his feelings for Katie. But it was time for a serious talk. "But that's not the issue here. I found out tonight that the reason I was kept from marrying Katie had something to do with Henry."

Ramon nodded. "I'm not surprised."

"What, exactly?" Victor asked.

Armando shrugged. "I don't know. At the time, Henry just told me to shrug it off and move on. He said Dwayne McCormack didn't think I was good enough for his daughter. He was just trying to send me a message. All that bullshit."

In a sad voice, Victor said, "Yeah, I remember."

Ramon's eyes were fixed on Armando, quietly waiting for him to continue.

"But according to Katie," Armando said, "there's some kind of history with Henry and the McCormack family. She didn't know what it was, but she heard her parents arguing. Her mom said something about how her dad shouldn't have made a deal with Henry years ago. She said it was like making a deal with the devil. They wouldn't talk about it in front of Katie, either. It was all really secretive. In fact, that whole thing is a big family secret for the McCormacks. They never talk about it. They just pretend it never happened."

Victor's brows knitted together. "Huh. All this time I just figured he was prejudiced. Didn't want her marrying a Hispanic guy."

Ramon let out a sarcastic chuckle. "Nah. Last year her sister married a guy named Eric Gomez. I think he's lived in Texas his whole life but he's Hispanic, for sure." He rolled his eyes. "You woulda thought it was the Royal Wedding or some shit. Had the roads blocked off. Signs everywhere. Henry went to it. Said it was really something. Hundreds of guests."

Armando and Victor looked at each other in disbelief.

"Wait a minute," Victor said. "Why are you just now mentioning this? The other night we had a little chat and you didn't say anything about Katie's sister marrying a Hispanic guy, or Henry going to the wedding…"

Ramon shrugged. "So? Didn't figure it mattered. Since when do you care about what happens around here, anyway?"

Gritting his teeth, Armando grunted, then said, "Okay, *now* I'm pissed. Ten years ago, I got hauled off to jail and left for dead in the desert because I wanted to marry Dwayne McCormack's daughter. And now I find out Henry, who lied to me all along, was off at the wedding of Dwayne McCormack's *other* daughter, having a great time like nothing ever happened. That really doesn't sit well with me."

Ramon nodded. "Yep. Henry and Dwayne always acted like nothing ever happened. Hell, I see Dwayne a couple times a year and we just shake hands and keep on goin'."

Armando's jaw dropped. "What the hell, Ramon? You were a real prick to Katie today but you're friends with her dad?"

"No." Ramon scowled. "We're not friends. It's just business. The Cattleman's Association quarterly breakfast. Dwayne knows a bunch of those guys and he's there keeping up appearances, I guess." His eyes darted between his brothers' indignant faces. "What? I got a business to run! I can't afford to be mean to people. I gotta maintain those relationships." He crossed his arms over his chest and gave them each a critical stare. "I know for a fact you both do it, too." He stopped at Victor. "You told me you met Cara at one of those snooty dinners. Same kinda thing."

Victor nodded and said, "Except nobody at that dinner ever left my brother for dead in the middle of the desert."

Armando shook his head at Ramon. "Is there something you're not telling us?"

Ramon snorted. "No."

Armando said, "What's the real reason Henry left eight months ago?"

Leaning forward in his chair, Victor waited for Ramon's response.

"You already know," Ramon said. "I bought him out of the ranch. He retired."

Armando quietly studied Ramon's face for any twitches of anxiety. A sign that he was lying. But Ramon was perfectly calm and collected.

Still, something didn't add up to Armando, and he knew Victor was thinking it too. Ramon always had a bit of a temper, but there was a bitterness inside him that was strange and unfamiliar. Out of the three brothers, Ramon was the only one who had lived at the ranch with Henry all these years. Turnbrook was a small town, and in addition to the quarterly breakfast, Armando knew Ramon must see the McCormacks occasionally. Given Ramon's temper, and his cold reaction to Katie today, it made no sense that Ramon would have the self-control to be nice to Katie's family all these years without blowing up at some point.

Victor gave Ramon a thoughtful look. "Next time Henry calls, keep him on the phone. Tell him we'd all like to speak with him."

Armando's jaw tightened. "Yeah. I'd just *love* to ask him a few questions."

Hesitantly, Ramon nodded. "All right. Next time he calls, I'll let him know. But it could be weeks."

"That's fine," Victor said. "We were already thinking of extending our stay for a while. Isaac really likes it here."

Armando felt happy for the first time in several minutes as he thought of his own reason for sticking around: Katie. "I was thinking about that too. I could use a long break. Might have to fly out for the day—"

Ramon shot him a wry grin. "You mean, you wanna stay here in my house? You just drop in out of the blue and expect me to give you a place to stay?"

"Yep." Armando sat back in his chair, hands folded over his lap.

Ramon flashed a subtle smile, then produced a deliberate, labored sigh. "I'm gonna have to put you guys to work, then. You earn your keep in this house. Hmm." He rubbed his chin. "There's a lotta shit to fix around here. We can start with the potholes out front..."

Victor groaned. "I'd rather just pay rent if you don't mind."

Armando laughed. "Me too."

Shrugging, Ramon grinned and said, "I guess we'll work something out." Then his face took on a serious look. "So, what are we gonna do about Dwayne? Henry? Are we all just waiting around for Henry to call? Or are we gonna take action of our own?"

Exasperated at the very mention of their names, Armando inhaled deeply and blew out a heavy breath. "I don't know. I don't wanna waste my energy on revenge."

They continued for another hour, discussing whether or not they should track down Henry or approach Dwayne. Armando struggled to hide the fact that his thoughts were elsewhere. All he cared about was convincing Katie to choose him over Mitch.

Maybe later he'd care about why they were ripped apart. They could never change the past, and Armando simply wanted Katie in his future.

* * * * *

Yawning, Victor crawled into bed beside Cara, who had already turned out the lights.

A few seconds later, in a sleepy whisper, she asked, "How'd it go downstairs?"

"Thought you were asleep." Victor put his arm around Cara's back as she curled up against him. He kissed her forehead and said, "*So* much family drama. Too heavy for bedtime conversation. I'll fill you in tomorrow."

"Mmm." Cara nuzzled his chest. "Good. So tired. Mom called when you were down there. That's enough family drama for me. She's upset we're staying for so long. She really misses Isaac."

"She and Tom could come down to visit. Stay here at the house."

"It's pretty crowded now, don't you think?"

Victor yawned. "Nah. It's just the three of us, plus Armando. There's another bedroom downstairs nobody's using."

"Yeah, but the house has probably gotten too crowded for Ramon. I'm afraid we're overstaying our welcome."

Victor kissed her forehead again, then said, "Don't worry about that. I can tell he's happy to have company." Victor knew Ramon would never admit it, but he saw Ramon's eyes light up when Armando said he wanted to stay. "Also, I was thinking it'd be nice for Ramon to have someone like Patty around. Not that I wanna just bring her down here just so she can work or something—"

Cara inhaled a quiet gasp. "No, you're right! I hadn't thought about it. She'd love that! Having you guys to cook for every night. I'm pretty sure she'll wanna overhaul the kitchen though. New pots and pans, appliances." She sat up a little, barely able to see Victor's eyes in the dark. "Have you seen what he's using to cook?"

Victor had a moment of laughter. When he calmed down he said, "It's settled then. I hope she can get down here, soon. Tell her I'll pay her. She just can't tell Ramon about it. When he's finished working at the end of the day, a good dinner'll be waiting for him. Patty insisted." He shrugged. "He gives her grief? I'll take care of it."

"What about when we all leave? He'll just be alone again."

"We'll worry about that when it happens. For now, I just need to make sure he's doing better without being obvious about it."

Cara settled against him with a yawn. "Sounds good to me. I'll call her first thing in the morning."

Victor rubbed her back. "And I might have a project for Tom, too."

* * * * *

It was Monday evening. Katie's last day off before returning to work, and two days since she saw Armando. She wanted to call him but resisted, at the urging of her sister, Chelsea.

Katie felt it was only right to give Mitch another chance, and tell him about her make-out session with Armando in person. Today she was worried. And not because she was afraid of what Mitch would say.

She was worried about being physical with Mitch tonight.

She had barely thought of him since Armando appeared in her life again. But she was too logical to consider their engagement to be over. After all, they had dated for over a year. Her family loved him. And he bought her a beautiful engagement ring. Certainly she wasn't flighty enough to forget about him just because the guy she fell in love with as a teenager magically reappeared.

Right?

Sitting on her couch, Katie took another sip of wine to soothe her nerves. Mitch was on his way over. Not long ago, she would have looked forward to his visit. She would already have the refrigerator stocked, ready to make him breakfast in the morning.

But now, she waited on pins and needles for someone who may as well have been a stranger.

Katie wore jeans and a nice blouse. Usually she wore something sexy when she was expecting Mitch but it would have made her feel like a fraud tonight. Perhaps her spark for him would reignite naturally. But she was certainly in no mood to seduce him. She spent a few minutes flipping through a scrapbook she made shortly after they got engaged. She stopped to study Mitch in each picture. He was handsome in his own right. Dark blond hair. Blue eyes. Tall. Nice build. All in all, a sexy guy.

At almost seven-thirty, Katie heard a knock at the door. She groaned, set her wine glass on the coffee table, then stood up and shuffled to the door to let him in.

Mitch was mid-yawn when the door opened. With his hand over his mouth, he said, "Hey baby."

"Hey you." She forced a smile. "Come on in."

He finished yawning and bent down to give her lips a very quick peck before walking in.

She relaxed a bit. That little kiss wasn't nearly as bad as she thought it would be.

Immediately, Mitch took off his jacket and hung it neatly over a chair, then loosened his tie and sat at one end of the couch. "Sorry it took so long to get here tonight. They shoveled more work on me today."

"That's good though, right? It means they believe in you. They think you can handle it. You're passing their test."

"No, I think they want me to pay my dues." He rubbed his forehead. "This all better be worth it someday." Then he let out a loud sigh and patted the couch next to him. "Come here. Sit down. Tell me what was so important you nagged me until I came over." He produced a wicked chuckle.

Katie knew that laugh. He was joking, but there was enough seriousness in his tone to let her know he truly felt nagged.

He seemed not to notice her hesitation when she settled in beside him and welcomed his arm around her shoulders. She closed her eyes and relaxed against his chest. He smelled good and his body was toasty warm. *So far, so good.*

"So?" he asked as he gently rubbed her back. "You gonna tell me why you wanted me over here? I'm gonna have to go home and go to bed soon."

"What?" Katie was glad, in a way. But she was also confused. She sat up straight and looked in his eyes. "This is the first time we've seen each other since Thursday. Don't you wanna spend some time together? I thought maybe we could order in and—"

He winced. "Katie, Katie, Katie. I tried to explain when you called earlier. I'm dead tired. That client in Dallas wore me out over the weekend. I just need a few nights alone in my own bed so I can rest up and do a good job at work." He cupped her chin. "Please don't be angry with me. I'm doing this all for us. For *you*." He grinned and continued in an easy tone, "I know it's hard now but it'll pay off someday. It won't be like this forever."

Katie nodded. Undeniably, she felt a deep sense of relief that Mitch was too busy to see her. But that relief turned to worry a moment later; her dilemma was left unresolved. She was engaged to a man she didn't love anymore. And if she wanted a chance to reignite her feelings, lack of time with him was surely not what she needed.

So, Katie looked into his eyes. If she had limited time with him tonight, she had to use it wisely. "I kissed my ex-boyfriend on Saturday." She gulped. "Actually, it was more than a kiss. We got a little carried away for a few minutes. But I stopped him. Then I left, and I haven't seen him since. I feel terrible about it. I'm sorry."

Mitch's eyes widened, then narrowed. He removed his arm from her shoulders and hunched forward in his seat, hands folded between his legs. Then he stared straight ahead at nothing. "Hmm."

"Well?" Katie asked. "Aren't you upset with me?"

"I don't know." He drew his hand to his temples, pulsing them with his fingers. Then he took a deep breath and said, "At least you told me about it."

"Okay." She waited for him to look at her, but he looked everywhere else instead, as if he was lost in thought.

Finally he met her gaze and said, "I'm not thrilled about it, but it's not the end of the world. It happens. You haven't seen each other in a while. There's familiarity. Maybe you had a few drinks or something." He shrugged. "I'll ask you not to do it again but I can overlook it this once. Everyone makes mistakes."

Alarmed by his reaction, she asked, "Has this happened to you before. Is that why you're so calm?"

Mitch groaned and looked away, sheepishly.

She gasped. "Was it after we started dating? Was it recent?" Another gasp. "Who was that woman I heard when I called on Saturday? I knew there was someone at the restaurant with you."

"Damn it, Katie! I'm way too tired for this conversation." He rolled his eyes. "The woman you heard was a stranger I met at the bar when I was waiting for the client to arrive. Just a lady I met in passing and we struck up a conversation. I don't even remember her name."

"Okay. What about my other question? Has there been anyone else since we got together?"

He paused for a few seconds before speaking. "Look, I'd only known you for a couple of months. It was a girl I dated in college. She sent me a message on Facebook that she'd be passing through the area. We met for drinks." Frowning, he shook his head. "I didn't plan for it to happen."

Katie's mouth dropped open. "Didn't plan for *what* to happen? Did you sleep with her?"

"No! We just kissed. And maybe a little more. In my car." Smirking, he added, "So, I guess we're even."

"No, we're *not* even. I feel terrible about mine and I didn't wait months to confess to you."

He gave her a glum look. "Katie, I wasn't sure about our future at the time. She and I go way back. It just happened. Probably the same way it happened with you and *your* ex."

Rapidly, she shook her head. "No. You told me you wanted to be serious with me two weeks after we met. What was I doing that night? Did you lie and say you had to work? Are you lying to me now? How do I know you're not cheating on me?"

Mitch groaned and turned his face up to the ceiling. "Why'd I have to open my mouth?"

She slapped her knees in frustration, then stood. "Get out of here." She lifted her arm, pointing at the door.

Mitch stood up next to her, his eyes and voice pleading. "This is all a misunderstanding. I'm not cheating on you." He gently placed a hand on the side of her face. "Don't break up with me over this.

I did a stupid thing a *long* time ago and there's nothing I can do to change it. But I wanna marry you, *now*. Soon, if you'll let me. I love you."

Tears welled up in Katie's eyes. If she had known about Mitch's encounter with his ex-girlfriend, she would have considered breaking up with him. And if she had, maybe she would be with Armando right now.

But, a tiny piece of her was jealous over Mitch and this other girl. It surely took place when Katie was completely smitten.

Confused and angry, Katie motioned toward the door again, this time in a softer tone. "Get out. I need time to think."

Mitch stared into her sad eyes, his face sullen. "Don't give up on me. Please. I forgive you for what you did because I love you. Please do the same for me."

"Just go."

He nodded, then gave her a peck on the cheek before heading to the door. As he stopped at the chair for his jacket, he said, "Let's have dinner in a few nights." He thought for a moment. "Thursday. I'll clear my evening and pick you up from work. I'll make reservations at someplace special. And I hope we can talk about setting a date." With a grin, he said, "That Cancun idea is really growing on me. Just us, a few family members. It's intimate, right there on the beach. We can do it soon. Please, think about it."

She pressed her hand against her stomach, nauseated by the idea of marrying him soon. Or at all.

Mitch let out a loud sigh. "I hate to leave you like this. Are you sure you don't want me to stay? I guess I could sleep here tonight. Your bed's not as comfortable as mine but—"

"No. Get out!"

"Okay. See you Thursday?"

Mindlessly, she shrugged.

Mitch put his hand on the doorknob. "I love you Katie." He blew her a kiss, then opened the door and left.

Katie rushed to the door to lock it. She then went back to the couch to have another glass of wine, but she was too sick with nerves to drink more than a few sips.

She remembered the night six months earlier when Mitch had almost gotten in a fist fight with a man who was flirting with Katie at a concert. But tonight, he showed practically no jealousy about the incident with Armando.

As she sat there in silence with nothing but her thoughts, she couldn't shake the feeling that Mitch was cheating on her.

She grabbed her cell phone, ready to call Armando, but quickly stopped. She didn't want him like this. Out of retaliation, rebounding from Mitch.

Heck, maybe she just wanted to be single for a while. Armando seemed ready to jump into a brand new relationship. That sure wasn't very practical. It would make all of her friends—and especially her family—think she was crazy.

Oh sweet Lord...her family.

Another thing to make her stomach feel sick. The idea of telling her mom and dad that she had chosen to break up with Mitch in favor of rekindling her romance with Armando Barboza, of all people. It would ruin her relationship with her parents, forever.

Then she suddenly burst into laughter as an image passed through her mind. The way-too-horrified expression on Mom's face. It was so sad, it was comical.

But a few moments later, it was just sad.

Katie sank back against the couch, sobbing as she had an epiphany. It was all perfectly clear now. Her choice was never between Armando and Mitch.

Her choice was between Armando and her parents.

CHAPTER 12

Tuesday morning arrived. Ramon left the house much earlier, at four o'clock, to head to another ranch he managed. Armando was in Ramon's office, sitting behind the desk, having a video conference on his laptop with some people in his home office. His suitjacket and tie presented a stark contrast to his jeans and bare feet, but his business associates could only see him from the waist up.

Victor and Cara were busy keeping Isaac entertained in the living room while they waited for their special guests to arrive. They thought it best for it to be a surprise to the young boy. For one, Isaac loved surprises. And second, if he knew he was about to see his Grandma, he would be too excited to sit still. So, they sat on the floor helping Isaac stack large blocks to build a brightly-colored fort. Victor and Cara shared a quick glance when they heard the car coming up the drive. Victor made sure to keep Isaac playing and sufficiently distracted.

Soon there was a loud knock at the front door, and Cara popped up to answer it. "Wonder who *that* could be, Isaac?" she asked with a suspicious grin.

"Huh?" Isaac turned to intently watch his mom as she went to the door.

As soon as it opened, Patty burst inside and gave Cara a hug. "It feels like I haven't seen you in years!"

Isaac ran to the door at the sound of Patty's voice. "Gwammah!"

Immediately, Patty let go of Cara and scooped Isaac up in her arms. "I've missed you so much!"

As Isaac and Patty hugged and talked, Victor came in. Patty gave him a kiss on the cheek, then headed into the living room with Isaac.

Tom, Patty's new husband, came through the door after her, holding a suitcase. He gave Victor and Cara a big smile. "Nice place you got here."

They greeted him warmly. Victor helped him carry the luggage to the downstairs bedroom next to Isaac's, where they would be staying.

A few minutes later they were all in the living room. Isaac—who had recently started to refer to Tom as "Gwampah"—ran up to sit in his lap and give him a hug.

Tom laughed. "Thanks, Isaac. Thought you forgot all about me."

"No," Cara said. "He's just excited to see his Grandma."

Isaac giggled and pointed to himself, proudly boasting to Tom, "I'm getting a baby bwothow fuh my buth-day!"

Patty gasped.

Cara and Victor, sitting on the loveseat, shared a stunned look. It was the first time in several days he had brought up his "baby brother."

Practically leaping off the sofa, Patty rushed over to Cara and Victor. "Really? Were you just waiting to tell me in person?"

As Patty bent down to hug her, Cara shook her head.

"No. I'm sorry, Mom," Cara said in a sympathetic tone. "Isaac's a little...uh...confused?"

Patty's face fell as she shrank away. "Oh."

Cara stood and led her mom across the room for a little privacy while the guys spoke with Isaac about the implications of having a brother. "Victor said Isaac started talking about it when he found out we were getting married. I've been afraid to ask how he connected marriage to having a brother. Victor and I've been reading up on how to talk to kids his age about sex."

"Aw," Patty said. "I told you he'd make a good father."

"I know." Cara nodded. "Do you have any idea how Isaac came to that conclusion?" She waggled her eyebrows at her mother.

Patty shrugged. "No idea. I promise." She let out a sad sigh. "Oh, but I already had my hopes up about another grandbaby. Are you sure you're not pregnant?"

"Pretty sure, yeah. Don't worry, we're talking about it. Victor definitely wants a family."

Patty turned her attention to the window, gazing at the clearing outside. "Have you thought about getting married here?"

"No."

"You should. It's lovely." She pointed. "You could put an arch right over there, in front of those trees. There's plenty of room. It'd be so beautiful."

"But I don't know anyone down here. The relatives would have to travel—"

"Oh, who cares? Let 'em travel. It's too pretty to waste."

In no mood to argue with her mother, Cara decided it was time to change the subject and show her the kitchen. So, she started across the room and motioned for Patty to come along. "Let me show you the rest of the house."

Patty followed Cara into the kitchen, immediately giving it

a hard once-over. "Hmm. Interesting. Looks a little run down." She looked up and down the counter at the paltry selection of appliances. "Oh no, this won't do."

Cara watched Patty float around the kitchen, going from cabinet to cabinet, then opening the refrigerator door. "You know, if you'd like to make a few…uh…*suggestions*…about this kitchen, Victor will gladly cover the costs—"

Patty raised an eyebrow at Cara as she closed the refrigerator. "Oh really, now? Is that why you invited me all the way down here? To get this dilapidated kitchen in order? Maybe have dinner on the table every night?"

"Uh…" Cara struggled for words. "No…"

Patty rushed to her, beaming. "I'd love to!" She folded her hands together, her eyes dancing around the room. "Oh, there's *so* much to do. New recipes. I'll need to go to the store right away to get started."

"Are you sure you're okay with this? We've got a full house here. It's a lot of work. We've been ordering take out."

"Are you kidding me?" Patty's eyes widened. "It's a dream come true! A big family. Lots of hungry men." She smirked and waved a dismissive hand. "Don't even worry about it."

Cara let out a quiet sigh of relief. "Okay, great. But I have to warn you. Ramon probably won't like you infringing on his turf. He really needs to hire someone to do the cooking and housekeeping but he's stubborn."

Patty shrugged. "It'll be all right. He knows we're here, doesn't he?"

"Yes. He didn't seem too happy about filling up the very last bedroom but he knew Isaac missed you. Victor thinks he's secretly happy to have a full house." Cara took a deep breath before changing the subject. "But anyway, about the housekeeping. We're hiring a service to come in during the day when Ramon's not here.

This house is too big and too crowded for one of us to do it. And God forbid one of these guys lift a finger. Armando and Victor have had maids for years."

Patty asked, "Have you thought about hiring Marcy? You know she keeps losing clients to some other office cleaning service."

"We don't know how long we'll be here and I didn't want her to miss out on some new business because she's out of town."

"Yeah, I get it. You really don't know how long you're staying?"

Cara briefly glanced behind her, then quieted her voice. "No. Both of Victor's brothers are going through some stuff. He wants to make sure they're both doing better before we leave. Says he feels like maybe he's neglected them for a long time."

Patty brought her hand to her heart, her lips in a sympathetic pout. "Aw. So nurturing."

They both turned to the sound of small feet running into the kitchen.

Isaac stopped at Patty, hugging her leg. "You gonna make me somethin' good, Gwammah?"

Patty opened her mouth wide in a quiet gasp. "Of course I am!"

Cara smiled. This house felt a little more like a home now.

* * * * *

When his conference call was over, Armando took off his jacket and emerged from Ramon's office to the echoes of excited voices filling the hallway. As he arrived in the foyer to turn to the living room, Isaac ran out of the kitchen toward him.

"A-mando!" Isaac reached for his hand, pulling him toward the kitchen.

Chuckling, Armando went where Isaac led him. He spent a few

minutes chatting with the vivacious Patty in the kitchen, then he went to the living room where Victor introduced him to Patty's husband, Tom.

After several minutes of greetings and pleasantries, Victor gave both men a serious glance and suggested they go to Ramon's office for some privacy.

They entered the office and closed the door. Armando sat behind the desk, while Tom and Victor sat in front of it.

Tom spoke first. "So, I guess this is regarding that job you told me about on the phone yesterday?

Victor nodded. "Yes."

Groaning a little, Tom said, "Well, I gotta tell you, I'm not sure how much I can help. The reason I'm good in New York and New Jersey is because I know people. I know exactly where to look for everything. But I've never been to Texas until today." Tom squinted at Victor. "Seems like a couple of guys like you should be able to pull some strings and find some information."

Armando spoke up for both of them. "We've both made some phone calls, called in a few favors. But this good ole boy network…" Armando rolled his eyes.

Victor let out a heavy sigh. "Yeah. My guy at the IRS says everything looks squeaky clean so far. And he's not the first person to tell me I might as well give up. We don't know how far back this goes."

Tom licked his lips and took a tiny notepad out of his back pocket. "Let's go back to the beginning here. I need to know what I'm dealing with. So, the guy who moved you to Texas. His name?"

"Henry Platt," Victor said.

The brothers took turns explaining that Henry found them in Mexico and moved them to Turnbrook, Texas to work on his ranch when Victor was twelve, Armando was ten, and Ramon was eight.

Victor and Armando shared an uncomfortable glance when Tom asked if Henry was romantically involved with their mother before she died. Armando reluctantly answered, "Yes, but in secret."

Next, they explained what happened to Armando ten years earlier. When Tom heard the part about Armando being kept in a holding cell then waking up in Mexico, his face took on a horrified look, but he continued taking notes.

They went on to explain that Henry left the ranch eight months earlier, after selling his remaining part of the business to Ramon, but they had their doubts about what really happened.

When they took a break, Tom shook his head. "I really don't think I'm the man for this job. I don't know where to start. Probably the courthouse. Find whatever public records I can find. Maybe I'll make up a reason to meet with Judge Dwayne McCormack, act like it has something to do with Henry. If he'll even meet with me."

Victor chuckled. "See? That's more than I probably would've thought to do."

"Yeah." Armando nodded in agreement. "You probably know how to tell if someone's lying, at least. Talk to people. Pay attention to how they respond. And whatever you do, don't tell anyone you know us. You're probably at an advantage. You're the Yankee from out of town, asking innocent questions." Armando shrugged.

Victor said, "Anything you find will be helpful. And don't feel like you have to spend all your time on this. Do this only if you want to. And please know, we don't expect a miracle."

"Good." Tom grinned. "Because the more you tell me, the more I have doubts about it."

"I'm sorry," Victor said. "Seriously, if you don't wanna help, it's okay. We'll pay for your time, regardless."

Tom shrugged. "It's okay. It'll be fun for me to get to know a new place. So, your brother Ramon can't know about this?"

Armando and Victor both groaned at the same time.

Victor said, "No. We told him we called some connections but he won't know we've told you a thing."

Tom's eyes flashed around the room. "Well, from what you've told me so far, I have a feeling there's some answers in his office right here about what happened eight months ago."

Armando shook his head. "We've already looked through everything. Even the stuff he's got locked up. Nothing."

Tom said, "Well, you may not know what to look for."

Armando chuckled. "You're right." Then took let out a deep sigh, hoping his brother wouldn't judge him too harshly for what he was about to ask. "I actually have another request. It's about Dwayne's daughter, Katie."

Victor almost smiled. Tom leaned forward, ready to take notes.

Armando continued. "She's engaged to this guy. Mitch Nelson."

Tom nodded and wrote his name down. "Okay."

Armando said, "He just became the youngest partner ever at the biggest law firm in San Antonio. One of the biggest firms in the state. I wanna know if Dwayne had something to do with it."

"Hmm," Tom said as he wrote.

Armando folded his hands together on top of the desk. "You see, Dwayne's an elected official, and I know Mitch is considering politics. I keep thinking maybe Dwayne didn't like me because I was born in Mexico. Can't run for President." Armando rolled his eyes. "But I really doubt it's something that simple."

Victor's head shook. "No, it's way more serious than that. I can't imagine anyone caring that much about politics to chase you down across the state and do what he did to you."

Sighing, Armando said, "I know. It's just a thought. Besides, Katie overheard that conversation about Dwayne making a deal with Henry."

Tom straightened his glasses, then started writing again as he said, "You never know. Might be a reason in there somewhere. You guys both U.S. citizens?"

Armando and Victor both nodded and said, "Yes."

"Hmm." Tom nodded. "Well, Dwayne might've helped grease the wheels. Might've done something that would get him in trouble for a long time. Immigration laws have gotten stricter the past few years but he might've pulled some strings back then to get you legal faster. And maybe he didn't want you marrying his daughter because he wanted a lot of distance between the families. Shady men with a lot to lose will do just about anything to keep their misdeeds from catching up with them."

"Huh." Armando put his arms across his chest and leaned back in his chair, thinking about what Tom said.

Victor nodded. "Yeah. You might be on to something." He looked at Armando. "I can't believe we didn't think about that."

Tom shrugged. "It's just a theory." He cleared his throat and said to Armando, "So, what's the name of that law firm where Mitch Nelson works?"

They discussed the case for a few more minutes until Cara knocked on the door to tell them lunch was ready.

After lunch, Armando took a few more conference calls. Then he prepared for his next move with Katie.

* * * * *

It was Tuesday evening, and Katie was just about to do her final walk-through of the restaurant when one of the servers whistled for her attention. With a knowing grin, he pointed at the front door.

Sure enough, it was a bouquet from the flower shop down the

street. The third one she had received today from Mitch. One bouquet awaited her when she arrived at work that morning. The second bouquet came at lunchtime. The third, and biggest, bouquet was a box filled with two dozen long-stemmed red roses.

Katie begrudgingly signed for it and turned around to the almost empty dining room to see the employees all laughing at her.

Jonny, a bartender, called out from behind the bar as she walked by, "Whatever he did wrong, I say you forgive the poor schmuck!"

Katie gnashed her teeth and swallowed her retort as she breezed by on her way to the back of the restaurant so she could toss this gift into a dumpster. She hadn't told anyone why she wasn't wearing her engagement ring today, or why she had received all those flowers. Rumors were spreading and she didn't care. Heck, she didn't even care enough to read the cards that came with all those flowers.

She used the same routine with each bouquet:

Remove the card.

Toss the flowers in the trash.

Rip up the card and toss into trash next to flowers.

She had kept her phone off all day as well. Surely, if Mitch had sent three apology gifts to her place of work, he was probably trying to call her. But her stomach couldn't handle the thought of talking to him. It wasn't so much about the girl he kissed, or the fact that she suspected he was cheating.

Katie's heart belonged to someone else.

But was she ready for the fallout? She contemplated waiting a few days before telling her well-meaning sister Chelsea, who would probably—for the billionth time—just tell her to give Mitch another chance.

The obvious choice was to call Armando and let him help her sort out her feelings. But he had already made his own feelings clear.

Katie stuck her palm to her forehead in a futile effort to stave off the impending dizziness that accompanied her nervous lack of eating, and the constant swirl of thoughts that left her mind spinning. All she wanted to do right now was get rid of those roses and get the heck out of that restaurant before Mitch showed up in person, causing every single employee to take up for him without knowing any of the facts.

As Katie charged through the kitchen, she was met by a pouting Jennifer.

"What?" Jennifer glared at the box tucked under Katie's arm. "*Another* one?"

Katie's tone was flat and cold as she brushed past the sulking blonde, hoping today wouldn't be one of those days when she would have to fix something for Jennifer that required working late. "Yeah. It's not a big deal."

Jennifer scowled at the back of Katie's head as she went by. "Maybe not a big deal to *you*. But most girls would *love* a man who sends flowers. Geez. What happened with you guys, anyway?"

"Don't worry about it," Katie replied over her shoulder.

Jennifer huffed and said something else Katie didn't hear as she pushed the loud metal door open and descended the stairs to the back parking lot.

Katie tore the card away before hurling the box into the dumpster. As she was about to rip it apart, she rolled her eyes and decided to read this one. After all, he had sent three bouquets. Maybe she should at least glance at one of the cards.

"You're the only one who matters, Katie.

You're the only one who will ever matter.

Love, Mitch."

A deep grunt of disgust escaped Katie's throat. That's the best he could do? She tore up the card and let the pieces float over the lid of the dumpster. From the light tone of his sentiment, he was completely clueless they were over for good.

Suddenly trembling, she pulled a hand to her unsteady stomach.

She knew she needed to talk to him. Break up officially. But she may need a few days to let the notion simmer. Summon the strength to break the news to her parents.

Then hope there was enough strength left over to deal with the repercussions.

Katie would have stayed outside to take some deep, calming breaths, but the air reeked of garbage, so she rushed back inside and filled her lungs with the pleasing smells of the kitchen. Tonight's dinner special would be what Katie considered timeless comfort food—mashed potatoes and beef tenderloin—and thankfully the smell of it didn't make her wretch, even though her appetite was nowhere to be found.

She stayed there for a few more seconds before heading out of the kitchen to check on a few things before leaving work for the night.

But on Katie's way through the dining room, she was met by a wide-eyed Jennifer, and her jaw tensed. "What is it?" Katie asked.

"Someone's here to see you. He's sitting at the bar." Jennifer's lips snapped shut and she turned away for a second, then quickly turned back. "Oh, and it's not Mitch." Then Jennifer sauntered off to a nearby table where a customer was flagging her down.

Trying to appear professional in front of the diners, Katie swallowed her complaint about Jennifer's lack of detail as she straightened her suitjacket with a big smile. She then rushed through the dining room, hoping whatever nuisance awaited her would go away quickly.

The bar was a little more crowded than usual this time of day.

It took her a moment, but when she saw the back of Armando's head, her heart swelled...then quickly ached. She inhaled deeply through her nose and gingerly slid onto the bar stool beside his.

Armando's brows went up and he gently turned to her with a mischievous smirk. "So, you decided not to call me?"

She shrugged. "You could've called *me*."

His head slowly shook as his eyes fixed on hers. "No, you never gave me permission. I'm determined not to overstep my bounds again."

Katie rolled her eyes and tried not to let her insides melt from his sexy, searing gaze...or the way his tight body filled out that perfectly-fitted Italian suit. "So, you just show up here where I work and ask for me? Is that not overstepping?"

One side of Armando's mouth quirked up in a playful grin. "No. Maybe I'm just a customer who needs to plan a party here at the restaurant. I told you to call me for a reason. It means the ball's in your court."

Armando then shifted his knees toward her. As soon as she felt them touch the outside of her thigh, without thinking, she shifted around in her seat until they were facing each other.

Her heart hammered inside her chest as Armando's eyes fell to her lap where she smoothed her palms anxiously against her skirt.

He inhaled sharply. "What's this?" He covered her left hand, his dumbstruck eyes rising to meet hers. "Do my eyes deceive me, or do I feel a naked ring finger?"

A shiver passed through Katie as the word "naked" passed Armando's lips. Somewhere inside her was a teenager, giggling inappropriately at naughty words. But right now, Katie was nowhere close to giggling. She was caught up in the feel of his warm skin against hers, and the way the words "naked" and "Armando" melted together and tickled her brain. She stared into his penetrating brown eyes and barely choked out, "I didn't wear my ring today." Then she swallowed and softly added, "I may never wear it again."

Armando's lips slowly spread into a broad smile. His eyes crinkled at the sides in a way that flooded Katie with memories. In high school, Armando was mysterious. Not quiet, but brooding, and very serious on the surface. But she quickly got to know who he really was. He was mature for his age, but he still possessed a sweet, boyish transparency. He loved with all his heart, and with reckless abandon. He was never shy to let Katie know how happy she made him.

Right now, she knew Armando was overjoyed—because of *her*. That smile was genuine and unassuming. He wanted her. He had always wanted her. And it would be so damn easy to give in and walk hand-in-hand with him out of that restaurant to a new life together...

But the cleared throat of Jonny the bartender plopped her right back down to Earth.

Jonny leaned across the bar with a sly nod as he asked Katie, "So, what'll the lady be drinking tonight?"

Katie gasped and pulled her hands away from Armando's, then looked around the restaurant. Several of the wait staff, including Jennifer—who should have been finishing up her shift in the dining room—were casting smug glances her way. Some were whispering to each other behind their hands. Her love life was definitely the talk of the restaurant today.

Katie's eyes were huge. She stood up and said to the bartender, "I'm not drinking," then to Armando, "I'm sorry. I..." Her mind went blank. She just knew she had to flee.

"What?" Armando gently grabbed her arm, his eyes sweetly pleading with her to stay. "Calm down. What's wrong?" He looked around the restaurant, following the paths of her frantic eyes. "Are we being watched?"

She waited for Jonny to walk over to another customer, then lowered her voice. "Yes. The whole restaurant's been talking about me all day. Mitch sent me flowers three times since I got here."

Armando shrugged. "So? Fuck 'em. Let 'em talk. You get off work soon, right?"

"It's not that." A thin layer of tears filled her eyes, burning her nose. "I just...I can't be seen with you."

Armando closed his eyes, his lips flattening. He shook his head slowly, then said, "Your parents."

Katie sniffled. "They know everyone."

He rolled his eyes then let out a single, solemn laugh. "God. After all this time."

She tucked her face down to hide her tears from her co-workers. "I know. It's like we're eighteen again. That same old crap with my parents."

Armando sighed heavily. "It's okay." Then he surprised her with his lighthearted tone. "I always wondered what it was like to travel back in time. Now I know...I guess."

Katie laughed as she wiped her tears away.

Armando wanted to touch her but he maintained his distance on the bar stool. "I probably shouldn't have come here but I didn't wanna just show up at your door."

Her voice was weak. "I secretly hoped you would, though."

"Aw, Katie," he whispered. His fingers knitted tightly together to restrain himself, he said, "I Googled your address. Vista Glen apartments? Unit 522?"

She nodded vigorously.

"See you there in an hour?"

"How 'bout twenty-five minutes?"

CHAPTER 13

Exactly twenty-five minutes later, with a smile on his face and a spring in his step, Armando bounded up the stairwell to Katie's apartment. His heart raced with more feelings than he could possibly decipher. His thoughts were chaotic, knowing full well the issue of her parents still hung over their heads. But that problem was the least of his concerns right now.

Armando knocked on the door.

In an instant, the lovely Katie—still wearing her clothes from work—opened it, waving him inside.

As Armando stepped through the doorway, he looked into her eyes and said, "I feel like I've waited a thousand lifetimes for this." Then he put his hands on her waist. In one move, he leaned down to kiss her and kicked the door closed behind him. Suddenly his hands were everywhere, roaming her back. Grabbing her hair. His body pushing hers backward in the direction of the sofa as his kiss strengthened.

When the backs of her calves touched the couch, Katie pulled away, blinking up at him. "Don't you wanna know what happened with me and Mitch?"

In a flat tone, Armando's quick reply was, "No. I don't give a fuck about Mitch." Then his mouth covered hers again.

She wiggled away, breaking the kiss. "We're not officially broken up yet. He thinks we just had a fight. He could even show up here this evening."

"Well, you wanna make it official, then? Give him a call. I suppose I can wait." He leaned down to nibble on her ear, whispering, "I'll give you exactly one minute to take care of that little issue before I rip your clothes off. Remember, sweetheart: you were mine first." He made Katie shriek with pleasure as he gave her neck a hard massage with his tongue, then went back to her ear. "This ain't cheating. I don't care what anybody thinks or says or sees. I don't care if he opens that door and gets an eyewitness account of everything I'm about to do to you. You were always supposed to be with me."

Katie let her head fall back as he kissed her neck again, then he reached for the top of her blouse to unbutton it.

As he reached the last button, Armando let out a light chuckle. "So I guess you didn't need that minute I was gonna give you?"

Katie shook her head as she reached up to his shoulders to take his jacket off. "No."

"Good. 'Cause I couldn't wait that long." Armando shrugged out of his jacket and let it fall off, then reached behind Katie, rubbing her ass until he found her skirt to unzip it. It quickly fell to the floor.

As she stood there in only her bra and panties, she reached out to unbuckle his belt and said, "I swear I didn't think we'd rush into this when I invited you over."

"Me neither, baby." He unzipped his pants as he crooked an eyebrow at her. "But you gotta remember, I was promised a honeymoon and I never got it."

Katie blushed, making no effort to hide her smile. "Yeah. Me too."

Armando pushed his pants and underwear to the floor then began unbuttoning his shirt. "Shit, I remember calling half the state of New Mexico looking for a honeymoon suite. No credit card. Too young. One guy told me I sounded like a drug dealer and he didn't trust me."

Katie frowned. "I know. I'm sorry. You have no idea how devastated I was. When all the…" She bit the side of her lip as her eyes darted nervously about the room. "Bad stuff started, I was sitting there in the car fantasizing about getting you alone. No one around to stop us." She stood still, her eyes a little misty. "I'll never forget it."

Armando tossed his long-sleeved shirt to the floor, then pulled his undershirt off over his head and tossed it to the side. Naked, and fully aroused, he took her gently by her shoulders. "Sweet, sweet Katie. What happened was truly horrifying. Traumatic. But right now all I can think about is loving you again. The rest of it barely registers as a thought."

When he cradled her cheek with his palm, she grabbed his wrist, holding it there against her face. She said, "I get it. I just can't believe you're here right now. Like this, in my apartment." She sighed. "But I want you, too. Maybe we just need closure." She nodded, affirming that statement to herself. "Yeah. That's why it's okay if Mitch doesn't know. I'm not a bad person. I can make it official later. Right now, this is about a fresh start. And closure for all that stuff in the past."

Armando smiled and weaved his fingers through her hair to the back of her head, then quickly changed course and moved both hands to the small of her back, pulling her close enough for his erection to press against her stomach. "There you go. Overthinking everything." He kissed her forehead, remember how he always found that quality of hers very endearing. "And you can call it whatever you want, as long as you know that 'closure' doesn't mean we're finished."

She shook her head rapidly, her eyes wide and scared. "No, no, no. I said it's about a fresh start, but closure first. Begin a new chapter."

He laughed, thinking back to their frequent long discussions when they were teenagers. Katie always had philosophies and ideas to discuss. Other guys may have found her annoying, but Armando always paid attention. He loved to hear her thoughts.

But right now, his greatest desire was to show his love another way. "Baby, you can call it a fresh start. Closure. Whatever you want." He bent his head down to kiss her, slowly brushing his tongue across her bottom lip until she moaned into his mouth. Then he pulled away, whispering, "I'll give you closure. I'll give it to you here on the couch." His eyes flashed around the room. "On that table over there. In your bed. In the shower." He gave her a brief kiss then pulled away, his lips going to her earlobe where he nibbled for a second. Then he whispered, "I'll give you all the closure you can handle."

Katie heaved out a breathless moan and melted in his arms. The time for thinking was over. She closed her eyes and savored the feel of his lips and tongue against her ear, then her neck, as his hands went to her to her back, unfastening her bra.

He tugged the thin straps off her shoulders and she let the bra fall to her wrists, then dangle to the floor. And now, standing there in just her panties, Armando embraced her, pulling her bare chest tight to his as he gave her a deep kiss. His tongue slipped between her lips, moving slowly at first. But when he felt her arms around him and her fingernails raking against his back, his kiss grew harder and more insistent. Her mouth met his with every movement, telling him she wanted more.

Armando's hands smoothed a straight line down her sides until he felt the elastic waistband of her panties. His finger gently dug against her soft skin to get under the cotton fabric. He bent his knees as he crouched down to pull them all the way to her feet, and she stepped out of them.

He trailed wet, warm kisses up her body...her knee, her thigh... she let out a deep moan when she felt his lips against the soft skin of her inner thighs.

When he heard her reaction, he stayed there kissing her, mere inches away from her most sacred area. It had been too long since he heard those breathy moans from her; he wanted to enjoy them before things got more intense, but he knew he couldn't wait long. He could smell her sweet arousal.

Then suddenly she squealed and almost fell forward, losing her balance.

"Oh no!" Armando stood up, steadying her in his arms. "Are you okay?"

Katie panted heavily, her mouth hanging wide open. A quick line of words spilled from her mouth. "Oh my God I can't believe we're together in my living room."

"Are you okay? Maybe I shouldn't have been so forward. I've dreamed of being with you again for so long. Do you need me to stop?"

Katie's eyes instantly widened. "No." Rapidly, she shook her head. "No. No, don't stop."

Their eyes met, and Armando knew she was experiencing the same kind of ethereal sensory overload as he was. He licked his lips, then leaned down for a fiery kiss, his hands going down to the small of her back, then sliding under her thighs, lifting her to his waist.

She wrapped her arms and legs around him at once, and they stayed there kissing, his erection pressing near her entrance.

Armando moved his lips away from hers, as he readjusted her body in his arms. "I assume that's your bedroom door." He nodded behind her.

"Yes," she said with a purr.

"Good." He began a slow walk with her in his arms, stopping every few steps to give her a kiss.

The bedroom door was ajar, so he pushed his way through and soon placed Katie on the side of her queen-sized bed, her legs dangling off the sides, her pretty face beaming up at him.

Memories and promises of what might have been mingled in Armando's thoughts. He spent a moment letting his eyes wash over her, enjoying the breathtaking sight before him.

Then he dropped down to the bed, hovering over her, his hands on either side of her shoulders. His bare thighs between hers. He leaned down to kiss her lips, then his mouth moved to her neck where he bathed her skin with his hot tongue. His hand covered her breast, holding and squeezing it.

"Yes...yes...I love that..." Katie moaned in his ear. Her hands slid up and down his back, finally settling on his butt to give it a firm squeeze with both hands as she pulled him closer.

Armando kissed her neck for a bit longer then whispered in her ear with a grin, "Don't you want me to take my time?"

"Maybe later." Katie closed her eyes, feeling his tip between her legs as he writhed on top of her. Wondering if he would take her at any second.

He sucked on her earlobe then kissed his way to her mouth, staying there until he felt her hips shift beneath him. He pulled away, panting, and said, "For the love of God, tell me there's a condom nearby."

Katie tossed her head back, giggling. "Uh-huh. Nightstand. Top drawer. Left side. You can probably reach one from here."

Armando narrowed his eyes at her in a mock display of aggravation as he stretched his arm to the nearby nightstand and opened the drawer. "Bad girl. Felt like you wanted to get me in there without a condom for a second."

Katie bit her lip. "No. I just wanted you. Remember? We used to do it without one all the time."

"Yeah." He produced a condom and immediately tore it open. His eyes widened at her. "We were pretty damn stupid at times. Thank God for a little maturity."

She propped up on her elbows as she watched him stand and unroll it down his shaft. "We weren't stupid, honey." She smiled, both at those sweet memories, and the intoxicating sight of his firm body. "We were in love. Young and wild and—"

"Dumb," he said, flatly. Then his face perked up as she spread her legs a bit wider. He put his arms under her thighs and lifted her to meet him. As he entered her, he watched her head fall back against the bedspread in ecstasy. He remained still, memorizing the moment, unable to contain his gigantic smile.

Katie was his again. Armando had reclaimed her.

He would surely remember this as one of the happiest moments of his life.

Armando started moving when she met his gaze. "I've never stopped loving you, Katie."

Her heart swelled. "Me neither, Armando. I love you." She paused for a moan as he worked deeper inside her. "I can't imagine *not* loving you."

There was so much more he wanted to say, but it was time to simply show her how he felt. He kept his fixed eyes on hers and rocked into her. After a while he took one of her legs and held it straight up in the air, kissing the top of her foot, then her ankle.

Katie's moans soon became shouts as he skillfully penetrated her. She watched his mouth hang open, hungry.

Armando went faster and faster, unable to hold back. With other women, that's what he would've done. But it wasn't possible right now. He had locked eyes with the love of his life, and he couldn't contain his passion.

Soon he was ramming into her with all his might as she screamed his name. Oh, the sound of her voice...the way her body writhed under him...the feel of her soft skin with every thrust...

"I love you!" Armando shouted just before he finished.

"I love you too!" Katie's entire body shook as she climaxed along with him.

* * * * *

A few minutes later, after Armando had disposed of the condom, Katie curled up against him in bed on top of the sheets, uncovered. The bedspread lay on the floor.

Armando's hard bicep cradled Katie's head. His other arm went around her, bringing her body against his as he planted gentle kisses on her forehead, nose, cheeks...finally settling on her mouth.

Katie's hand slid up and down his back, which was a tiny bit sweaty from making love to her. She reveled in his arms and the subtle fragrance of his cologne as she felt the hard lines of the muscles in his back.

She moved her hand to his side, then to his stomach.

He shivered and let out a tiny chuckle, breaking their kiss.

"Sorry." Katie winced. "You're ticklish. I forgot."

Armando's brows furrowed. "I'm not *that* ticklish anymore."

Katie pulled away a little, scanning his chest and abs as she contemplated how she hoped to get to learn everything about him all over again. Her eyes settled on a mark several inches above his hip. "*Ooh*, I remember that scar."

Armando sighed and rolled away a little, looking down at his body. "Yeah. At least the one on my chin went away. Mostly."

Katie's eyes went to his chin. It bore a scar that was now so tiny, you had to know it was there to see it. "I'll never forget how worried I was when I heard about your accident. You came to school with all these bandages like you were dying."

"I know. It could've been a lot worse."

A tiny rush of excitement passed through Katie as she thought back to their junior year, when they were mere friends with unspoken crushes on each other. Armando and Ramon had wrecked an old pick-up truck on the ranch. The truck was totaled, but luckily neither boy was seriously injured aside from a lot of soreness and a few wounds requiring stitches. When Armando came back to school a couple of days later, several girls who had been vying for his attention used his injuries as an excuse to vie even harder. Laurie Haskell made him cookies. Tiffany Hunt offered to carry his books to every class for him. Armando was flattered by their actions, but unaffected. By the way it appeared to Katie, she thought she had no chance with him, with so many other girls around. It would be several months before he confessed he had only liked her all along.

Katie asked, "So, how'd that accident happen, anyway? You'd never tell me."

Armando rolled his eyes and huffed an annoyed breath out of the side of his mouth. "It was so stupid, it's embarrassing. Ramon thought he was a stunt driver or something."

"Well, I guess he thought wrong."

"Ain't that the truth. He didn't even have his driver's license yet."

Katie bristled at the thought of Ramon. "He really hates me, doesn't he?"

Armando inhaled deeply before speaking. "I told you the other day, he's going through something. That's why he's a jerk."

"No, it's because he hates me. He'll always hate me for what happened." She frowned.

"It doesn't matter what my brother thinks. You let me take care of that." Armando cupped her cheek. "How about tonight we don't talk about any of that bullshit. Your family, my family. It's been ten fucking years. It's time we do what's right for *us*."

Katie's bottom lip slowly began to tremble. "I don't know. It just seems like no one's on *our* side. It scares me. I wish it didn't."

Armando gave her a sympathetic look, his hand moving to her back. His voice was gentle. "Why? A lot's changed since then. I'm not trying to sound arrogant but I consider myself the one with the upper hand this time. I don't care how many powerful friends your dad has all over Texas. There's nothing he can do to me. To *us*."

Katie shook her head as her eyes welled up with tears. "He can freeze me out. Never talk to me again. I know my dad can be an asshole sometimes. And Mom's not much better. But they're the only parents I have. I wouldn't mind moving away and only seeing them a few times a year but I don't know if I could handle being cut out of their lives completely."

Armando let out a defeated sigh. "Yeah. I get it. But maybe it won't come to that."

She sniffled as a few tears fell down her face. "I hope not but after the talk I had with Mom last week…" She paused to take a deep breath and wipe her cheeks with her fingers. "If you really want me, it has to be a sure thing. My entire life will change. I'm sure of it. I can't give up my parents over an impetuous fling."

Armando pulled her closer, looking deep into her eyes. "This isn't a fling for me. This is me coming home to my best friend. To the love of my life who I've thought about every single day since that afternoon when we were torn apart. I regret like hell that I didn't come back sooner but I fucking hate *regret*. I'm not gonna live my life that way. I just wanna be happy, and you make me happy, Katie."

Overwhelmed, Katie laughed as thick tears rolled down her cheeks.

He brought her close, letting her cry against the crook of his neck for several minutes until her tears lessened, and she pulled away enough to look in his eyes.

Katie inhaled very slowly, then said, "It's happening so fast. A week ago I was engaged to someone else and now I'm here in my bed, in *your* arms. It feels like I'm stuck with my back against the wall, watching the room spin around me. Wondering what'll happen when it stops."

Armando gently replied, "You're dizzy."

Katie let out a soft chuckle. "Yeah."

He cradled her in his arms, one arm under her head, the other against her back, pulling her closer. "My sweet Katie. I know there's a whole lot that doesn't make sense right now. Hell, what happened to us back then didn't make any sense either. But I love you. And you said you loved me, too. Right?"

She nodded silently.

He continued. "Well, maybe love doesn't have to make sense. For years I've wondered why I couldn't fall in love with someone else. But now I know why." He brushed his fingertips along her jaw. "It was you. It's always been you. No other woman stands a chance." He paused to kiss her forehead. "Have you considered that maybe we still have these feelings for a reason? Maybe it's a gift. A second chance. Yeah, what happened back then was traumatic. Believe me, waking up on the side of that road and not knowing how I got there was probably the lowest moment of my life. But how much good would it do me to cry about it now? To live my life in fear or anger, pissed off at the world because someone hurt me? Why can't I just be thankful that when I was young, I fell in love with the most amazing girl in the world? And ten years later, I found her again and knew for sure I was still in love with her. That doesn't have to be a bad thing, does it? We can just take it as a gift, because that's what it is. To me."

Katie was still, her eyes locked on his. Her natural logic was no match for that speech.

As tears spilled down her face once again, Armando tightened his arms around her and pulled her into a passionate kiss.

Katie stopped crying immediately. It suddenly felt like she and Armando were the only people on Earth. The room stopped spinning. The chaos and fear in her mind quieted for now. She returned his kiss, desperate to show him how she felt.

After a few minutes, she felt his hand glide down her stomach, then lower. She instantly parted her thighs for him, and soon felt his fingers fondling her.

He kissed her for a bit longer then broke from her lips and kissed her chin, her neck. He spent a few minutes reacquainting himself with her breasts, his tongue moving in slow circles around her hard peak. She wove her fingers into his thick brown hair and let herself moan as loud as she wanted. Her appreciative sounds made him work even harder.

When he let go of her nipple, Armando kissed a fast trail down her stomach, then surprised her by changing course and flopping onto his back, his head falling just beneath the pillow. Before she could respond to his sudden action, he gave her a big smile and said, "Get up, baby. I want one knee *here*," he patted the bed beside his left shoulder, "and one knee *here*."

Katie let out a hungry moan and immediate got on her knees, crawling up a few paces until her knees were near his shoulders.

Armando looked up at her with a wink as he took one of her knees and guided it across him. Then he said, "Hold on to the headboard, okay?"

Before she could say, "Okay," to him in agreement, she felt his mouth engulf her as her hands touched the headboard. She tossed her head back and hollered up at the ceiling.

Armando cupped her bottom, grabbing her and holding her

hips as close to his mouth as possible. He continued on, unable to get enough. Hoping she wouldn't get off too soon so he could enjoy this as long as possible.

Katie arched her back, screaming and writhing on top of him. She maintained her balance by keeping hold of the headboard, otherwise the sheer pleasure coursing through her may have caused her to fall. She didn't remember his tongue being so agile, and she was unprepared for her body's reaction.

Unconsciously, she wiggled her hips against him as her screams grew louder and louder. For a passing moment she considered her neighbors on the other side of the wall. But that thought escaped her head with the next stroke of his tongue.

And before she knew it, she had let go of the headboard as her orgasm rolled through her. Armando held her firmly to make sure she wouldn't fall as her body lost control. She screamed, "Armando! Yes! I love you!" over and over until her body went limp.

Armando carefully helped her down and placed on her side. "You okay, baby?" he asked.

She gave him a dazed look as she panted for air, then she closed her eyes.

He smiled. "I'm gonna let you recover for a little while." He left her for a few minutes to go to the bathroom then the kitchen.

When he returned, he brought with him a glass of water. "Thought you could use this."

Katie sat up and took the glass. "You read my mind. Thank you." She took a long gulp of water, then said, "Wow. I don't think anyone's ever gotten that reaction out of me before."

His brow lifted in a show of mock arrogance and he said, "I'm sure you haven't." Then he thought for a moment. "Hey, wait a minute. What about me? In high school? I'm pretty sure my technique's improved a whole lot as time went on."

Katie placed the glass on the night stand, then scooted along the sheet to sit beside him. "You were always good, to me. Even if we never had sex again I'd still love you. But I'm sure as hell not gonna complain about the perks of being your..." She paused. "Girlfriend? Is that what I am?"

"You're much more than that to me. But yeah, I guess that's the title."

"Holy crap." Her heart raced, and not in a good way. "I really gotta break up with Mitch. Soon."

"Hmm." Armando rubbed the back of his neck, thinking. "You sure about that?"

"Excuse me?" She lifted a brow. "You wanna share me or something?"

"No." He took her chin and looked in her eyes. "No. Absolutely not." He let go of her chin. "But I was just thinking. Maybe it'd be best, for *you*, if you gave it a little time before the official break up."

"Huh? How's that best for me?"

"Well, you were probably right earlier when you said it's gonna change your life when everyone finds out we're back together. Your parents like Mitch, right? Don't rush yourself. It'll only stress you out. We can be secretive for a while. And maybe you'll feel better about *us* after we've spent more time together. I wanna prove to you you're not a fling. I want you to have no doubt."

She smirked. "Okay."

Sensing her skepticism, he continued. "I plan on seeing you a lot. Hell, it's been a long time. I wanna get to know you again. So, I'm gonna stay at the ranch for a while longer to be near you. But there'll be times, like this Friday, when I have to fly to Los Angeles for the day." He shrugged. "And, I was thinking maybe you could take Friday and Saturday off to come with me? If not, I can get back here that night. But I'd love to show you my house. Take you to some of my favorite restaurants. And we wouldn't have to sneak around there."

Katie smiled and rested her head on Armando's shoulder. She was quickly reminded of the previous weekend when Mitch went to Dallas and refused to let her tag along. But Armando wanted her around. And she definitely wanted to be around him. "I'll see what I can do on short notice. I haven't taken a day off in a long time so it might be all right."

Armando kissed the top of her head. "Good."

She sighed. "Well, how long do we keep this up? It's like high school all over again. Sneaking around. Hiding from my parents and everyone else. Do I just let Mitch think I've forgotten about him? He sent me flowers three times today. He's not gonna give up until I tell him to give up. And if I don't tell him, he'll probably call my parents and have them talk to me."

"Shit." Armando groaned. "Well, here's what you can do. Call him tomorrow. Tell him you need a while to sort out your feelings or whatever. Don't let him think it's over for good just yet. That should buy us a little bit of time."

Katie rolled her eyes. "Yeah. Probably doesn't even matter. I've barely seen him in weeks. He's working all the time. Using any reason to be away from me, it seems."

Armando shook his head. "What an idiot. He has no idea what he lost."

Katie grinned. "Thank you."

"Now, if he starts pressuring you to get back together, let me know and we'll figure out our next move. Does that make sense?"

"I think so."

"Good. And as far as your parents." He sighed, shaking his head. "We'll figure it out. In fact, Victor and I've been making a lot of phone calls. Calling in some favors. Trying to figure out what the hell happened to make your dad so violently angry about us getting married."

She huffed. "Yeah, well, good luck with that. Daddy's smart. Does his dirty work with a handshake. No paper trail. No proof."

"Well, we're gonna try. Maybe if we figure out what happened, we can then figure out how to keep your parents from freaking out."

Katie's eyes filled with tears, and Armando drew her close. In her heart, she knew she would choose him, even if it meant angering her parents for the rest of their lives.

But silently, she prayed it was a choice she would never have to make.

CHAPTER 14

The next day at work, Katie was tired after her steamy, late night with Armando. But from the way she smiled, it looked like she had all the energy in the world.

It was also the second day in a row that she left her engagement ring at home. But today, unlike yesterday, she was oblivious to the petty gossip at work. She simply bounced around the restaurant, happy and full of life. New memories of Armando raced repeatedly through her mind. She could barely contain her excitement, knowing she would see him again tonight.

To make her day even better, her manager immediately agreed to let her have Friday and Saturday off, since there were no events scheduled for those days, and Katie had put in so many extra hours lately. She sent Armando a text message that she was free to go away with him for the weekend.

But then, right after lunchtime, Jennifer approached her, smirking and handing her a box. "Here. The first gift of the day."

Katie felt a twinge of disgust in the pit of her stomach. Mitch had barely been a thought to her today, until now. She took the box and opened it. "Okay. So today it's chocolates instead of flowers, I guess."

Jennifer pressed her lips together in anger for a second then said, "You should really learn to treat your man better or you just may lose him entirely."

Katie put her hand on her hip. "Excuse me? You realize I'm *your* boss, right? I can let a lot of things go but I can't tolerate you disrespecting me or anyone else. Especially in front of the customers."

Jennifer glanced around at the almost-empty dining room. Her tone was sarcastic. "What customers?"

Katie headed to the bar, wondering when Jennifer would finally do something bad enough to get herself fired. She took the card from the box of chocolates as she opened it, displaying it at the corner of the bar. She flagged down Jonny the bartender and said, "These chocolates are for anyone who wants them." He nodded, then she went to the door.

After her reunion with Armando, she had a feeling she needed to start reading Mitch's cards and stop sweeping it all under the rug. If she was going to keep her new relationship a secret, she would have to be smart about it, and that meant no surprises. So, she walked outside the front of the restaurant for a little privacy and opened the card.

"These past few days have been torture without you. I can't wait to see you at dinner tomorrow. Love, Mitch."

Dinner? It took Katie a moment to remember their conversation on Monday night. It had only been a few days but it felt like it happened so long ago now. On his way out, Mitch said he wanted to pick her up after work on Thurday—tomorrow—and take her someplace nice for dinner where they could hopefully discuss setting a wedding date. She hadn't agreed to dinner, but he had obviously assumed as much.

Katie tapped her toe against the pavement, knowing she couldn't put it off any longer. Armando was right. She had to call him today. Now. She walked a little farther away from the front door to a bench, then took her phone out of her pocket and sat down to dial Mitch's work number.

He answered on the second ring. "*Finally! I've missed you so much.*"

"Uh...okay. Look, I never agreed to have dinner with you tomorrow. And that's the only reason I'm calling."

"*What? Don't you miss me? At all? I've completely left you alone, aside from the gifts. I was hoping you'd eventually call and tell me you missed me, too.*"

"No. I'm only calling to tell you we're not on for dinner. That's all."

"*I don't understand. Are you breaking up with me?*" His voice got weak.

She then realized it would be harder than she thought to keep Mitch in the dark for long. She suddenly felt badly, like she would be leading him on if she told him what Armando wanted her to say. But she quickly thought back to the argument she and Mitch had on Monday, and she summoned the strength to say it. "I need some time to think. To sort out my feelings. I'm not ready to see you right now."

Mitch let out a sigh, then paused. Quietly, he said, "*I was afraid you'd say something like that. Please don't break up with me.*"

Katie felt her facade crumbling. She hadn't expected him to sound genuinely upset. "I don't see the big deal, really. You've been working so much, I thought you'd probably be relieved that I wanted to take a break."

"*What? A break? No! Didn't you hear anything I said the other night? I wanna marry you. Soon! I'm tired of waiting. For all I care we can go down to the court house. I don't need a wedding.*"

"No." Katie looked around to make sure she was still alone outside before letting herself burst into tears. Then she tucked her head down and said, "I can't marry you. It's over. I'll drop the ring off at your office."

He gasped. "*Holy shit, Katie. I can't believe this! You'll drop the ring off at my office? That's cold. What the hell?*" He was quiet for a moment. "*Is this because you think I'm cheating? I'm not. I'd never do that to you. You can't just break up with me over that. Please. Give me another chance. I'll do anything.*"

She sniffled. "I...can't. I just can't."

"*No. No! What happened? What'd I do? Let me make it right. I'll spend more time with you. I'll do anything you want. Please tell me what I need to do. You're the only thing that matters to me, baby. The only thing. Come on. I'll leave work right now and come over there. I—*"

Katie panicked. "I'm not in love with you anymore!"

She couldn't hear his response over her own hysterical sobbing. How was she to know he would beg her for another chance? His words made her heart ache. He obviously had a right to be confused. Angry, even. One week they were happily engaged. The next week, they were not.

After she calmed down a little she held the phone tightly to her ear and asked, "Are you there?"

He breathed into the phone for a few seconds before responding. "*Yeah. I'm here. I don't get it, Katie. What happened? Tell me the truth. Is there someone else? Or did I leave you alone for too long?*"

"Mitch, I—"

"*Look, whatever it is, we can fix it. If there's someone else, at least give me a chance to compete. I wanna win you back.*"

As she searched her thoughts for anything to say, he continued.

"*I neglected you, didn't I? Fuck, I'm so stupid. I should've taken you to Dallas with me last weekend. Even if we only saw each other for an hour it would've been worth it.*"

She took a few slow breaths, trying to stop her tears. "Listen Mitch, I'm sorry. I know this isn't fair to you. But I'd rather break it off now than get a divorce later. I don't think I've ever loved you."

He suddenly let out a growl. "*It's that guy from high school, isn't it? The one you kissed. Shit, of course that's it. I can't believe it took me this long to catch on. Damn it Katie! Give me a chance to win you back! Who is this guy, anyway? At least give me a name. I think I deserve that much.*"

Oh my God! Katie thought. There was no way out of this situation but to stretch the truth, and she hated herself for doing it. "It doesn't matter how it happened—I've realized lately that I'm not in love with you. And I can't marry someone I'm not in love with. And you shouldn't be engaged to someone who's not in love with you. You deserve better than that."

Mitch took an extremely long pause, then said, "*Fine. But this isn't over for me.*" And then he hung up.

As soon as the phone went silent, Katie wiped her hand against each of her eyes, then called Armando.

Breathless, he answered on the fifth ring. "*Hi baby.*"

She sniffled, choking back her tears. "I'm sorry to bother you. I know you're busy."

"*Oh no. What's wrong?*"

"I panicked."

His voice was soft. "*Shit. What happened?*"

"Mitch." She paused for an unsteady breath. "I called him. It didn't go how I expected, at all. He wants me back. Doesn't even care if I'm cheating. Wants to win me back."

Armando paused and asked, flatly, "*Is that what you want?*"

"No! I want you." Katie glanced around, quieting her voice as a few customers entered the restaurant. "I love you. I don't want him back."

He let out a sigh of relief. "*Good. You had me scared for a second.*"

"He figured out that it had something to do with the ex-boyfriend I kissed the other day."

"*What? You told him you kissed me?*"

"He doesn't know your name. Look, it's a long story and you said you didn't wanna know what happened with me and Mitch. I didn't confirm his theory. I just told him I'm not in love with him and he needs to move on. The whole conversation really took me by surprise. I figured he'd just back off when I told him I wanted some time to think."

"*Yeah, me too. I guess he's not as dumb as I thought. He knows a good thing when he has it. But he's not taking you away from me. That won't happen to me again.*"

Katie produced a soft chuckle. "No. It won't."

"*Well, what happened? Did you break up with him officially?*"

"Yeah. But he begged me not to. Pleaded. It was horrible. I feel like such a heartless witch."

Armando laughed a little. "*Sweetie, the fact that you feel so bad about it kinda proves you're not heartless.*"

"I don't know. That's how I feel. You should've heard him go on. The last thing he said to me was, 'this isn't over.' He's not giving up. I don't know what to do." Her voice cracked.

"*Shh,*" he said in a soothing tone. "*It's okay. I wish I could be there to comfort you right now. It's gonna be all right. I know it hurt to break up with him but you did the right thing.*"

"I'm afraid to go to my apartment tonight. What if he shows up? What'll I do?"

"Don't let him in. What's he gonna do? Break the door down? Then you call the cops. It's simple."

"It's not that. I don't think he's a threat or anything. I just dread hearing him knock at the door. What if he knocks and knocks and I have to deal with him? I don't wanna have that conversation again, telling him to leave because it's over. I've never heard him so persistent."

"Are you sure you don't think he's dangerous? Like, he'd threaten you or hurt you? Sit outside your apartment to see who's coming and going?"

"I think he's harmless but he might be jealous enough to stalk me a little. He really wanted your name for some reason."

"Just come straight over here after work tonight, okay? Keep a look out in case he's following you. If you want I can arrange someone to pick you up."

"No, I'm not scared of him."

"Well, maybe you should be. Okay, I just made up my mind. I'll be in touch before you leave work about finding a way to get you here, unnoticed. Don't argue with me about it. It's a done deal."

"Okay. No arguments. I can't wait to see you tonight."

"I can't wait to see you either. I gotta go, but give me a call if you need me. I can make time for you. I love you."

"I love you, too."

* * * * *

Katie made it through the rest of her day at work with no more gifts or contact from Mitch. And she practically held her breath all day, wondering if her parents would call. But thankfully, they didn't. And that meant Mitch hadn't gone running to them about the breakup. But she knew she had to tell her parents...soon.

How quickly she would tell them about her new relationship with Armando? She had no idea.

But Katie was on her way to the ranch from work, traveling according to Armando's instructions. First, she had to drive to a specified parking lot five miles from work. She left her car there and hopped into a chauffeured Chrysler sedan that Armando rented from a San Antonio limousine service. The driver was friendly but quiet as they rode to the ranch, mostly in silence.

When Katie arrived at the door, Cara answered, happily welcoming her inside to sit with her in the living room.

"Armando's in a conference call," Cara said. "He should be finished in a few minutes. So, you're having dinner with us?"

"Yeah. I hope that's okay."

"Oh, sure. It's perfect. My mom's at the grocery store right now getting some last minute items for dinner. She's staying here for a while and she loves having so many people to cook for." Cara scowled. "Personally, I don't get it. She lives for cooking, but I hate it."

Katie nodded, relaxing a bit as she listened to Cara's small talk. "I understand. I like to cook sometimes but I definitely wouldn't call it something I love." She paused, glimpsing around the room, suddenly feeling nervous again. "So, is Ramon here?"

"No. He'll probably be gone for a couple more hours." Cara gave her a sympathetic frown. "The guys filled me in. Look, don't let Ramon bother you."

Katie shrugged. "How? This is technically *his* house, right? It's sorta hard to feel welcome inside a house where you know the owner doesn't like you."

"It's not that he doesn't like you. He's just angry about what happened to Armando. But he wants his brother to be happy. And if Armando wants you here because you make him happy, Ramon will just have to accept it."

Katie shook her head as she stared away at nothing. "Feels so weird. Sitting here in this house after all this time." She looked at Cara. "Do you know if Armando's staying in his old bedroom?"

"Yes. He is."

Chuckling, Katie said. "Wow. I can't believe it. This has to be the strangest couple of weeks of my entire life." She turned around to the sound of footsteps in the hall, then stood when Armando entered the room.

Armando flashed Katie a warm smile. "Hey beautiful." He walked up to her and pulled her into his arms.

Katie glanced nervously at Cara.

Armando waved a dismissive hand in Cara's direction. "It's okay. She knows. She's cool."

Katie half-smiled. "It's a little unfair that *you* can tell people but I can't."

Armando shrugged. "Well, tell your parents not to be such jerks and we can shout our love from the rooftops."

Katie was about to reply when her phone rang in her purse with a personalized ring tone that instantly made her head hurt. "Oh no. It's Mom."

"So?" Armando asked. "Do you wanna answer it or not? It's up to you."

Katie sighed. "No use burying my head in the sand anymore. I'd rather not be surprised later." Katie pulled her phone from her purse and hurried outside to the porch before answering. "Hi Mom."

"Hey Katie-bug. I won't keep you. Just wanted to confirm we're all still on for lunch tomorrow."

"Uh…" Katie winced. She had forgotten about her dad's new idea of a weekly lunch every Thursday at the restaurant "Uh, no. We're not."

"Oh. Is Mitch working out of town again?"

Katie sucked her bottom lip between her teeth, dreading the words she was about to say. But she knew she had to tell Mom the truth before Mitch did. "No." She inhaled a deep breath through her nose and quickly said, "I broke up with him."

"What? No! You can't be serious!"

"Yes, I'm absolutely serious."

"Why, though? Are you okay? Are you sick? Not feeling well?"

Katie gritted her teeth. "Did you really just ask if I'm 'sick?' Like, out of my mind, sick? Because Mitch is the best I'm ever gonna get and I should just settle, even if I'm not in love with him?"

Her mother let out a breath. *"That's not what I meant. I just wonder if maybe you're not thinking clearly right now. I remember how happy you were when he proposed. You were in love. And now, suddenly, you're telling me you're not?"*

"No, I'm not in love with him."

Her mom simply breathed into the phone, quiet.

Katie waited for a response, her anger increasing as she thought about all those biting, snarky comments from Mom about her finally getting married. Finally doing the "right thing." Katie was soon boiling inside, ready for the insults and unsolicited advice.

But, to her surprise, Mom's tone was calm. She said, *"I think we need to have this conversation again in a few days after you've come to your senses. There's no reason to panic just yet."*

"Well, whatever. But I guarantee I won't change my mind."

"I guess we'll see, won't we?" Mom chuckled. *"I'm sorry hon, but I only had a minute to call you. Your dad and I have a banquet to attend tonight. I'm not gonna tell him what you just told me. It'll only upset him. But I'll be in touch soon."*

And then the phone went silent.

Katie rolled her eyes, unsure whether she should be pissed off or relieved. Then she stood and walked into the house, heading to the living room.

Armando stood from his chair when he saw her. "That was fast. What'd she say?"

Cara's eyes were wide with interest.

Katie tossed her phone into her purse, then slumped down on the loveseat. "Not much. She didn't take me seriously at all. Thinks I'm gonna come to my senses and get back together with Mitch. And she's not even gonna break the news to dad. She's just gonna go on like we didn't have that conversation."

Armando shrugged then sat next to her, draping his arm around her back. "Well, maybe that'll work in our favor."

Shaking her head, Katie said, "I don't know. I figure she'll talk to Mitch, because she obviously thinks he's the more level-headed one. He'll give her some theories. Tell her about me kissing a nameless ex-boyfriend from high school." She patted Armando's knee. "And that's when she'll figure it out."

Cara asked, "Are you sure? Didn't you have any other boyfriends back then?"

Katie sighed. "None that mattered. And Mom knows it."

They all heard a car driving up the long driveway. Cara stood and looked outside. "Well, there's *my* Mom." Then she scuttled off to the front door.

Armando squeezed Katie closer to him and gave her temple a long kiss, then whispered in her ear. "Don't worry. We'll get through this. I love you."

Katie looked in his eyes, weary, but hopeful. "I know. I love you, too."

With his hand cupping her face, he kissed her lips until they heard the sound of footsteps trudging up the stairs to the porch. Armando pulled away and said, "Come on. Let me introduce you."

As they walked to the foyer, Katie heard an unfamiliar woman's voice say, *"Did you put those lasagnas in the oven like I told you?"*

Cara answered, "Yes I did. They'll be ready on time," as she came through the door carrying a bag of groceries.

Then an attractive older woman with dark hair pulled up on top of her head walked in. She appeared as though she was about to speak, but stopped when she saw Katie, her eyes brightening. "Oh, hello! You must be Armando's friend."

Armando took the bags of groceries from Patty's arms as he introduced her to Katie. Then Isaac came through the door, huffing strenuously, his little eyebrows furrowed like he was working hard with the two small bags he carried.

Armando went back down the hallway to the office to finish some work. Katie was grateful to busy herself by helping Cara cut up the fresh vegetables Patty bought at the grocery store. Isaac sat on a stool, barely able to see over the island in the kitchen. He chimed in once in a while as Patty gave Katie the details of her recent wedding. After a while, Isaac grew restless and went to the living room to watch cartoons.

When Isaac left the room, Cara craned her head to make sure he was where she could see him on the couch. She softly said, "Hey, about that day care you told me about? The one where your sister works?"

Katie said, "Yeah?"

Cara focused on the carrot she was slicing. "We drove past it yesterday. Isaac flipped out when he saw all those kids playing outside. He misses that. I called them but they haven't called me back yet. Are you sure they have an opening? They looked busy."

Katie nodded. "From what Chelsea tells me, yeah. I'll give her a call and speed up the process. Or you could drop by in person. Tell her I sent you."

Cara said, "I may do that. I was afraid to say anything in front of Isaac in case he remembers you from the other day, when you said your sister works at the day care. Armando swore all of us to secrecy about your...uh...situation?" Cara shot Patty an odd glance, but Patty was oblivious, her attention focused on a tray of garlic bread she was arranging. "Anyway, I was afraid my son would say something about you and Armando to your sister. Does she know yet?"

Katie let her knife fall to the cutting board and drew her hands to her stomach, her eyes closed. "Oh my God. I don't even wanna think about telling Chelsea."

Patty's mouth fell open in a slow gasp. She rushed over to Katie, putting an arm around her shoulder. "Oh honey. I wish you could see it like I see it." Patty raised her other hand in the air in dramatic fashion, her voice dreamy. "Forbidden love." She pulled her hand to her chest. "It's *so* romantic."

Katie sighed. "Yeah. In a way, I suppose."

Cara widened her eyes. "Mom's a dreamer."

With a tired grin, Katie said, "She's a lot nicer than *my* mom."

Patty gave Katie a hug, then let go of her and smirked at Cara as she walked past her to the stove. "I don't know how I raised such a cynical daughter." Then, her attention turning back to her garlic bread, Patty said to Katie, "I think maybe you should give your family the benefit of the doubt. All any mother wants is to see her children happy."

Katie quickly shook her head. "No. My mom reminded me last week. I think she might strangle me when she hears about me and Armando."

Cara looked at Patty. "You heard the story, remember? About how her family broke them up in high school? Do you really think they'd *ever* be happy about them getting back together?" Then Cara winced at Katie. "Sorry to be so blunt."

Katie took a deep breath. "It's okay. You're absolutely right about that."

"Well…" Patty's lips pursed, angry. "I can tell you one thing. If that had happened to one of my brothers back in Jersey, the person responsible wouldn't have lived to tell about it. On my mother's side I'm related to some," she winked at Katie, "wealthy Sicilians, if you know what I mean." She arched a brow.

Cara shook her head at Katie, silently mouthing, "No."

Patty smirked at Cara. "Yes, it's true." To Katie, she said, "You know that show, *The Sopranos*? It's loosely based on some distant cousins of mine."

Cara groaned and shook her head at Katie, mouthing, "No."

Katie laughed, but stopped when she heard a car drive up. She rose from her seat to look out the window. "Who's that?"

Patty looked outside. "Oh, it's just Ramon."

Under her breath, Katie muttered, "Great. Just great." She gave her full attention back to slicing the the pile of vegetables in front of her.

CHAPTER 15

Katie steeled herself, concentrating fully on the cucumber she was slicing. She braced herself for Ramon's coldness—the same coldness he had displayed those rare times when she saw him around town.

She wished she and Armando could just go to Los Angeles tonight instead of enduring this awkward evening. But unfortunately, she had to work tomorrow.

Isaac ran to the front door to greet Ramon as soon as he walked in. "Wuh-moan!"

Ramon smiled and ruffled Isaac's hair. "*Hombrecito*. You take good care of the cows for me today?"

"Uh-huh!" Isaac replied.

Katie smirked inwardly, astonished that Ramon could actually sound like a decent human being.

Ramon walked into the kitchen with Isaac in tow. His eyes met Katie's for a split second but his expression was blank. Katie expected him to be dirty from ranch work all day, but his jeans and T-shirt were clean. His boots looked well-worn, but polished. He patted Cara on the shoulder and said, "Hey there," then walked over to Patty as he sniffed the air around him. "Smells good in here."

Patty beamed at him. "I hope you like lasagna. I've made plenty."

"That's nice of you but you didn't have to do that," Ramon said. "You're a guest here."

"Oh, don't be silly," Patty said. "It's the least I could do. You're letting me stay here with my daughter and grandson."

Ramon's eyes skimmed the appliances on the kitchen counter. "Are those new?"

Silently, Cara cast a sly glance over her shoulder at Ramon, then Patty, then she grabbed another pepper to slice.

Patty nodded and placed a gentle hand on Ramon's back. "Yes, I hope that's okay. They were all on sale and I thought, why not? I'll be here for a while and I love to cook."

"Huh." Ramon's eyes fell all around the kitchen, noticing a few things that seemed different than they way he had left them that morning. "Well, I guess that's all right. But," he grimaced, "I wish you didn't feel obligated to do all this. You're supposed to be on vacation."

Patty's eyes widened. She patted his back. "I don't feel obligated. I enjoy this."

Ramon grinned. "Well, thanks." Then he covered his mouth as he produced a big yawn. "Excuse me. It's been a long day. I gotta go check on everything out back before I call it quits."

Patty said, "Well, dinner'll be waiting when you're ready."

Isaac gasped. "Can I come? Pwease?"

"We need to ask your mom," Ramon said, tilting his head to the side, giving Cara a pleading look.

Cara's worried eyes passed between Ramon and Isaac. She hesitated, then said, "Yeah, I suppose."

Ramon nodded at Isaac and said, "All right. Come on."

In seconds they rushed out of the kitchen and down the hall to the back door, chatting like old friends.

Cara smiled at Patty and said, "Worked like a charm."

Katie asked, "What are you talking about?"

"Well," Patty said, "I'm staying here under somewhat false pretenses, to cook and make Ramon's life a little easier. Give him some motherly love."

Nodding, Cara said, "Yeah. And it's working much faster than we thought it would."

"Why?" Katie asked. "To make him less of a jerk?"

"Yes," Cara said, flatly.

Patty shot Cara a scolding glance. "He's a sweet boy. He just needs a little love, that's all."

As Cara was about to reply, Armando walked in, making a beeline for Katie.

Katie dropped her knife and smiled when he came up behind her, his arms around her waist. He brushed her hair off her shoulder and gave her neck a quick peck. She closed her eyes and let the sensation from his lips rush through her...wishing they were alone.

Cara and Patty acted like they weren't watching.

Armando kissed Katie's cheek and pulled her closer. "Sorry about that. Been in meetings most of the day." He reached into his pocket and produced a credit card, which he slipped into Katie's hand. "Here. Tonight, maybe you and one of these ladies can go shopping after dinner. You need something to wear to work tomorrow."

Katie's face scrunched up in confusion. "Huh? I can just go to my apartment in the morning before work."

Armando shook his head. "No." His voice softened. "I'd rather you not go back there until I think it's safe." He kissed her cheek again.

Rolling her eyes, Katie said, "You're *really* overreacting about Mitch. He's not that kind of a guy."

Armando shrugged. "Well, humor me, then. Besides, even if he wouldn't hurt you, he might be jealous enough to camp outside your door and beg you to get back together. And who knows what your parents might do. We don't need any more stress. I think it's best you just stay out of that apartment until we get back from L.A. on Sunday night. I've got a security guy looking after it in the meantime."

"What?" Katie's jaw dropped and she looked up at him over her shoulder. "That's excessive."

Armando cast her a doubtful look. "No, it's not. I'll do anything to keep you with me. After all we've been through, do you really think I'd take a chance on losing you again?" He smiled. "Trust me, it's not excessive. It's caution. So, just go shopping tonight. Get anything you need to last you through the next few days. If you must have something from your apartment, I'll send someone to get it for you. But you're not going back there. And tomorrow morning I'll have someone drive you to work and bring you back to the ranch."

Katie fumbled with the credit card in her fingers. "Okay...I guess..."

Patty chuckled. "Honey, if a man gives you a credit card and tells you to buy whatever you want, you take it and buy *whatever* you want."

"No," Katie said. "I'll only use it for what I really need, I promise."

Armando smiled down at her. "It's okay. Spoil yourself a little."

Cara glared at Patty with a groan. "And Mom? Remember. You

keep your mouth shut. No long talks with random strangers. A lot of people around here probably know Katie's family. Word travels fast."

Patty's voice was sad. "But that's how I met my husband." Then she closed her eyes and raised a hand like she was taking an oath. "But I've learned my lesson. I promise, my lips are sealed." Patty opened her eyes and saw their confusion, so she explained. "You see, my new husband is the man Victor's ex-girlfriend hired to spy on us."

Armando and Katie both said, "What?" at the same time.

Katie now understood the odd glances Cara gave her mother when they spoke earlier about keeping their secret.

Patty nodded. "Yes. Tom took a seat next to me one afternoon at the park. Such a sweet, handsome man. He started talking. I started talking." She shrugged. "How was I supposed to know he was a private investigator?"

Cara said, "He quit that job the very next day to be with Mom."

"Yes," Patty said. "He's a wonderful man. We hit it off right away."

Armando cleared his throat. "Please promise me you won't strike up any random conversations here in Turnbrook. People are nosy, especially if you're from out of town."

Katie nodded. "Yes. And everyone around here knows Ramon, at least in passing. And they *all* know my parents. If they hear you're staying in this house—"

Patty interrupted. "I swear, I understand. Not a peep outta me."

* * * * *

Tom and Victor arrived at the house just before dinner. Victor took Katie and Armando aside and told them they needed to have a talk afterward.

Dinner was not as awkward as Katie previously feared. Ramon was too tired to do much besides shove food into his mouth. And there was enough conversation to keep her sufficiently distracted from her worries, even if her appetite was non-existent.

As the others cleaned up after dinner, Victor signaled for Katie and Armando to come down to Ramon's office.

When they entered the room, they saw Tom sitting behind the desk. He nervously ran a hand through his gray hair, then adjusted his glasses. "Have a seat," he said.

Katie and Armando sat in front of the desk. Victor sat on a stool close by.

Tom started with, "Since we just met at dinner, let me formally introduce myself." He gave Katie a gentle grin and leaned forward, his fingers knitted together on the desk. "Tom Sutton. Retired cop. Part-time investigator. Proud newlywed." He cleared his throat. "Victor and Armando asked me to look into some things. You're probably already aware."

Katie gave a little shrug. "Somewhat, yeah. I don't know the specifics."

Tom nodded. "Basically, I'm trying to answer some questions about the past. Victor and I've spent most of the day researching public records. Seeing if we can find a starting point."

Victor interjected, "Haven't found much so far."

"Nope," Tom said. "And you're probably wondering why you're here. So, now that you have a little bit of background, I'll tell you." He continued to speak as he opened a drawer and pulled out an electronic tablet, tapping the screen with his finger. "Armando also wanted me to do a little research on Mitch."

"Oh Lord." Katie's stomach churned.

"It's okay," Tom said. "Since you already broke up you may not even care about this anymore. But it's only right that I inform you anyway."

Armando's eyebrows shot up.

Katie groaned.

Tom let out a heavy sigh as he handed the tablet over the desk to Katie. "In short, he's cheating on you."

Katie set her mouth firmly as she shook her head and reached forward to take the tablet. "I had a feeling. We had this big argument about it on Monday night. I feel like such an idiot." She sighed. "Oh well. It's over now…" Her voice trailed off as she examined the first picture. "Is this in the back seat of his car? It's hard to see anything."

Tom nodded. "Yeah. I'm only allowed to take pictures in public places. Those are along the street or in a parking lot. There's twenty-five pictures, total. All today. I gotta tell ya, it was too easy. He's a bold one."

Katie flipped to the next picture, and gasped. "Oh my God!"

"What?" Armando leaned over to see.

Katie gritted her teeth and went to another picture. This time she growled, then shouted, "You've *got* to be kidding me! It's Jennifer!"

Armando's eyebrows knitted. "Who's Jennifer?"

Pausing long enough to make eye contact with him, she said, "She's the absolute worst employee at the restaurant. If she was any worse, I would've already fired her. The only thing she's really good for is flirting with the male customers." She snorted and went to the next picture. "What the hell? Kissing in broad daylight?"

Tom's eyes widened and leaned back in his chair. "Like I said. He's a bold one."

Katie's cheeks reddened as her anger increased. "It makes

so much sense now. I bet they were together in Dallas over the weekend. That's why she called out sick on Saturday. And that's why she's been so jealous of all the presents he sent me at work this week." She brought the tablet to her lap for a moment and stared off at the wall. "How could I have been so stupid? I remember one night weeks ago I was complaining about her to Mitch and he was all like, 'don't fire her' and I didn't even catch on. It was right there in front of my face the whole time." She looked at Tom. "Do you have any idea how long it's been going on?"

Tom shrugged.

Victor said, "I was with Tom for a while when he took some of those. Seemed like they were familiar with each other, not like a new relationship at all."

"Yeah." Tom nodded. "That's what I was thinking. That argument this afternoon…"

"This afternoon." Katie shook her head as tears of rage filled her eyes. "It was after I broke up with him. He went straight to her."

Confused, Armando asked, "What's wrong? Are you jealous or something?"

Katie scoffed as her eyes met his. "Hell no, I'm not jealous. I'm pissed! After the way he played my emotions today? Begging me for another chance? He made me feel terrible for breaking up with him and the whole time he was…" She looked down at the tablet and saw the next picture of Mitch and Jennifer clearly making out. "Oh my God!"

She put the tablet on the desk and stuck her palm against her forehead. "Oh no. No, no, no. I can't believe this. I spent all weekend trying to be faithful when I knew I didn't love him anymore. I tried to do what was right. And he's been cheating on me. Probably for a long time." She sniffled. "Why would he do this? If he wanted her all along, why didn't he just break up with me?"

Armando softened his voice in an effort not to provoke more anger. "Do you think it had something to do with your dad? Political connections?"

"Maybe." Katie stared straight ahead. "Yeah. Maybe he was just using me for that all along. Wow. I'm the dumbest person in the world."

"No." Tom shook his head. "Don't say that about yourself. This happens to the best of us and I see it all the time. There's a million theories about why people cheat. Chances are, he wants to marry you for the right reasons. But there's something about having a girl on the side that makes him feel good about himself. Maybe he's told himself all along he'd stop when you got married. And please, don't get me wrong. I'm certainly not taking up for this guy." Tom gave her a sympathetic look. "But you're not stupid."

"Thanks for saying that." Katie nodded, then reached forward to take a tissue from the box on the desk. "Is it okay if I ask you to email me those pictures?"

"Sure," Tom said.

Katie then thought about some good that would result from Mitch's cheating.

It lessened her guilt over breaking up with him.

And it would certainly close the meddling mouths of her friends and family—especially her mother.

* * * * *

The next day at work, Katie was determined to make time pass quickly until the end of the day when she could start her long weekend with Armando. So, she busied herself with any task she could find.

She also tried to stay the hell away from Jennifer, but it was nearly impossible. Katie considered Jennifer "almost bad enough to fire," but never found enough reason to actually do it. And she refused to fire her today out of spite. Katie had no intention of confronting Jennifer, at least, not yet. Today she simply wanted to be away from the perky blond server, lest she lose her temper in front of the customers.

Katie planned to work through her lunch hour today. There was no point taking an hour to sit there, stewing in her anger over Mitch and Jennifer. Or watching the minutes crawl by as she counted them down till six o'clock, when a driver would take her to the private jet bound for Los Angeles. Katie just wanted this day to be over.

At twenty minutes till noon, her phone vibrated in her pocket. Her heart raced, hoping it was Armando.

But it was Lisa, her mother.

Katie took a deep breath and walked to a quiet corner. She answered with an unenthusiastic, "Hi Mom," hoping to get this over with, quickly.

"Hey sweetie. You free for lunch today?"

A knot instantly formed in Katie's stomach. "No. I'm working through lunch."

"What?" She uttered a disgruntled sound. *"Well, too bad. I'm already on my way."*

"No! I'm busy, Mom."

"Well, I'm determined to speak with you today and I won't take no for an answer. I'll just follow you around the restaurant while you work if I have to."

Katie smirked, having a sudden idea. This could be the perfect time to show her mother some pictures she'd recently obtained. "You know what? Let's have lunch. But not here. Across the street at Cafe Spera."

"Fine with me. See you at noon."

After her mom hung up, Katie slipped her phone into her pocket with a sense of relief. Soon, Mom would see the pictures, and realize there was no hope for Katie reconciling with Mitch.

When Katie entered Cafe Spera at approximately one minute after noon, Lisa was already there, her gold bangle bracelets jangling as she waved at Katie from a table for two.

Katie went to the table and gave her mom a big smile as she sat down across from her. "Hello Mom."

Lisa cocked a brow. "My, my, my. Aren't we happy today?"

"Yes, as a matter of fact."

"Hmm." Lisa eyed her daughter suspiciously as she took a quick sip of her ice water. She set the glass down on the table and said, "So, I'll assume that means you've taken Mitch back?"

Katie let out a labored sigh and closed her eyes, trying to keep her anger at bay. "Did you come here to have lunch with me, or to insult me?"

Lisa's tone gentled. "How in the world is that an insult?"

"You assume the only reason I'm happy is because I must have taken Mitch back? You have no idea what you're talking about."

Lisa shrugged. "What? I can't imagine why any woman would give up a guy like him. You need to snap out of this little rebellious phase before he moves on to someone else."

Katie chuckled. "Have you spoken to him?"

"No, not yet. I wanted to speak with you first."

Nodding, Katie said, "So you *do* plan to meddle."

Just then, the friendly male server came to take Katie's drink order. As soon as he left, Lisa responded with, "It's not meddling. It's helping. Now tell me what happened. Let's get things back to the way they should be."

Katie shook her head and reached into her pocket for her phone. The pictures were saved in their very own folder. She touched the screen a few times, then handed the phone to her mother. "Here. This is what happened."

Lisa gave Katie a wry grin as she took the phone. Her eyes then narrowed at the picture. "Okay. What am I looking at?"

"You can't tell?" Katie took a deep breath, then let out a long sigh. She made sure the first picture her mother saw was one of the clearest, but apparently it wasn't good enough. "Tap the right side of the picture to go to the next one."

Lisa tapped the screen. Then she tapped again. Then again. She spent at least five seconds on each picture until she came to the last one. And then, she calmly handed the phone back to Katie. Her voice was quiet, but firm. Her eyes widened. "Get rid of those."

"Excuse me?" Katie snapped.

Lisa looked her daughter straight in the eyes and repeated, in a loud whisper, "I said, get rid of them!"

"What?" Katie's jaw dropped. "Why the—"

Lisa looked around the restaurant as if she were afraid someone was listening, then she leaned forward as far across the table as possible and said, "Do it! In case Mitch ever runs for public office. Something like that could ruin him forever."

"Mom! He cheated on me!"

Lisa's nostrils flared as she glanced around the restaurant again. "Keep your voice down."

Katie felt like she'd been punched in the stomach. She stared silently at her mom as the server dropped off her water and said he'd be back in a minute to take their orders. When Katie spoke, her voice was weak. "I can't believe this. You don't even care that he cheated on me?"

Lisa gazed sympathetically into Katie's eyes for a moment, then smirked. Her voice was just loud enough for Katie to hear.

"Sweetie, sometimes you need to look at the bigger picture. I've met that girl. She's a dingbat. Probably his last fling before he marries you. She's nothing to him."

Katie shook her head in disbelief. "I don't understand—"

"Think about it. Years from now, you'll be married to a senator and she'll probably still be waiting tables somewhere. There's nothing to be jealous over."

"I'm not jealous! This isn't a competition between me and Jennifer. My fiancé cheated on me, Mom." Katie's eyes widened. "He lied to me. Repeatedly. He might be sleeping with more women for all I know."

"Have you talked to him about it?"

"No. Why should I?"

"You can still work it out. It may not be as bad as you think, Katie-bug." Lisa grinned, softly. "Trust me. Sometimes people cheat. And sometimes the best thing you can do is forgive 'em."

"Oh really? Has Daddy ever cheated on you? Would you forgive him if he did?"

Lisa shrugged. "That depends. But this isn't about me and your dad. It's about you and Mitch. And you both have a bright future ahead of you. Now please, talk to him. We can talk to him together if you want. It's time we start planning your wedding."

"No. I have no desire to be a senator's wife, or a governor's wife. Or the First Lady." Katie stood up and walked around the table, staring down her nose at her. "Mitch and I are over. For good. You and Daddy will not dictate my love life, ever again. I've had it with this bullshit. Goodbye, Mom."

And with that, Katie turned on her heel and walked out of the restaurant. Her phone vibrated with her Mom's call as soon as Katie crossed the street, but she ignored it. She then ducked inside a coffee shop to hide as she called Armando.

He answered quickly. "Hello? Katie?"

"Yes." The sound of his voice unlocked a torrent of emotions that suddenly made her choke up. "I uh...," She sniffled, "I'm leaving work early. Now."

"Okay. I'll send the car. What's wrong? Did something happen?"

Katie inhaled as deeply as possible and did her best to calm down. "Lunch with Mom. I'm done. I don't give a damn about losing contact with my family anymore. Take me away from here."

"All right. Anything you want. I love you."

She smiled, tears of joy rolling down her face. "I love you, too."

Katie hung up and called her manager to tell him she had to leave work immediately to start her long weekend. He heard her crying and simply said, "That's fine." She then sneaked over to the restaurant to meet the driver at the usual spot. Her anger mounted as she stood in front of the restaurant, wondering if her mother would exit Cafe Spera and try to speak with her again, but she didn't.

CHAPTER 16

Katie and Armando left for Los Angeles two hours after she left work. He immediately took her out for a long, luxurious dinner at one of his favorite restaurants, then brought her to his house in Malibu for the night.

She was relaxing in Armando's arms on a loveseat on the patio of his beautiful home, marveling at the view of the sunset over the ocean, when his phone rang.

When he saw it was Victor, he answered. "What's up?"

Victor took a hesitant breath and said, *"Hey. Sorry to bother you, but we have a little situation. Katie's sister is here. Said she's been trying to get in touch with her all day."*

"Shit." Armando groaned. "Is it just her sister, or the whole family?"

Katie's eyes grew wide with worry.

"It's only her sister. And I didn't confirm Katie was with you."

"Okay. Hold on." Armando put his hand over the phone and said to Katie, "Chelsea's at the ranch. I guess she showed up there after she couldn't reach you?"

Katie winced, her body tensing. "That's not good. Let me go get my phone. It's probably dead by now."

"That's okay. Stay here." Armando said to Victor, "Hey, can you let her use your phone so they can talk?"

"*Sure. She's in the living room. Hold on.*" Victor was then silent. About thirty seconds later, Chelsea's voice came through the phone. "*Hello?*"

Without saying anything to Chelsea, Armando handed his phone to Katie.

Katie said, "Hello?"

Chelsea grunted. "*I knew it! What the hell's wrong with you?*"

"Nothing. I'm happy! Am I *not* allowed to be happy for once in my life?"

"*So, you did it. You broke off your engagement. For Armando. Who you haven't seen in ten years.*"

"It's more than that. I—"

"*Yeah, I know. I heard about Mitch cheating. Mom told me.*" Chelsea paused for a breath. "*Oh, and I haven't told anyone about our talk the other day. She has no idea you're with Armando.*"

Katie chuckled. "You're more than welcome to tell her. I don't care what they think anymore. I'm over it."

"*Oh no. I'm not saying a word. You're on your own with that.*"

"Well? What do you want, then? Did you call to beat up on me and tell me what a horrible person I am because I won't take 'Mitch the cheater' back?"

"*No.*" Chelsea's voice got sad. "*Mom told me what she said to you at lunch. It's unreal, even for her. We argued about it for an hour before I came over here to look for you.*" She paused. "*I was worried. That's all. I heard you left work early. We've all been trying to reach you.*"

"So, no one knows you're at the ranch?"

"*Nope.*"

"Okay. Well…" Katie thought for a moment. "I'll send Mom and Dad text messages to let 'em know I'm all right and I'll be back on Monday morning. I'll talk to 'em sometime next week about Armando."

Armando grinned and rubbed her back.

"*Oh, good Lord.*" Chelsea sighed. "*Fine. You do what you gotta do. And if you want me around for that talk with Mom and Dad, I'll be there. For the record, I'll be dreading it every second until then.*"

"I know, and I'm sorry. But this is something I have to do." Katie looked at Armando as she told her sister, "I never stopped loving him."

Chelsea let out a sad little chuckle. "*That's crazy.*"

"I know. And I don't care."

With a resigned sigh, Chelsea said, "*Okay. Have an amazing weekend. Love you.*"

"Love you, too." Katie hung up and handed the phone back to Armando.

Swiftly, he put the phone in his pocket then pulled her in for a kiss.

Katie reached up and wove her fingers in his thick, wavy hair as his tongue made slow circles around hers, knowing she had made the right decision.

* * * * *

It was Saturday. For the second morning in a row, Katie woke up naked in a huge bed, forgetting for a moment how she got there. When she opened her eyes, she saw the unfamiliar decor and smiled. The faint smell of coffee filled her nostrils. She heard Armando taking a shower and thought about joining him. Instead, she yawned, closed her eyes, and fell back into her peaceful slumber.

A little while later, she awoke to the feel of Armando's bare chest against her back. His arm was around her stomach, pulling her close as he nuzzled her ear and whispered, "Wake up, sleepyhead."

Katie giggled softly. "But your bed's so nice…"

"I know." Armando kissed her temple. "But I have a surprise for you. There's a jet waiting. Gotta get ready."

Katie jolted completely awake. "What? Where are we going?"

"Cabo."

"Why? I just got here. I thought we were gonna lay around all day."

Armando laughed. "But you did that yesterday while I was at work."

"Yes. And it was awesome."

He laughed some more and kissed her ear, then whispered, "Don't tell me you'd really rather hang around here than have a tropical getaway with me."

"I already feel like I'm on a tropical getaway. The ocean's right outside."

"Come on. Let me spoil you. I've dreamed of this for years."

"You have?"

"Yes. Waking up on a Saturday morning, leaving town on a whim. With you."

Katie melted inside. "I can be ready in fifteen minutes."

A few hours later, Katie was standing in the living room of a beautiful private villa perched from a cliff in Cabo San Lucas. As Armando walked around the house to do a quick inspection, Katie opened the glass doors to the veranda and was instantly wrapped up in the comfortably warm breeze, her jaw dropping at the sight of the ocean way down below. A portion of the beach was private, but off to the side a few vacationers lounged in the sun.

To her immediate left was a hot tub, where she dreamily imagined kissing Armando as they sipped champagne and watched the sun set on the ocean below.

Armando came outside to join her. "Everything appears to be all set. The bed's made. The fridge is stocked. If I've forgotten something, let me know."

Katie's eyebrows lifted. "No, I'm pretty sure you've thought of everything." She let out a nervous chuckle.

"What's wrong? You don't like it here?"

"No, from the little I've seen, I love it here. It's breathtaking." She smiled, shyly. "It's just...wow. I don't know what to say. I guess my head's spinning. I still think of you as the guy I used to sneak off with after school and now you're living this life. Flying wherever you want, whenever you feel like it. You have all these fancy houses."

Armando shook his head. "This place is a rental. I don't own it." His eyes widened. "But I can buy it if you want."

Katie laughed and put her arms around his waist. "No, that's not what I meant. You've already done so much for me. I love it, and I appreciate it, but I really just need *you*. It wouldn't matter to me if you dug ditches for a living and we lived in a tent."

Armando beamed. "I know. And that just makes me wanna take you more places and buy you more things." He sighed. "Look, I've been successful. And I wanna reap the rewards with the woman I love. Hopefully, this is just the beginning."

Armando cupped each side of her face and pressed his lips to hers. As his tongue slipped into her mouth, his hands moved to her hair, his fingers gently grasping her silky red tendrils.

Katie held him close and let herself enjoy it. He kissed her in a way that made her feel like the most desired woman in the world. And she knew that to him, she was.

She felt her body lift in the air as they kissed. She marveled at the easy way he carried her. His body was lean and muscular, not bulky. He was deceptively strong for his looks. The thought made her quiver. Mmm...such a powerful man he had become, in so many ways.

Katie soon found herself sitting on a large chaise lounger as Armando broke the kiss and quickly scooted in beside her. Soon they were lying on their sides, kissing once again. Katie quickly unbuttoned his linen shirt until his chest was bare. Her hand glided across his hard abs and chest as her breath went weak from the feel of his lips and tongue against hers.

As his body curled into hers, she felt his manhood pressing against her. She gently raked her fingers over it, then unbuttoned his pants. As his zipper slowly gave way, she wiggled her hand inside his underwear. Her fingers curled around his blazing hot skin as he moaned into her mouth.

He took her wrist and moved it over her head as he flipped her onto her back.

She broke the kiss and said, "Can anyone see us up here?"

He smiled. "No, my love."

"Good." With her free hand, Katie reached down to lift up her shirt. Armando instantly went for her shorts to unbutton them as he reached into his pocket to retrieve the condom he had placed there earlier.

In moments, they stripped off each others' clothes.

Katie lay naked on her back with Armando between her legs and hovering over her, shielding her eyes from the searing noonday sun.

She grinned up at him and said, "I love you."

He bent down to give her a kiss, then whispered, "I love you too." And then he pressed deep inside her.

Her entire body bucked against him. She shouted, "Yes!" as he went faster and harder, encouraged by the sound of her moans.

The warm, gentle breeze from the ocean encompassed them as they made love.

The sound of the waves crashing below mimicked what Katie felt happening in her body. Waves of pleasure built slowly from every touch of Armando's body. She reached out to touch his chest as he reached down to cradle her thighs, working himself deeper inside her.

Armando's head fell back as her mouth fell open. "Yes! Yes...oh yes!" she shouted repeatedly, holding nothing back.

It didn't take long for her to climax when he took her from that position, hitting every part of her just right. She yelled his name, professing their love in the wide open air. And soon she heard him moan louder as his breathing quickened. He threw his head back, screaming her name until he couldn't form words.

And then he lowered her leg and got down on his elbows, locking her body under his as his mouth descended on hers.

When it came time to stand up, Katie glanced at the cliffs surrounding them. "Are you sure no one can see?"

He nodded. "Yeah." Then his face screwed up. "Well, unless they have a telescope, I guess."

He laughed as Katie sheepishly grabbed her clothes from the patio and ran into the house as fast as possible.

Armando retrieved his boxer shorts from the ground and put them on, then strolled into the house. "Are you hungry?" He asked. "I sure am."

Katie quickly put on her panties and T-shirt then followed him into the kitchen where he took a plate of cold shrimp out of the refrigerator. "Where's all this food from, anyway?" she asked.

"Mostly from a restaurant a few miles away." Armando took a moment to chew a shrimp and swallow, then he extended the plate to her. "One of my favorite places. Oh, let me know later if you wanna go out for dinner or have it delivered. Either way's fine with me."

Katie flashed him a coy grin as she took a shrimp from the plate. "I don't think I wanna leave this house at all. Especially the patio. We could just stay there the entire weekend for all I care. I love the privacy." She popped the shrimp into her mouth.

Armando blushed slightly as he set the plate down on the counter. "So, I guess my technique's improved a bit since high school?"

Katie inhaled a tiny gasp and put her hand on his back. "You were always good!"

He laughed until he nearly snorted. Calming down, he said, "No. I was terrible. You just didn't know any better."

"Don't say that! I thought you were great. When I look back, I don't have anything bad to say about it. Quite the opposite." She let out a dreamy sigh. "Remember that night of the Winter dance?" Her eyes twinkled as she smiled.

Armando looked into her eyes, his voice soft. "Of course I do."

"I always wondered if that was really your first time. Seemed like you knew what you were doing."

He smirked. "Yes. It was absolutely my first time. And no, I had no idea what I was doing."

She reached up and put her arms around his neck. "It was the best night of my entire life. I wrote every single detail I could remember in my diary. I read it sometimes." She frowned. "Thankfully, I was able to hide it or Dad would've thrown it away. He threw away those pictures of us. You know, the ones we had taken that night at the dance, to prove we showed up?"

Armando's eyes narrowed, thoughtfully. "Yeah. I know." Then he looked off at the wall as if he was intensely concentrating. "I have something for you. Go to the living room. I'll be right back."

Katie took the plate of shrimp with her to the living room and placed it on the coffee table as Armando went to the bedroom.

After a few minutes, he reappeared, still wearing only his boxer shorts, carrying something tucked under his arm.

Katie strained to see what it was, but he hid it until he sat down beside her.

He cleared his throat as though he was anxious, then presented it to her.

Katie took it from his hand—a small photo album. She looked in his eyes, knowing what was inside before she opened it. "Is the picture in here?"

Grinning, he said, "Open it."

Her eyes welled up when she flipped the cover open. And there it was, on the first page. Katie in her powder blue dress, wearing a wrist corsage. Armando in a nice black suit, the most handsome she had ever seen him. They were posed in the position the photographer had posed all the couples who had waited in that line. Facing each other, holding hands.

Katie's voice broke as she said, "I'm so happy you kept it."

"Me too."

She stared at it for a while longer then flipped to the next page and immediately laughed. It was a goofy picture of both of them in Katie's mom's car on one of their many clandestine dates. "I forgot about this!" She quickly turned to another page where there was a just a picture of her. She turned to the next one, showing Armando and Katie with some of their friends at a restaurant. "I'm so glad you have these. I had nothing left. Nothing."

He nodded. "So, who's the jackass with the camera phone *now*, huh?"

She laughed. "Yeah, you thought you were so cool back then, didn't you?"

He smiled and put his arm around her shoulder, drawing her close as she flipped through the rest of the pictures.

When Katie arrived at the last page, she gasped and brought her hand to her mouth. "Oh my God." She had expected to see a picture, but instead, there was a sparkling diamond ring, adhered to the page with a piece of tape.

Armando removed the tape and took the album from Katie's hands, gently placing it on the coffee table.

Before he stood up, Armando looked into her eyes and said, "I was gonna wait till later and be more formal but I just couldn't wait anymore. This is long overdue."

Katie's hand went to her chest, her eyes filling with new tears as she listened to him continue.

He said, "If you say 'yes' to me, I'll take that to mean nothing can tear us apart again." His voice was earnest. "And I mean, *nothing*. I need you. I love you. I'm always gonna love you." And then he stood up, shoving the coffee table away to give himself ample room. He locked eyes with her and dropped down to one knee, extending the ring in his open palm. "Katherine Grace McCormack. My beautiful, precious Katie. Will you please be my wife?"

Katie's bottom lip trembled as tears fell down her cheeks. The word she wanted to say stuck in her throat. She forced herself to take a few deep breaths, then said, "Yes."

Armando's eyes held tears of joy. He quickly slipped the ring on her finger, then stood and reached down to pull her up beside him.

She buried her face against his collarbone, tears spilling onto his bare skin. The proposal was unexpected, but it was perfect. She cried with a happiness she had never felt before.

CHAPTER 17

The weekend passed too quickly for Armando and Katie. They woke up early to take a private jet to San Antonio so Katie could get back to work.

And now, on this Monday morning, Armando was driving Katie from the airport to her apartment.

"Please, call in sick again today," Armando said as he reached for her thigh to give it a gentle squeeze. "You don't need that job anymore anyway. Let's just run away and get married. Today."

Katie shivered at his touch. "I wish I could, but you should've heard my boss when I called in late this morning. I'll turn in a two week notice today. It's the right thing to do." She yawned. "I wish I could've slept in, though. I'm exhausted."

He produced a sly chuckle. "Hmm. Maybe I should've let you sleep instead of keeping you awake all night."

She giggled. "No, I'll go to bed early this evening. I'll be just fine."

Armando nodded. All weekend they had a silent understanding to live in the moment. Even though they were engaged now, there was no talk of what would happen when they came back to Texas. He sensed that even though Katie was finally ready to tell her parents about their love—no matter the consequences—it would still be more difficult than he could possibly understand. Instead of adding to her stress with talk of setting a date, or quitting her job immediately to move to California and live with him, he stayed in the present. Basking in their rekindled love.

The more he thought about it, the more he knew it was a gift. Old love becoming new again. Their feelings growing and deepening in ways they never would have experienced if they hadn't been torn apart years earlier. And he refused to do anything less than treasure each moment with Katie. No reason to talk about how different their lives would've been if they had stayed together.

They were together now. Nothing else mattered.

When they pulled into the parking lot at Katie's apartment complex, she gasped.

"What's wrong?" Armando asked.

"Cars...oh no..." For a second it looked like she could hyperventilate. "My parents are here. Or at least, my dad is."

Armando's eyes quickly scanned the parking lot. He immediately pulled into the first empty spot, turned off the car, then took her hand. "It's okay, sweetheart. Don't be scared. They can't stop us anymore."

A thin layer of tears formed in her eyes. "I know. But I don't like this." She craned her neck to look farther down the parking lot, then around the side of the building. "What? That's Mitch's car!"

Armando rolled his eyes with a loud groan. "That's just great."

Katie turned in her seat, staring straight ahead through the windshield. "What the hell are they doing here? Waiting for me upstairs? What about the security company you paid to watch it for me?"

"They only come by every few hours." Armando's head shook

gently. "You don't have to go up there, you know. You can come back home with me." He put the key in the ignition, ready to start the car again.

She inhaled deeply and said, "No. I'm not gonna put this off anymore. And I'm sure if I don't face them now they'll just bombard me at work. That's the last thing I need." She took her phone out of her purse to look for missed calls; there were none.

"Okay." Armando turned around to look at the apartment building for any sign of the people Katie dreaded seeing. "I'll come with you."

She shook her head rapidly. "No. Not yet. I wanna see what they have to say first."

"Are you sure? I don't know if I like the idea of you going up there alone."

Her eyes met his. "I'm sure. It's not because I'm scared of what they'll do to you. I just need to do this by myself. I'll call if I need you."

Armando held her gaze, nodding. "All right."

A smile flickered across her lips for a moment, and Armando reached behind her head and pulled her forward to give her a long, fervid kiss. When he let her go, he looked in her eyes, his face inches from hers. "I'll always love you, Katie. No matter what happens up there, even if you lose your family forever. I'll always be with you."

Her beautiful face lit up, and tears spilled down her cheeks. "I know. And I'll always love you, too." She took off her engagement ring and placed it carefully inside a pocket in her purse. "I promise, I'll tell 'em we're engaged *soon*." Her eyes met his. "I mean it. But one thing at a time." She gave his lips a quick peck, then opened her door and hopped out, like she was ready to get this over with.

Armando watched her in the rear-view mirror. She rushed across the parking lot and to the stairs. When he couldn't see her anymore, he got out of the car and ran across the lot, keeping his eyes open and alert. *Surely she didn't think I'd just sit out in the car waiting for her, did she?*

He ran up the metal stairs, taking them two and three at a time, trying to be as quiet as possible. Echoes of angry voices suddenly filled the air as he neared the top. He instantly recognized Dwayne's and Lisa's. And he assumed the male voice he didn't recognize was Mitch. He hung back in the stairwell, out of sight.

The angriest person was definitely Lisa, whose shrill voice pierced the air. She shouted. "We were worried about you! You just take off and leave all weekend without telling anyone where you're going?"

Katie said, "I'm twenty-eight years old, Mom. I'm way past the age of checking in with my parents when I go out of town. Besides, I sent you a text message. And none of you called to tell me you were gonna show up here this morning."

Dwayne's voice was surprisingly calm. He said, "Honey, you know better than to think I take one of those little messages seriously. I needed to see you and know you were all right. Especially after everything that's happened."

"Well," Katie said, "As you can see, I'm fine. And if y'all don't mind, I need you to leave so I can get ready for work."

Lisa said, "Work can wait. The four of us need to sit down and get things straightened out before you take off and leave town again. Worry everyone to death."

"You're unbelievable," Katie said. "For one thing, I have absolutely nothing to say to," she pointed at Mitch as her eyes stayed on Lisa's, "*him*. We're through. End of story."

Mitch said, "Come on, Katie. We can put all this mess behind us. Whatever you did, it doesn't matter to me. I'm ready to start my life with you."

Katie scoffed. "Excuse me? Whatever *I* did? Have you already called Jennifer today? Do you have plans to meet in your car for a quickie at lunch?"

Mitch's face instantly reddened. He stared off at the wall in silence.

Dwayne asked, "What are you talking about?"

Katie looked at her dad. "He's cheating. Didn't anyone tell you?"

Lisa glanced up and down the hall then whispered, "Shh! Someone might hear you."

Katie huffed out a sarcastic chuckle. "Oh, so *now* you care about the volume of the conversation."

Dwayne stammered for a moment then said, "Nobody told me about that." He glanced at Mitch, then stared at Lisa. "You knew about this?"

Lisa rolled her eyes and quietly said, "It's not a big deal. He's a catch. He's probably got women throwing themselves at him all the time. And Katie works so much. It'll change after they get married and she can quit her job and spend more time—"

Katie interrupted her. "Wait. You think I work too much? Are you serious? It's *my* fault that my fiancé cheated? Because I'm not constantly taking care of his," she cleared her throat, "*needs*? You're the one who's out of her mind."

Dwayne let out a sinister laugh, then said, "Well, I ain't gonna put up with some guy cheatin' on my little girl. Mitch, I suggest you get on outta here before I do something to you we'll both regret."

Lisa sighed. "You're overreacting, Dwayne."

"No, I'm not!" Dwayne grabbed Lisa's shoulder. "I don't put up with that shit and you know it. Some guy out there messin' around, bringin' home diseases?" He shook his head. "Not to *my* daughter. No way in hell."

Katie pressed her lips together, trying to keep herself from crying. She was touched, forgetting that Daddy actually stood up for her sometimes. Her voice on the verge of cracking, she softly said to her father, "It's because of his possible career in politics. She wanted me to delete the pictures because it might hurt his career later."

Mitch inhaled a deep breath and stared down at the floor. Lisa rolled her eyes and fidgeted with her watch.

Dwayne took his hand from his wife's shoulder and asked her, "Why do you care so much about whether or not he has a political career? That's no reason to badger Katie into marrying a guy who—"

Suddenly fuming, Lisa interrupted him with, "I want her to go on to something more than just the wife of a district judge! It barely even counts as an election!"

"I see." Dwayne's jaw set firmly as he nodded slowly, his eyes fixed on hers. "Didn't know I was such a disappointment."

Katie summoned a bit more anger at the mention of Lisa's true agenda. "So, you wanted to live through me? Because you had aspirations of being married to someone with higher standing, to impress your friends? Is that what it is? The glamour of being a governor's wife?"

Lisa's silence spoke volumes. So, Katie pressed on as her mom's eyes bored into hers. She gave her mother a smug grin and said, "Is that the real reason you made me break Armando's heart? Because you thought he'd never run for public office and make you proud?"

In the shadows, Armando's pulse quickened as he waited for their response.

Dwayne's face grew sullen. He took a deep breath, then shared a glance with Lisa.

Lisa shook her head. "That had nothing to do with it. And now's not the time—"

"Well, what was it then?" Katie shrugged. "Must've been something pretty damn bad for you to leave him for dead in the middle of nowhere."

Dwayne's eyes widened, but he said nothing.

Lisa extended her hand toward Katie in a calming gesture. "Let's not overreact here."

Mitch's eyebrows knitted as he asked, "Who's Armando? Is he the ex-boyfriend you kissed last weekend?"

Lisa brought her hand to her chest, staring at Katie, then quietly uttered, "What?"

Then they all turned to the sound of footsteps behind them as a man in a suit came out from his hiding place. He cleared his throat and firmly stated, "I'm right here."

Katie's hands flew to her mouth, covering it as she gasped. But Armando looked in her eyes, holding her in a gentle gaze as he slowly walked toward her, calming her. She kept her eyes only on him, ignoring whatever reaction her parents were having. When he came near he smiled and held out his hand, and she gladly took it. Together they stood, facing her parents.

Lisa's nostrils flared. Her eyes were set on Katie as if Armando wasn't there. Her voice was soft but unmistakably angry. "You selfish little girl."

Katie was about to scream at Lisa, but her eyes flashed to Dwayne, and Katie did a double take at what she saw.

He simply stared at Armando, his eyes glistening with tears.

Armando gave him a thoughtful stare in return.

Lisa shrugged as she looked Armando up and down, then turned to her husband. "Well? Aren't you gonna do something?"

Dwayne shot his wife a cold glance, then he looked at Mitch. "You need to get outta here, boy." He nodded behind them at the stairwell, his voice stern. "Go on. *Now*."

As Mitch headed for the stairs, Katie sensed it was time for privacy. She fished her keys from her purse and opened the door as fast as she could.

Everyone filed into the apartment in silence. First Armando, then Dwayne, then a hesitant Lisa, who glowered at Katie as she walked past.

Dwayne waited until Armando took a seat in the corner of the couch, then he sat close by in a recliner. Lisa pulled a chair from the dining room and sat beside her husband, hands folded in her lap.

Katie cozied up next to Armando, holding his hand.

The room was silent as Dwayne closed his eyes, thinking. When he opened them, they were glossy. He put his elbows against his knees, leaning forward, fingers laced together.

Lisa's eyes narrowed at Dwayne as she waited for him to speak.

Dwayne sniffled and drew the back of his hand across one eye. Then he took a long, deep breath, looking in Armando's eyes. In a gentle voice, he said, "I'm sorry."

Lisa's jaw dropped.

Armando squeezed Katie's hand, unprepared for his apology. But he was especially unprepared for his sincerity.

Dwayne continued. "Son, if I'd known your Mama was sick, I never would've…" His voice trailed off as he sniffled again. He reached into his suit pocket for a handkerchief, which he wiped across his face.

Lisa rolled her eyes and shook her head.

Katie and Armando stared at Dwayne, both of their hearts racing, stunned by his emotional display.

After a little while, Dwayne put the handkerchief away, appearing calmer. He cleared his throat and looked again at Armando. "What I did to you was wrong. There ain't much else I can say about it. Thought I was doing the right thing, protecting my family." His eyes flashed to Katie. "If you still make my little girl happy after all this time, then—"

"No!" Lisa slapped her legs with her hands. "You can't be okay with this!"

Armando stared straight in her eyes and said, "Why the hell not? Katie and I both deserve an answer."

Dwayne nodded, his face solemn. "I agree."

Lisa huffed out a stubborn sigh.

Katie said, "Mom, stop doing this. Daddy's fine with it! Haven't we been through enough?"

Lisa gritted her teeth, glaring at her daughter. Then she straightened her skirt and stood up, pacing back and forth in a nervous display Katie knew all too well.

Dwayne watched his wife for a second, then turned to Armando and Katie. "We may need to have this talk another time. After everyone calms down a bit."

Armando watched Lisa pace the floor. "With all due respect, sir, I'd like to know right now. It changed the course of my life and I feel like I've waited a million years to hear it. I already know it has something to do with a deal you made with Henry. Please tell me what it was."

Lisa bristled at the mention of Henry's name.

Dwayne gave his wife another glance, then his eyes focused thoughtfully on Armando. "Do you know where he disappeared to?"

"Who, Henry?" Armando shrugged. "No. He checks in with Ramon once in a while. He's traveling. That's all I know."

Dwayne scoffed. "Traveling. Well, when he finally gets his skinny ole ass back to that ranch, you tell him it's time me and him had a talk."

"A talk about what?" Armando asked. "You gotta give me more than that. If it's something bad enough to make you break us up the way you did, it's probably something my brothers and I need to know about. We've been trying to figure it out and we're not gonna stop."

Dwayne inhaled sharply, then exhaled, a glum look on his face as his eyes darted around the room everywhere but at his wife. After a long pause, he said, "What story did Henry tell you about why he moved you and your family over the border, to his ranch?"

Lisa stopped pacing to glare at Dwayne.

Confused, Armando said, "I don't know what you mean by 'story.' I met him when I was eight and he got lost in our village. I gave him directions. He said he never forgot how nice I was. He came back a couple years later and tracked us down, offered our mom a job. So we moved."

Dwayne's lips pursed, thoughtfully. "You ever think there's something not quite right about that story?"

Through gritted teeth, Lisa whispered, "Dwayne!"

Dwayne continued, ignoring her. "You ever wonder why he'd let a strange woman and her three boys move right into that nice, big house of his?"

Armando gulped. "No. But we didn't have anywhere else to live, and Henry's ranch didn't have living quarters."

Dwayne nodded. "So I guess you never really questioned it, then."

"At first we did, maybe, but we were kids," Armando said. "Henry was good to us. Mama was happy. We weren't struggling anymore. That's all we cared about."

"Well, son," Dwayne said, "Henry Platt lied to you."

Lisa grunted in frustration and brought her hand to her forehead.

Armando's eyes widened. "About what?"

Dwayne gave Armando a sympathetic frown. "He knew exactly who you were when he met you."

Armando felt the hair on his arms stand up as a nervous twinge fluttered in his stomach then spread through the rest of his body. "How?"

"Dwayne!" Lisa shouted.

Sighing, Dwayne looked at his wife, then back at Armando. "Like I said. You let me know when Henry comes back. There's a whole lotta shit he's gonna have to tell you himself." His head shook. "But I can't."

"Yes, you can," Armando pleaded. "I had no idea. I beg you, please tell me. I can track Henry down if I have to."

"Well, you do that," Dwayne said. "And I'll be ready to talk. But for now, that's all I can say." He paused, sighing. "That, and I'm sorry."

Lisa threw her hands up in the air, then muttered at Dwayne, "I can't believe you. I'll see you in the car."

"Mom, wait!" Katie opened her purse, frantic. "I need to show you something." When she found her ring, she turned to Armando with a big smile and she slid the ring onto her finger, right where it belonged. Then she lifted her hand, displaying the ring with pride. "We're engaged!"

Lisa shot Katie a mean look. Her eyes then settled on Armando for the briefest moment. And then, with a loud huff, she gave her husband one last glance before opening the door and slamming it shut behind her.

Dwayne snorted and waved his hand toward the door in a dismissive gesture. "Don't worry about her." Then he stood, gazing down at Katie. "You have my blessing."

Katie rose from her seat, her bottom lip trembling. She held back her tears and softly said, "I'm shocked. After what happened I—"

"I know." Dwayne nodded. "I know." Then he put his arms around her and pulled her in tight. "I know, darlin'."

Hesitantly, Armando rose. "Thank you, sir. It means a lot to have your blessing."

Dwayne hugged Katie for a little while longer before letting her go and turning his attention to Armando. He extended his hand. "Again, I'm sorry."

Armando's heart raced, his thoughts whirling in a hazy cloud of disbelief. He was about to shake the hand of a person who had done him so very wrong. Maybe Armando should hate Dwayne. But he remembered his mother's words. *Revenge will end up killing you.* So, Armando took Dwayne's hand, shaking it firmly. "Thank you."

Dwayne stared into Armando's eyes. "I know it doesn't make any sense right now. But like I said. You get Henry, I'll give you answers."

Armando sensed Dwayne's genuineness. He knew he was dealing with a man whose handshake was as good as getting it in writing. Armando nodded in agreement. "I'll do that."

Half-smiling, Dwayne let go of Armando's hand and said, "Welcome to the family." Then he stood back and addressed the couple. "I'm gonna leave you two alone now. There's a big fight with my wife in my future. Better go get it over with."

Armando instantly thought about the fight he had with Dwayne ten years earlier. He surprised himself by letting a statement fly out of his mouth, "I have a feeling you're gonna be just fine, sir."

Dwayne gave him a knowing look, and chuckled. "Yeah. And hey, no more of this 'sir' stuff. Just call me Dwayne. All right?"

Armando nodded. "All right."

Dwayne patted Armando's shoulder, then gave his daughter another hug and a kiss on the cheek before saying goodbye and heading out the door.

When the door closed, Katie turned to Armando. Their eyes locked for a moment, and then they both burst into tears.

Armando held her as tight as possible, stroking her hair.

Katie went weak against him.

They both felt a huge weight had been lifted, and they were finally free to live their lives as husband and wife. Exactly how they had always intended.

CHAPTER 18

Exactly three weeks from the day Armando proposed, Katie was in her wedding dress, arm-in-arm with her father as they walked down the sandy, makeshift aisle, to the love of her life. Her red hair was piled atop her head, with flyaway pieces hanging down, blowing with the gentle ocean breeze.

They were in Cabo San Lucas, on the beach below the villa where Armando proposed. They had such a lovely time there that weekend, he decided to buy it, and was in the process of doing so.

No more waiting, they decided. This wedding was long overdue. So the planning was quick. Katie wasn't so concerned about what dresses she or the bridesmaids wore. As long as she would finally be Mrs. Armando Barboza today, she was happy.

Her mother, Lisa, took about a week to get over her anger with Katie. Or, at least she acted like she was over it. Katie suspected her Mom was just grateful she could brag to her friends about her daughter marrying such a successful man. But regardless of the reason, Katie was thrilled to have some peace in her life.

However...

Two days earlier, when Dwayne and Lisa arrived, they broke

the news to Katie and Chelsea of their separation and pending divorce. The decision was made less than a day after they learned of Katie's reunion with Armando. Their argument began when they left her apartment and ended in the wee hours of the following morning, both of them hoarse from screaming.

Privately, after Lisa went to her hotel room, Dwayne confided in his daughters that the greatest reason for the divorce was Lisa's lack of respect for him. He encouraged Katie to always be honest with Armando, and to never let an issue fester until it boiled over. He said he learned more about his wife the day of that argument than he learned in their entire thirty years of marriage. No matter the reason for their divorce, the girls were less than thrilled about the news, but they both understood and wished their parents well.

Since the wedding was planned so quickly, Katie and Armando ended up with just over twenty guests, but to them, that was plenty. In fact, they had an inside joke that maybe the secret to having a small, stress-free wedding was to have it in another country on less than two weeks notice. Thankfully, many of the guests in attendance were the most treasured people in their lives.

Katie's matron of honor was her sister, Chelsea. And because Katie had thrown herself into work the past few years, she had inadvertently let a few of her closest friends slip away. As a result, Cara and Patty stepped in as bridesmaids. One of Katie's college friends was able to attend the wedding at the last minute, but Katie was positive it was only because she had seen pictures of Armando's single brother, Ramon. Katie did her best to warn her that, no matter how gorgeous he was, he had been a total jerk to her for the past ten years. Armando found the idea hilarious, considering how much Ramon reveled in his bachelorhood.

Armando stood at attention in front of the minister alongside his two brothers as he awaited his bride, a full-wattage smile on his handsome face.

Katie smiled back at him, her heart blooming with joy. This moment was so much more than a "dream come true." Katie felt as if everything that had happened in her life had prepared her for this moment. And even though she despised what her father did to Armando, deep inside she wondered if she and Armando would appreciate each other nearly as much if it had never happened.

Her eyes drifted from Armando for a moment as she took a glimpse of the bridal party. The ladies smiled at her, looking beautiful in their powder blue dresses. Beside Armando were Victor and Ramon, standing in a line, all of them wearing lightweight beige suits that were similar to the color of the sand. It warmed Katie's heart to see the dashing brothers together like this, beaming at her. Even Ramon held her gaze for a moment and gave her a soft grin.

When the minister asked, "Who gives this woman to be married to this man?" Katie teared up when her father said, "Her mother and I do," and kissed her cheek. Even though Katie would have married Armando without their approval, it felt a million times better to be open about their love.

The ceremony was quick. Armando and Katie kept their vows simple. A mere promise to spend the rest of their lives together was all either of them needed.

The wedding ring Armando slipped on her finger was made of solid gold, with one tiny diamond chip—the same diamond from the treasured engagement ring Armando gave her in high school. She knew the old ring was going to be used to make her wedding band, but this was her first time seeing it. Her heart fluttered and she blinked rapidly to try to make her tears go away when she saw it on her finger for the first time.

Armando kissed her like they were the only two people in the world. Sounds of cheering and music all faded into the background. Katie's heart swelled with the realization that she was now his wife. She suddenly felt like a teenager again. Her mind's eye flashed back to that day, before their worlds were shattered. Sitting there in his car, holding his hand as he sped through Texas, was the most thrilling time of her life. Until now. She remembered gazing at him, memorizing his face. And knowing, deep within her soul, that she would be his wife.

She just didn't know it would take ten years to happen.

* * * * *

Victor smiled at Cara as he hooked his arm around her elbow, escorting her down the aisle behind Katie and Armando as the recessional music played. They both nodded at Isaac, who sat on the front row beside Tom, eagerly waving to get their attention. Chuckling, Victor said, "I think he's getting anxious for that baby brother."

Cara blushed and bit her lip as she looked down at her sandaled feet. "Yeah. About that. Maybe we should set a wedding date soon. I'd rather not have to wear a maternity bridal gown. Isaac'll ask too many questions."

With a gasp, Victor drew her closer and said, "Are you pregnant? Now?"

When Cara's eyes met his, Victor slowed his pace.

Cara said, "I don't know for sure. Maybe."

Victor felt his eyes well up with joyful tears. He took a deep breath and tried to concentrate on walking his fiancée down the rest of the aisle. "Only *you* would give me news like that at a moment like this." He laughed.

"I'm sorry. We've been so busy with this last-minute wedding trip, I didn't even realize it till this morning. I've been dying to get you alone."

"It's fine, *querida*. We'll get you to a doctor as soon as possible. And no alcohol for you at the reception."

Cara nodded. "Okay. Please keep it to yourself. I'd hate to get everyone's hopes up."

"Of course." Victor glanced over his shoulder at Patty, who chatted with Ramon. "So, do you wanna get married here in Cabo? It's beautiful. And I'm sure they'd let us use the property."

"I don't know. The idea of having the wedding at the ranch is starting to grow on me. That is, if Ramon wouldn't mind."

Victor smiled and paused long enough to kiss her forehead. "You have no idea how happy you just made me."

* * * * *

Patty's eyes danced among the wedding guests as she held Ramon's arm. She let out a hopeful sigh and said, "What a beautiful place to get married."

Ramon nodded as they walked along. "Yep."

"Oh, come on." Patty gave his arm a light smack. "It's a beautiful wedding. You're next, you know. Or, well, you're next after Victor and Cara…"

Ramon snorted. "*Next*? For what? A death sentence?"

Patty's eyes rolled. "You just haven't found the right woman."

At that very moment, Ramon noticed an unfamiliar girl smiling at him out of the corner of his eye. He assumed it was Katie's single girlfriend Armando told him about before the wedding. Ramon straightened his posture and made sure to walk past her with blatant disinterest. "No such thing as the right woman. Some men just aren't the marrying kind, Patty."

Patty noticed the girl who was gazing at Ramon, and gave her a friendly grin as they marched by. "No, she's out there. I don't think she's here at this wedding, but she's out there." She ignored his deep groan as she thought about Marcy.

EPILOGUE

Three years later

Armando and Katie had an annual tradition of taking an extended vacation for their anniversary. They spent the first few weeks in their villa in Cabo San Lucas, then they came to Turnbrook to visit their families. This year, they would stay long enough to attend Isaac's seventh birthday party, which was a few days away.

Katie was six months pregnant with their second child: a girl. This morning, they left their two-year-old son, Carlos—named after Armando's paternal grandfather—in the care of doting grandpa Dwayne and his soon-to-be wife, Yolanda.

Armando brought the car to a stop in the mall parking lot and turned to Katie. "So, what to buy for a seven-year-old boy's birthday?"

Katie patted his thigh. "Just think about the stuff you liked when *you* were seven."

"My life at seven was a lot different from Isaac's, I can assure you."

Katie shrugged. "It's nothing to stress over. He'll be happy with anything."

"Yeah." Armando breathed deeply and took Katie's hand, his voice laden with sympathy. "You can stay out here if you want."

Katie raised a brow. "I'm pregnant. Not *helpless*."

"I know, honey." Armando flashed her a warm smile and leaned over to kiss her as his hand gently caressed her swollen belly.

Inside, Katie smiled to herself as they kissed. Armando was always too protective, but he was so darned sweet about it.

Soon, they strolled hand-in-hand through the mall to the first toy store they found. After twenty minutes of deliberation, Armando held a large basket full of toys as they stood in line at the register.

Katie leaned against him. "This is fun. Isn't it nice to buy gifts in person, for a change? Instead of sending your assistant or ordering online?"

Scoffing, Armando said, "What are you talking about? I buy stuff in person all the time for you and Carlos. You know that."

Their friendly argument continued until they reached the counter, where a blond-haired sales associate stared at Katie, her mouth gaping.

Caught off guard, Katie's thoughts took a moment to settle. When they did, she politely said, "Hi Jennifer," as Armando placed the basket of toys on the counter.

Jennifer swallowed, hard, and plucked a toy from the basket to scan it, no longer looking at Katie. "Hi. You move back to town or something?"

Katie glanced at Armando, who seemed oblivious. "Uh, no. We're just here visiting family." She cleared her throat and decided to ask another question to hopefully make this awkward encounter pass quickly. "So, you don't work at Cortez anymore?"

"No," Jennifer said, her voice carrying a hint of sadness. "I left right after you did."

"Oh." Katie mindlessly put her hand on her baby bump and chose to be quiet instead of asking more questions. Aside from the occasional fleeting thought, Katie hadn't thought of Mitch or Jennifer in years. And she had the feeling, given Jennifer's tone, that Mitch had something to do with her leaving the restaurant.

As Armando handed her his credit card, Jennifer asked, "So, when are you due?"

Determined to give her as little information as possible, Katie said, "A little over three months from now."

With a weak smile, Jennifer looked in Katie's eyes and said, "Congratulations. Is it your first baby?"

Katie shook her head and said, "No. We have a two-year-old boy."

"Oh." Jennifer nodded, her eyes lighting up for the first time during their conversation. "So do I."

Katie grinned and chose not to ask any questions. Even though Jennifer looked the same as she did three years earlier, it was obvious her demeanor had changed. She no longer appeared as the happy-go-lucky girl Katie once knew. Maybe motherhood had matured her. Maybe there was strife between Jennifer and her son's father...and maybe that father was Mitch. Regardless, Katie just wanted to get out of that store with a minimal amount of information.

Katie said, "Goodbye," to Jennifer and took Armando's hand as he lifted the bag of toys from the counter.

They had just set foot outside the store when Katie heard Jennifer's voice behind her.

"Wait!" Jennifer said. "Katie, wait."

Katie and Armando stopped. Katie turned around and said, "Yes?"

Jennifer's eyes filled with tears. She hesitated, then said, "I'm sorry."

Katie was unexpectedly choked up at Jennifer's sincerity. "It's okay. I forgive you."

"Really?" Jennifer asked, her bottom lip quivering.

"Yes." Katie forced a grin and swallowed against the lump quickly forming in her throat. "Yes, I do."

Jennifer nodded and said, "Good." Then she let out an abrupt chuckle as she took a tissue from her pocket to blot her eyes. "And for what it's worth, he'll probably always be a cheater." She sighed. "But at least he pays child support."

Armando's eyes widened.

Katie instinctively placed a hand on Jennifer's shoulder and said the first thing that came to her. "Well...good luck."

"Thanks." Jennifer nodded and went back into the store.

After she left, Armando put his arm around Katie's waist as

they headed through the sparse crowd to the parking lot. "Shit," he said. "I didn't realize it was her until she said that thing about cheating."

Katie exhaled an unsteady breath and tried not to cry. "Yeah."

"You okay?" Armando stopped walking, pulling her over to the wall to be out of the way of traffic.

Katie drew in a deep breath through her nose, sniffling, then reached into her purse to scrounge for a tissue. "I'm fine. It's probably just the mom in me, or the pregnancy hormones. I feel bad for her."

"Listen, I've always heard if someone will cheat *with* you, they'll probably cheat *on* you." Armando's eyebrows arched. "She should've seen it coming."

"So?" Katie found a tissue and brought it to her eyes. "It *still* makes me sad for her. And for her...little boy..." Her voice cracked.

Armando pulled Katie close as she sobbed against his chest.

When she finished, she pulled away and wiped her face. "I'm sorry," she said. "I didn't mean to do that in public."

Armando kissed her lips, then draped his arm around her back as they walked on. Gently, he said, "You know I don't care what anyone thinks."

Katie let out a sigh of relief. "I know. I love you."

"I love you, too."

In silence, they headed out to the parking lot. Katie was afraid to speak again, lest her hormones launch her into another fit of despair.

A few minutes later, as Armando started the car and prepared to back out of the parking space, Katie said, "Do you think we'd be together right now if I never got engaged to Mitch? That's why you came back to find me, right?"

Armando removed his hand from the gear shift and kept the car in park. He turned his body to face her. "I thought of you every single day when we were apart. I would've come looking for you, eventually. Your engagement was the kick in the ass I needed, I guess." He shrugged, then took her hand and repeated something he had told her many times. "We should've found each other sooner, but I'm not gonna mourn those lost years. Regret will only eat away at your soul. I'm with my true love, *now*. She's carrying my baby girl, *now*." He placed a tender hand on her stomach. "And Carlos. What would our lives be without him?"

Katie laughed as tears welled up in her eyes. "I love you more than you'll ever know."

Armando moved his hand to her cheek and leaned across the seat to give her a long, deep kiss.

When he pulled away, she smiled at him, her tears now almost dry. She held his gaze and said, "It feels like those ten years never even happened. I barely remember them anymore."

Armando nodded. "I know."

"Is it weird that I forgot about Mitch?" Katie's eyes narrowed thoughtfully. "You came back into my life and *poof*." She snapped her fingers. "It was over. I didn't want him anymore--"

"Shh." Armando placed a finger against her mouth, then quickly moved it away to kiss her before his lips went to her ear. He whispered, "You felt that way because you were always mine." He kissed her ear. "And you're always gonna be."

Katie sniffled and let her forehead rest against Armando's. "I know. You're right. I shouldn't be upset about it now." She groaned as she brought a tissue to her eyes. "It's these stupid hormones."

Armando chuckled softly. "It's okay."

He waited until she was sufficiently calm before pulling the car out of the parking lot and heading down the road. To lighten the mood, Armando said, "I hope your dad's house is still standing after Carlos has his way with it."

Katie laughed. "Me too. I don't think Dad knew what he was getting himself into. At least Yolanda's there to help. And they haven't called us. That's a good sign."

"Yeah." Armando nodded. "So, are you sure you wanna go see your mom this afternoon? Are you really up for that, without me around?"

Katie shrugged. "I'll be fine. She'll be so distracted with Carlos, she'll barely notice I'm there. Besides, I can always come back to Dad's house if she pisses me off."

Armando shook his head and let out a long sigh. "I don't know. I should come with you. I'll let Victor know--"

"No." Katie's voice was firm. "Henry's expecting both of you today. We may not be here again during visitation days for a few months."

Armando sighed as he stared off at the highway in front of them. "I know. I just hate the thought of you going off to your mom's while I'm at the prison." His eyes rolled. "It's probably only gonna put both of us in a bad mood. It's so depressing to see Henry like that."

"I know." Katie placed a hand on his knee. "But later on tonight, you come back to me. And *poof.*" She giggled as she snapped her fingers. "It'll be like it never happened."

Armando smiled and put his hand on top of hers. "You know... you're absolutely right."

THE END

Coming Soon: The final book in the Barboza Brothers Series:

More Than a Maid

Ramon and Marcy's story begins.

Victor and Cara begin their lives together as husband and wife.

The full story of the Barboza Brothers and the nature of their relationship with the mysterious Henry Platt is revealed.

Add your email to Reeni's mailing list at http://www. reeniaustin.com to receive a notification as soon as the book goes live.

ARE YOU ON THE LIST?

Go to http://www.reeniaustin.com and your email to the
mailing list to be notified when Reeni's latest book is available
for purchase.

MORE ABOUT REENI AUSTIN:

More work by this author can be found under the name "Shaina Richmond." Look for her 900 page erotic romance book, "Safe With Me," at most major eBook retailers.

Visit:
http://www.shainarichmond.com
to learn more about the Safe with Me series.

CONTACT REENI

http://www.reeniaustin.com

http://www.facebook.com/ReeniAustin

(page intentionally left blank)

(page intentionally left blank)

www.ingramcontent.com/pod-product-compliance
Lightning Source LLC
Chambersburg PA
CBHW030918120626
46554CB00001B/194